# SHADOW
## ~ OF THE ~
# DRAGON

### PART ONE - KIRA

# KATE O'HEARN

A Catalogue record for this book is available from the British Library

ISBN-13: 978 0 340 94528 5

Typeset in AGaramond by Avon DataSet Ltd,
Bidford on Avon, Warwickshire

Printed in Great Britain by
Clays Ltd, St Ives plc

The paper and board used in this paperback by Hodder Children's Books
are natural recyclable products made from wood grown in sustainable
forests. The manufacturing processes conform to the environmental
regulations of the country of origin.

Hodder Children's Books
a division of Hachette Children's Books
338 Euston Road, London NW1 3BH
An Hachette UK Company
www.hachettechildrens.co.uk

For Mom,
We miss ya!

# ABOUT THE AUTHOR

Kate O'Hearn was raised in the heart of New York City. Throughout her life, she has always had an active and vivid imagination. As a child walking down 5th Avenue, she would envision herself soaring among the city's canyons on the back of a wild dragon.

While in Florida, looking over the sea, she could imagine living amongst the whales and breaching in the heavy swells.

At night, a star studded sky was yet another playground.

These dreams and ideas never faded. Instead they grew until they spilled over into the books she loves to write.

*For more information visit:*
www.kateohearn.com

*Paradon's Eye*

# CHAPTER
## ~ 1 ~

'I don't want to get married!'

'You don't have a choice!'

Kira watched her father's blazing eyes as they bored into her. There was just no reasoning with him when he was like this. Turning desperately to her mother seated at the end of the table, she pleaded, 'Mother, please. I can't get married, not now. I'm too young.'

Instead of an answer, her mother shut her eyes and lowered her head as tears trickled silently down her cheeks.

Kira turned back to her father. 'But Father, please, I don't know anyone called Jurrie. How can you expect me to marry someone I've never even met?'

'You haven't met him, but I have,' her father answered. 'He's a good lad and will treat you well. We couldn't have found a better match for you.'

Kira sat back in her chair and folded her arms across her chest. She couldn't believe her parents would do this to her. 'Why now?' she demanded. 'Why do you have to do this to me now when we've got the harvest to bring in?'

'Why?' her father repeated. 'You ask me why?' Rising from his chair, he ignored his crutch as he hopped one legged over to an old parchment that had been mounted on the cottage wall above the cooking hearth. Tearing it down, he hopped back to the table and slammed it down in front of Kira.

'First Law, that's why!'

Kira gazed down on the faded parchment. She had never been taught to read, but she knew exactly what it said. The six points of First Law had been drummed into her head for as long as she could remember. Saying nothing, she looked back up to her father.

'First Law,' he repeated. 'After all these years, do I still have to teach it to you?' Before Kira had the chance to say no, her father picked up the parchment and started to read aloud.

'Point one,' he read. 'Girls are not allowed to leave their homes unless escorted by their father, brothers or husbands and may never travel any further than their neighbouring village. Point two: Girls are never to be educated. Point three: Girls are not allowed to hunt, fight or engage in any activities that are considered boyish. They may not dress as boys and must never carry weapons of any sort. Point four: Unmarried girls are never allowed to visit the palace or approach the king.'

Kira reached up and grasped her father's arm. 'Father, I know the First Law—'

'Obviously you don't!' he cut in. 'Otherwise you would know that the next point is all about you.' Shaking her hand off his arm, he continued to read aloud. 'Point five: Girls must be matched to the boy or man they are to marry by the age of twelve. They must be married before the age of thirteen. The day after the marriage ceremony, their husbands must send confirmation to the king.'

Putting down the parchment, he returned awkwardly to his seat at the head of the table. 'Kira, you are twelve. Your mother and I have waited as long as we possibly could, but there is no getting around it. First Law was written specifically for girls. You are a girl. Like it or not, you are. And one way or another, you will marry Jurrie before next summer!'

'Please, Kira,' her mother timidly put in. 'Listen to your father. He knows what's best for you. He knows what's best for all of us.'

Kira shook her head and leaned closer to her mother. 'Marrying a stranger isn't what's best for me. I don't want to get married. I want to go to the palace to work in the dragon stables and learn to be a dragon knight just like father was before his accident with Ariel.'

'Kira, no!' her mother cried softly as her nervous eyes darted back to Kira's father.

'What did you just say?' he demanded as his dark eyebrows knitted together in a deep frown. 'Did I just hear you mention dragons again? How many times do I have to tell you? You are never to mention those monsters in this home again!'

Kira watched her father's temper getting ready to blow. But as angry as he was, she felt her own temper starting to flare. 'Father, it's just not fair! Next season Dane gets to go to the palace and learn to ride them. What do I get? A husband. But I don't want it. If I can't go to the palace, then I'll go to the Rogue's Mountain and tame Ferarchie!'

'Ferarchie?' her father cried. 'Ferarchie?' Turning furious eyes to her mother, he threw his arms in the air in exasperation. 'Where does she get these insane ideas?'

He looked back to Kira. 'You listen to me, little girl. Ferarchie is the meanest dragon to ever curse this earth. He kills. That's all he does. He kills and he eats anything or anyone who comes near him. As long as he flies wild in those mountains, they're cursed. Swear to me you will never go anywhere near them.' Slamming his fist violently down on the table, he caused a vase of wild flowers to tip over and roll off the side. 'Swear it!'

Kira watched her father's face turning red with rage. In all her life, she'd never seen him this angry before. Not even when her brother Dane broke his favourite axe. Terrified, she weakly nodded. 'I'm sorry Father. I swear I'll never go to the Rogue's Mountain to see Ferarchie.'

An agonized moment of silence passed between father and daughter. Finally he sighed. Softening his tone, his imploring eyes pleaded with her. 'Kira, please, of all the rules in the king's First Law, the last one is the most strictly enforced.' He reached for the parchment again and read aloud. 'Point six: Under no circumstances are girls ever to be allowed anywhere near dragons.'

When he finished, he put down the parchment. 'The penalty for breaking any one of these points is a trip to Lasser Commons for execution. But the penalty for breaking the last one is slow torture and death.'

'But Father—' Kira pleaded.

'No buts,' he said softly as he raised a calloused finger to her lips. 'Listen to me, please. Dorcon has been waiting years to get back at me for what he thinks

I did to him. He's been searching for any opportunity to discredit me with the king. If he can't get me directly then he'll get at me through you. You must do as First Law states or Dorcon will be here in a flash to take his revenge on all of us.'

'What does Lord Dorcon have to do with me?' Kira asked. 'That fight was between the two of you. Not me.'

'Dorcon hates me,' her father explained. 'That means, by extension, he hates you too. I'm sure if he had his way, he'd see all of us sent to Lasser.'

'Your father's right, Kira,' her mother put in. 'Lord Dorcon is an evil man. It wouldn't do well for your father's reputation if he had to come here because of you.'

Kira turned on her mother in complete disbelief. 'You're worried about Father's reputation? What about me and what I want?'

'What about you?' her father challenged as his temper flared again.

'I don't want to get married!' Kira argued. 'And it's not fair for you to make me!'

'What do you know about fair!' he harshly demanded. 'It wasn't fair when my own dragon turned on me and ate my leg. It wasn't fair when Dorcon got promoted over me because I could no longer fight. Kira, life isn't fair.'

'But I don't want to go—'

'You don't have a choice!' he shouted. Then he paused and his voice went suddenly cold. 'Now you will do exactly as your mother and I say. Next spring, whether you like it or not, you will marry this boy. It's the First Law. To break it is to die.'

Kira's eyes suddenly flashed with anger equalling her father's. 'Just because the king hates girls and makes up these stupid laws, doesn't mean we should follow them blindly. I don't want to get married! Do you hear me? I don't want it and you can't make me!'

Kira quickly stood, casting her chair backwards. 'I won't do it!' Turning from her parents' shocked faces, she ran from the table and fled the small cottage.

Outside, she raced past her youngest sister who was playing with the chickens in the yard and straight into the grain field. It was late in the season and the tall stalks of grain rose well above her head. As she ran, the sound of her full skirts brushing against the drying grain made a strange hushing sigh, almost as though the field itself was crying especially for her.

Kira ran blindly. She couldn't believe her parents would do this to her. She didn't want to get married.

She wanted to work with the dragons at the palace stables. Suddenly that dream seemed even more remote.

When she could run no more, Kira walked. Wandering alone, she tried to figure a way out of the arrangement. There had to be something she could do, some place she could go where being a girl wasn't such a curse.

Furious at the injustice of it all, she wandered to the edge of her family's property. In the distance she could see the Rogue's Mountain rising majestically above her. Taking a seat at the outer edge of the field, she stared at the tall mountain and waited.

This was her secret place. The one place she could go to be alone with her thoughts. A place where on very rare occasions, she could watch Ferarchie flying wild in the skies over the mountains and envy him his freedom.

'Kira?'

Startled, Kira turned and looked into the flushed face of her youngest sister. 'Shadow, what are you doing here?'

Elspeth sniffed and wiped her nose on her sleeve. 'I heard you shouting. So I followed you. Please don't be mad at me.'

Kira looked at her sister and sighed. Elspeth had

been like a shadow to her since she first learned to walk. There was nowhere she could go that Elspeth couldn't find her. And in truth, there was nothing that Kira wouldn't do for her.

'I'm not mad at you,' she said, softening her tone. 'Come here and sit down.' Patting the ground at her side, Kira put her arm protectively around her sister's narrow shoulders. 'I was shouting because Mother and Father said something that made me very cross.'

'What?'

Kira sighed again. 'Well, they said they've made a match for me. That they have found a boy in the next village whom I must marry. So, next spring, they're going to send me away to live with him.'

Elspeth's eyes flew open wide. 'You can't leave here!'

'I must. It's the law.'

'Then I'm coming too.' Elspeth folded her thin arms determinedly across her chest. 'They can't separate us.'

'Shadow, listen to me, please,' Kira begged, feeling it tear at her heart to tell her sister she couldn't go. 'Mother needs you here. She relies on you. Who else would feed the chickens or count the new kittens in the barn? What would happen to all the other animals? They need you here too. You're the only one they'll talk to.'

Elspeth's eyes filled with tears as she sniffed. 'But I don't want you to go.'

Kira gazed back up to the mountain. Softly she said, 'I don't want to go either.' Sitting huddled with her sister she pointed up at the mountain. 'Do you see up there?'

Elspeth followed Kira's finger. 'Uh-huh.'

'That is the Rogue's Mountain. He lives up there. The Rogue is free. But you and me? We're not. The king hates us, so he makes us do things we don't want to do.'

'Why? What did we do to him?'

'Us? Nothing,' Kira answered thoughtfully. 'The king has always hated girls. Mother says that his father did too, and his father before him. No one knows why, but all the kings do.'

Elspeth sniffed again and looked up at the mountains. 'Maybe we should go there then.'

Pulling her sister closer, Kira studied the mountains and wondered what it would be like to have Ferarchie's kind of freedom. Or to live in a land where girls could travel on their own if they wanted, where they weren't forced to marry boys they didn't know and where they could be whatever they wanted to be, not just what the king told them to be.

Tears began to sting her eyes as she desperately

tried to fight her destiny. Her parents said she had to marry a stranger from another village. But deep in her heart, she knew she couldn't do it. There had to be another way.

As the balance of the day passed slowly away, Kira sat quietly with her sister watching the mountains. She felt drained and defeated. There just wasn't anything she could think of to change her fate.

When the sun finally passed from overhead and started to descend in the western sky, reluctantly, Kira knew it was time to take her sister home. She stood and reached for Elspeth's hand. 'Come on, Shadow, we should be getting back.'

Climbing slowly to her feet, Elspeth pointed to the sky. 'What's that?'

Kira turned and followed her sister's finger to a large dark shape in the distant sky. Suddenly all thoughts of her upcoming wedding disappeared.

'Ferarchie,' she sighed, enviously watching the dragon soaring in the setting sun.

'But I thought you said the Rogue lives up there?'

'He does. Ferarchie is the Rogue. That's his real name. The name he had before he escaped and became wild.'

'Then that's the bad dragon Father doesn't like to talk about?'

'That's him!' Kira said proudly. 'When I was your age, before Father had his accident with Ariel, he told me a story about how when he was a boy, he'd worked for the man who'd raised and ridden Ferarchie.'

Kira paused and reached for a tall stalk of grain and broke it off at its base. Drawing it like a sabre, she stabbed the air and other stalks of grain. 'His master would tell him amazing stories about fierce battles fought and won with that one dragon.' Turning on Elspeth, she stabbed at her with the fluffy end of the stalk until her little sister giggled uncontrollably. 'But Ferarchie was mean and he was dangerous, maybe the most vicious dragon the kingdom has ever possessed.' She stopped and held up her finger. 'He was also the most intelligent.'

'How did he get free?' Elspeth asked, ducking behind Kira as she held her stalk of grain up high and pointed it at the soaring dragon.

'Father said that when his master was killed in battle, Ferarchie went mad! He killed a lot of men and dragons on both sides of the battle and then escaped. When he settled in the mountains they stopped calling him Ferarchie and started to call him the Rogue. He's lived there ever since. Sometimes, the king sends knights up to try to kill him.'

'Why?' Elspeth asked.

'Because the king hates rogue dragons almost as much as he hates girls. But this rogue dragon always wins. Now legends are built around him.'

As Kira watched the Rogue riding the thermals in the sky, once again she envied him his freedom. 'I wish I could break free too, Ferarchie!' she sighed heavily.

'Me too,' Elspeth agreed, mimicking her sister's sigh.

When the dragon finally passed from sight behind the mountain, Kira reluctantly drew her eyes away. She playfully ruffled Elspeth's hair. 'Come on, let's get home.'

# CHAPTER
~2~

Walking side by side, Kira held on to her sister's hand but was only half listening to her light chatter. She was lost deep in thought. Despite the love she felt for her parents, she was about to defy them. There was just no way she could ever marry a boy she'd never met.

'Kira, do you smell that?' Elspeth asked.

'Smell what?' Kira asked, coming out of her thoughts.

'That. That smoke.'

Kira stopped and realized that she could smell a fire. Looking around she saw great plumes of smoke rising in the sky ahead of them. Suddenly frightened, she squeezed her sister's hand.

'That's coming from home. Come on. Shadow, run!'

Racing through the field the air was becoming thick and clogged with acrid black smoke. When they neared the edge of the grain field, Kira suddenly stopped. She heard raised, angry voices and the sound of her mother's terrified screams.

Throwing herself to the ground, Kira tugged Elspeth's hand. 'Shadow, get down!'

'Kira, you're hurting me—'

She clamped her hand over Elspeth's mouth, leaned forward and whispered in her ear. 'Elspeth, listen to me. There are bad men at the cottage, you must be quiet!'

Perhaps it was the tone of her voice, or the use of her real name that put the fear in her sister's eyes. Whatever it was, it worked and Elspeth stopped struggling.

'I'm going to take my hand away. When I do, will you promise to be quiet?'

Elspeth's large frightened eyes blinked at Kira as she nodded.

When Kira removed her hand, she drew her sister carefully forward. 'Now, keep low and whatever you see, for heaven's sake stay quiet. All right?'

Elspeth silently nodded.

'Let's see what they want.'

Creeping closer to the edge of the field, Kira and Elspeth's eyes met a terrible sight. Their cottage was alive with flames. Not far away from the raging fire, a line of knights was holding their brother and sister. In the early evening light, the glow from the fire turned the knights' heavy silver armour into liquid gold.

At the very end of the line, a knight carried a tall staff with a large flag at the top. The king's crest was blazoned on the fabric and flipped wildly in the wind created by the huge fire. Across from the knights holding Dane and Kahrin, Kira saw several more knights supporting her father on his one leg while others held on to her crying mother.

Kira strained to hear what they were saying above the fire's roar, but she could only make out fragmented bits of the conversation.

'Dorcon, you know full well I've already served the king,' her father was shouting. 'I lost my leg in his service, isn't that enough? My duty to him is over. Finished!'

'One's duty to the king is never finished,' said Lord Dorcon smugly as he waved an armoured finger in front of her father's face. 'You should know that.'

'But the harvest, we must bring in the harvest!'

'There isn't going to be a harvest for you, Darious.'

*So that was Lord Dorcon*, Kira thought as she watched the tall knight standing before her father. She could see all the things her father had told her about his rival. Stories of how vicious and ambitious he was.

But above all else, how vain. As she studied his immaculately polished armour with all of its decorations, she understood what her father meant.

She also recalled her father saying how jealous Lord Dorcon was because he'd always been the king's favourite knight. Looking at him now, Kira saw that Lord Dorcon remembered everything too.

Kira turned away and stole a quick glance over to Elspeth. Her sister had fresh tears in her frightened eyes and she was trying to force her tiny fist in her small mouth. Kira realised Elspeth knew who Lord Dorcon was as well.

In despair, her eyes were drawn back to the knights holding her family. They then passed to where the only home she had ever known was going up in flames. Kira wanted to cry. She wanted to shout. But she was too frightened to do either. Instead she glanced back to Elspeth and held up her hand. 'Stay here. I can't hear what they are saying. I'm going to get closer.'

When Elspeth nodded, Kira crawled up to the edge of the field. Terror knotted her stomach as she watched Lord Dorcon lean closer to her father's face. 'You, your wife and son are to be taken to the palace. There's a long and hard war coming and you are being ordered back into service.'

Kira's father shook his head. 'Take me then if you must, but leave my family alone. We've done nothing wrong. You can't just come here, burn everything and force us to go with you.'

'You are so wrong, Darious. By order of the king, I can.'

Kira had always hated Lord Dorcon from the stories her father told. Now she hated him more for burning down her home, and even more than that, for the fear she saw on her father's face.

'By order of King Arden,' Lord Dorcon continued, 'all retired knights, their wives and sons are to be escorted to the palace and put back in service. The king knew you wouldn't want to come back, especially after what happened with Ariel. But with no home left and your family kept at the palace, you will have no choice but to serve, and to serve well if you want to keep them safe.'

'But what about my girls?' her father demanded. 'You didn't mention my daughters. If we must go, they are coming with us.'

Lord Dorcon laughed. But it was a cold and mirthless sound. He started to shake his visored head. 'Ah, yes, your girls. Well Darious, I'm afraid your lovely daughters are not going to the palace with you. Believe me, it will be my greatest pleasure to personally escort them to Lasser Commons.'

'What!' Kira's mother cried as her hands flew up to her mouth. 'Lasser Commons? No you can't! Please, you can't send my daughters to that horrible place—'

Stepping away from her father, Lord Dorcon turned to his men. 'You there, Captain Darious has two other girls, Kira and Elspeth. They are coming to Lasser with me. Find them.'

'Father, they can't do that!' Dane shouted as he kicked at the knights restraining him. But the more he fought, the tighter they squeezed his arms. 'Let me go!' he finally cried, squirming in their grasp. 'You're hurting me.'

Lord Dorcon glanced back to Dane and studied him for a moment. He then walked over to where he stood.

While Kira watched, her brother stopped struggling and stood defiantly before the tall knight. She had to stifle a scream when Lord Dorcon suddenly whipped his armoured glove across her brother's face and caused blood to flow from the corner of Dane's mouth.

'Have no illusions, boy,' Lord Dorcon said coldly, poking a sharp finger in Dane's chest. 'I can and will do anything I please. My orders are to take your sisters to Lasser. That's what I intend to do.' He turned back to his men. 'The girls are probably frightened by the fire and hiding. But they won't venture too far away. Start with the barn and then search the fields.'

'You leave my family alone!' Kira's father shouted as he started to struggle against the knights restraining him. 'They've done nothing wrong!'

Ignoring him, Lord Dorcon barked at his men, 'I said find them!'

While several men left to search the barn, Lord Dorcon directed his attention back to Kira's father. 'Darious, I've always known about your nasty little habit of teaching your eldest daughter things that no girl has a right to know. You've been talking to her about dragons. Showing her how to hunt and how to make fires. I also know that Kira behaves more like a boy than a girl. Any one of these actions is a full breach of the First Law and punishable by death. But as you were in the king's favour, he ordered me to keep an eye on you but otherwise leave you alone. That ends now. War has come back to the kingdom. Your daughters are unmarried. They will join all the other unmarried girls being delivered to the gates of Lasser.'

'But Lasser Commons is a prison for murderers,' protested Kira's mother. 'You can't send my girls there.'

Lord Dorcon glanced over to Kira's other sister,

Kahrin, before answering. 'Lasser is indeed for murderers. But now it's also for all unmarried girls.'

'But Kahrin is only nine and Elspeth seven,' her mother begged. 'They are too young to have matches. And . . . and . . . Kira already has one. Jurrie. He's from the next village. We could hold the ceremony today—'

'No, no, no, it's too late,' cut in Lord Dorcon. 'They are unmarried, so they all go to Lasser. Now stop your whining you foolish woman or I'll have you sent there as well!'

Kira watched the exchange between Lord Dorcon and her parents continue. Even though she couldn't see his covered face, she knew from the tone of his voice that he was enjoying himself.

He finally turned from her parents and looked back to where his men were emerging from the barn. 'Well?'

'Nothing, my Lord, they're not in there.'

'My Lord . . . ?'

Kira suddenly felt eyes resting heavily upon her. She looked up and saw an armoured knight pointing directly at her.

'Sir, I think that's her.'

Everyone turned. Kira heard her mother's anguished cry and then Dane and Kahrin calling out to her. But it was her father's voice she heard the loudest.

'Run, Kira!' he shouted, renewing his struggle against the knights. 'Take Elspeth and save her! Get away from here! Go!'

'Get her!' cried Lord Dorcon as he started to run forward.

Seeing the line of huge knights charging towards her, Kira stole a final glance back at her despairing family. Then she dashed over to Elspeth. Catching hold of her hand, she dragged her little sister to her feet.

'Come on, Shadow, we've got to run!'

Clutching hands, Kira and Elspeth raced deep into the grain field. Running as fast as their legs could carry them, they heard the large knights crashing through the field behind them. But the knights were wearing armour not designed for running. Keeping low, the distance between them soon broadened until the knights lost the way completely.

With her heart racing, Kira didn't know which way to go. But her instincts told her that she and Elspeth stood a much better chance if they stayed in the large grain field instead of moving out into the open.

'Kira, please . . .' Elspeth cried as she stumbled. 'I can't run any more.'

Stopping, Kira crouched down and drew Elspeth

close to her. 'I think we've lost them,' she panted. 'Let's wait here a moment to catch our breath.'

Watching her sister's frightened and flushed face, Kira saw tears in her eyes. 'I'm scared,' Elspeth whined between gulps of air. 'I want to go home.'

'We can't,' Kira whispered, still trying to regain her own breath. 'And keep your voice down. We don't want them to hear us.'

Lifting her head, Kira listened for the sounds of the knights. She could still hear them shouting and clumsily crashing through the field, but they were far in the distance.

'But what do they want?'

'Shh, they'll hear you,' Kira hushed. 'Those bad men are taking everyone away. We've got to be quiet or they'll take us too.'

'Where? I want to go with Mother and Father.'

Kira looked into her sister's pained eyes. 'Lord Dorcon has taken them to the palace to be with the king.'

'Then why can't we go there?' Elspeth's voice broke as she started to hiccup.

'Because Father said we had to run. He thinks it's dangerous at the palace. And Father is always right, isn't he?'

Elspeth frowned and pouted. 'But you always

wanted to go there to be with the dragons.'

An angry bitterness clutched Kira's heart. She shook her head. 'I was wrong, Shadow. I never want to go there. Neither do you. King Arden is no friend of ours.'

'Then what are we going to do?'

Kira sighed and sat back on her haunches. She hadn't a clue what she was supposed to do next. 'Well,' she answered very softly as she put her arm protectively around her little sister, 'I guess we wait here for a while, then we go back.'

'Back where?'

'Home,' Kira answered. 'Or what's left of it.'

# CHAPTER
## ~3~

Kira and Elspeth remained huddled together until it was long past dark. Around them the temperature was quickly dropping and Kira could feel her sister starting to shiver. Neither of them was dressed for staying out in the cool night air.

As she strained her ears to listen, all Kira could hear was the sound of the autumn breeze blowing eerily through the grain. Owls hooted in the distance. But deep in the field, there were no more sounds of the king's knights.

'Come on, Shadow, I think it's safe now.' Climbing stiffly to her feet, Kira drew her sister up beside her.

'Are we going home now?' Elspeth asked tiredly.

'Yes,' Kira answered, dreading the thought of what they would find when they got back there.

'Are all the bad men gone?'

'I hope so.'

By the pale light of the full moon hanging sullenly overhead, Kira saw Elspeth's haunted expression. A small part of her wondered if it would have been better to let the knights capture them. But she quickly cast the thought aside, remembering the terrified expressions on her parents' faces when they found out they were to be sent to Lasser.

Both girls said little as they picked their way home. But right before they emerged from the grain field, Kira saw the final confirmation that staying hidden had been for the best. Creeping up to the outer edge of the field, they found a large patch of scorched earth.

A rock settled in the pit of Kira's stomach. 'He did this,' she said softly, as she kicked at the smouldering embers.

'Who?' Elspeth asked.

'Lord Dorcon. While we were hiding, he tried to set fire to the field.'

'Why?'

'Because he was angry and wanted to hurt us.' Seeing Elspeth's frightened expression, Kira didn't say more. She was just grateful that the rainy weather of the past few days had kept the grain too wet to burn.

They finally emerged from the field, and looked over

to the cottage. What they found nearly broke Kira's heart. It was all gone.

Fresh tears came to her eyes as she and Elspeth quietly crossed over to the remains. Standing together, shivering in the cold night air, they gazed silently upon the ruins of their home. Finally, Elspeth broke the silence.

'It's gone,' she said quietly in a voice hushed by shock. 'All burned down.'

Rage smouldered deep within Kira as she regarded the charred remains. In the centre of the cottage, glowing embers crackled and sparked as they rose lazily into the night sky.

Kira reached down and caught hold of Elspeth's hand. 'Come on, Shadow, let's see if we can find something warmer for you to wear.'

With the moon's light to guide them, they walked carefully around to the rear of the cottage. Not far ahead was the washing line where Kahrin and their mother had hung out the laundry earlier that day. Everything was still there. Kira pulled down her father's heavy jumper and quickly drew it over Elspeth's head. It hung down past her sister's knees and her hands were swallowed up in the sleeves.

Despite their situation, or maybe because of it, when

she looked at Elspeth, she started to laugh. 'Well, at least you won't get cold any more.'

Instead of laughing, Elspeth started to cry.

'Oh, Shadow, I know. I'm frightened too.' Pulling her into a hug, Kira squeezed her tightly.

Elspeth wiped a long sleeve across her nose. 'Where do we go now, Kira?'

*Where do we go now?* Suddenly it struck her. In that flash of an instant, Kira's childhood ended. She was now solely responsible for her little sister. 'Well, the first thing,' she said, sniffing back her own tears of despair, 'I need you to gather the rest of the clothes down from the line. I'm going to see if there is anything else left.' Lowering herself down to one knee, Kira reached forward and kissed Elspeth on the cheek. 'Can you do that for me, Shadow? Can you gather the clothing together?'

Elspeth wiped her sleeve across her nose again. 'Uh-huh.'

'That's my girl.' Standing, Kira started towards the barn then glanced back to her sister. 'Don't go near the cottage. The fire isn't out yet and I don't want you to burn Father's good jumper.'

'I won't,' Elspeth said miserably.

Walking up to the barn, Kira saw the large stone

shell and glowing embers from within, but no more than that. Nothing remained of their previous life. Her hands started to shake, but not from the cold. She couldn't believe that Lord Dorcon and his knights had done this to her family. Could he really have been so jealous of her father?

Picking her way through the barn's remains, she tried not to let her eyes linger too long on the charred bodies of all the farm animals killed by the fire.

'They didn't save you because of me,' she muttered bitterly.

Finding nothing to salvage, Kira left the barn. She walked back to the clothes' line, and took down Dane's leather trousers. But as she started to put them on under her skirt, Elspeth caught hold of her arm and cried, 'No, Kira, it's against First Law for you to wear Dane's clothes. You'll get in trouble.'

'I don't think we have to worry about that any more,' Kira said gently as she drew the cold leather trousers up her bare legs and tied them closed at the waist.

Elspeth said nothing more. Kira wondered if her sister had any idea of the full extent of trouble they were in. Or the penalty they faced if they were to be captured now. She pushed the uncomfortable thoughts aside, and quietly helped Elspeth gather the rest of the items down from the washing line. It was lucky that their mother and Kahrin had washed a couple of bed covers earlier in the day. They would come in very handy.

When they finished, both girls put on as much clothing as they could wear. Kira then tied the rest up in a bundle and slung it over her shoulder. Taking her sister's hand, they searched the cottage and barn a final time for anything from their previous life. But there was nothing left to find.

With a heavy heart, Kira squared her shoulders. 'Come on, Shadow, there is nothing for us here now. Maybe they left our neighbours alone.'

Elspeth said little as they slowly walked through the night towards their neighbour's property. The moon had long since passed from overhead and was now sitting on the distant horizon. When they arrived, they found the same devastation. The cottage and barn were nothing more than burned-out wrecks.

They picked their way around the remains. But there was nothing left to find. No food and no shelter, just dying embers from an empty shell, looking sad and desolate in the moonlight.

'What's that?' Elspeth said tiredly, pointing ahead of her.

Kira followed her sister's finger, and caught sight of moonlight glinting off something shiny on the ground. Crossing to it, she bent down and picked up a long dagger in a jewelled sheath. Turning it over, she realized this wasn't too unlike the one her father had. It had been a gift from the king after the accident with his dragon.

'It's a knight's dagger,' Kira explained as she held it up for her sister. Then stashing it in her belt, she said, 'We might just need it.'

'For what?'

'I don't know. But I'm keeping it anyway.'

'Can we go to bed now?' Elspeth asked quietly.

Kira saw the way Elspeth was swaying on her feet and struggling to keep her eyes open. 'Sure, Shadow,' she said gently. Gazing around the area, Kira drew her sister towards the woodpile.

Kira removed the bundle from her shoulder, and used the extra clothes and bedcovers to make a small nest. Sheltered against the tall woodpile, Elspeth fell asleep the moment she put her head down.

Exhausted, Kira curled against her sister, feeling lost and frightened. What were they to do now? Where were they to go? In all her life, she'd never spent a single night away from her family. Now they had no home and nowhere to go.

Moving closer to Elspeth, she tried to block out the sounds of the night, but they refused to be hushed. Terrified for their grim future, the deep sobs she'd been fighting so long finally overwhelmed her. Putting her arm around Elspeth, Kira cried herself to sleep.

Just past dawn, the harsh sound of shouting and horses' hooves woke both girls with a fright. Glancing quickly around, Kira helped Elspeth burrow deeper into the woodpile. A few moments later, she saw armoured knights astride their high warhorses moving slowly along the narrow trail that ran beside the remains of their neighbour's cottage.

'What is it?' Elspeth asked.

'Not now, Shadow, we have to stay really quiet.'

Kira soon lost count of the number of mounted knights filing past. Next she saw four horses pulling a large carriage that looked like a big cage. It was filled with people crying and begging to be released. But the knights were ignoring them. Behind the first carriage followed a second, then a third and finally a fourth. At the very end of the parade, armoured knights rode in escort.

'Did they take Mother and Father away in that?'

Elspeth asked as she raised her head and peered over the woodpile.

'I don't know,' Kira answered truthfully. 'Maybe.'

Both girls remained motionless long after the carriages disappeared into the distance. Only when they couldn't hear them any more did Kira dare to breathe a nervous sigh of relief. 'I think it's safe now,' she said softly.

'Kira, I'm hungry.'

'Me too,' she agreed. 'Come on, maybe we can find something in the daylight.'

Kira gazed around and listened for the sounds of knights. Instead she heard only nature. Birds were singing the last of the season's songs. Insects were preparing for the winter and in the distance, a lonely cow was mooing to be milked. But there was no one left to milk her.

'I wonder if the king is going to send out men to collect all the animals?' Kira said absently as they moved forward.

'Like they did at our farm?' Elspeth asked innocently.

Kira looked sadly at her little sister and lied. 'Uh-huh.' She knew Elspeth had a very special relationship with animals. She loved them. More importantly, they seemed to love her right back. Knowing all of this, how could she ever hope to tell her the truth of what she'd discovered in the remains of their barn?

'Come on, Shadow,' Kira finally said, casting away the terrible memories. 'Let's see if we can find something to eat inside the cottage.'

Picking through the remains of the burnt-out home they found nothing. Kira looked over to what was left of its barn. It appeared that the back half of the stone building had somehow managed to survive the fire. They started to search through the debris. Much to their surprise and delight, Kira found a barrel of stored potatoes and a smaller one of carrots and onions.

She handed Elspeth several carrots. She could never have imagined how sweet and good a raw vegetable could taste until that moment.

When they had eaten their fill, Kira opened her bundle of spare clothing and pulled out two long woollen skirts. Tying a knot in one end of each skirt, she fashioned two sacks.

She handed one to her sister. 'Here, fill this with as many carrots and potatoes as you can carry. We don't know when we might find more food.'

'Aren't we going to go and find Mother and Father?'

'No, Shadow, I already told you. The knights

took them away to the palace. Father said we should run away.'

Kira watched her sister's confused face. She could see that Elspeth still didn't quite grasp what had happened to them. 'But I want Mother—'

'So do I, but King Arden has her.'

'Why can't we go to the palace and ask him to give her back?'

'Shadow, listen to me,' Kira said tiredly. 'I told you yesterday. The king hates girls. He won't let us near the palace.'

'But what about Kahrin? You said he had her too.'

Kira was caught in the deception. Sighing, she knelt down beside her sister. 'I'm sorry, but I lied to you. The truth is Lord Dorcon has taken Kahrin to Lasser Commons. When they catch us, they are going to take us there too.'

'But Lasser is a very bad place! Mother always says so.'

'It is. That's how I know King Arden hates us. He's sending all the little girls there.'

Tears returned to Elspeth's eyes. 'I don't want to go to Lasser. I want to be with Mother and Father.'

Kira pulled her sister into a fierce hug. 'I don't want to go there either. Which is why Father told us to run away.' Kira wiped the tears from Elspeth's cheeks. 'And why we have to be extra careful.'

'But if we can't go to the palace, where can we go?'

Standing, Kira put her hands on her hips and looked around. She slowly shook her head. 'I really don't know. But I do know that we can't stay here.'

'What about the village?'

Kira had considered that. She hoped that they could find a safe place to hide. But if the knights were really gathering all the unmarried girls together and sending them to Lasser, they would have emptied the villages as well.

'I don't know, Shadow,' she said thoughtfully. 'Maybe the knights are already there. They might be waiting for us.' Turning in a circle, Kira frowned. There had to be some place safe for them to go.

Finally her eyes settled on the one place she knew Lord Dorcon or the king's men would never follow them. The trouble was, it was also the one place her father had forbidden her from ever going. But what choice did they really have?

'I think I know where we can go.' Kira finally turned back to her sister and pointed. 'Up there.'

'The mountains?'

'The Rogue's Mountain,' Kira finished. 'No one

would dare follow us there. We could be safe.'

'What about the Rogue?'

'Yes, the Rogue is there,' agreed Kira. 'But at least the king's knights won't be. We'll be safe.'

At least, she hoped they'd be.

# CHAPTER
## — 4 —

Dane stood at the small window and stared out over the torch-lit courtyard. He watched as the portcullis was raised and a line of tired knights entered. Behind them, he saw the horse-drawn cages that carried more of the villagers to the palace to work for the king.

There was an eerie silence from the villagers, as though they'd lost the will to call out for help, help they knew would never come. And as he watched the cage doors open and the people climbing down into the courtyard, their exhausted and defeated faces revealed nothing but despair.

Soon the palace guards took over from the escort knights and started to yell at the villagers. Herding them into long lines, they explained the many rules of the palace, finishing with the threat of death to anyone who dared break even one tiny rule.

But the fear Dane saw on the faces of the people

below was nothing compared to the fear he'd seen around him from the other boys who were also training to be dragon knights. These were boys who knew they were likely to die in battle very soon.

Turning his eyes from the window, Dane looked over the bunk beds in the crowded dormitory. Most of the younger boys had the covers drawn over their heads, hoping to hide the sound of their lonely tears. But it didn't work. He could hear them all.

Dane didn't cry. He couldn't. He was too angry. Instead he found himself unable to sleep as his thoughts remained constantly with his sisters. Kahrin was at Lasser. She'd committed no crime, but had been taken to the prison anyway. As for Kira and Elspeth, their fate was unknown. Rumours around the palace said that Lord Dorcon was hunting them down, intending to kill them when he caught them.

Letting his eyes drift back to the window, Dane made a silent pledge. If the rumours were true and Lord Dorcon so much as touched his sisters, then no one could stop him from killing the evil knight at the first opportunity. Lord Dorcon had been a dark shadow hanging over his family his entire life. That shadow had now become a living nightmare.

Suddenly at the end of the dormitory came the

crashing sound of the doors bursting open. The dorm master entered carrying a torch. A foul expression darkened his filthy face.

'Oy,' he shouted angrily. 'I can hear you girls whinin' all the way down the corridor. What kind of dragon knights you lot supposed to be if you spend all your time cryin' for your mummies? Now shut it and get some sleep.'

Dane watched the unwashed and toothless dorm master striding up the aisle and kicking the beds of the boys who'd been crying. But when his watery eyes came to rest on Dane at the window, he crossed over to him.

'You, boy, what you doin' there?'

When all new recruits were speaking to their superiors, they were supposed to lower their eyes. Dane flatly refused. Instead he stood before the dorm master and said, 'I couldn't sleep.'

'I don't give a flyin' rat's tail if you can sleep or not. Back to bed. Just 'cos you're the captain's son, don't give you no special privileges with me. Unless you expect me to bring you somethin' warm to drink before bed?' As he spoke, the dorm master moved a step closer and blew his foul breath into Dane's face. 'Is that it, boy? You want me to bring you a nice warm drink?'

'No, sir,' Dane answered coldly.

'Good!' the dorm master boomed. Turning away from Dane, he shouted at all the boys in the dormitory. ''Cos the sooner you brats learn that I runs this place, the better it'll be for all of you. Now get to sleep and don't none of you start cryin' again or there'll be hell to pay!'

The stink of the dorm master lingered in the air long after he had left the dormitory. Leaving the window, Dane slowly walked back to his bunk.

'You really the captain's son?' came the hushed voice of the boy from the bunk above his.

'Yeah, so?' Dane challenged.

The boy held up his hands. 'Nothing. I'm just surprised to find out you're the captain's son and still stuck in here with the rest of us.'

'Where else would I be?'

'With your father, I'd have thought.'

Dane leaned his head against the side of the bunk and sighed heavily. 'No, they won't let me. The only time I get to see him is during training at the stables. They won't even let me see my mother. I know she's here somewhere, but I don't know where.'

'It's different for me,' the boy said lightly, leaning over the side of the bed to speak. 'I don't have any family to miss. It's always been just me. I'm Shanks-

Spar, by the way. You can call me Shanks.'

Dane looked at him and nodded. 'I'm Dane.'

'How long have you been at the palace?' Shanks asked.

'Not long. A few days.'

'You come in one of those big cages?'

'No. Because of my father, we had an escort.'

'You're lucky. The way I see them treating the people in the cages, I sure wouldn't want to be in one of them.'

'Lucky?' Dane repeated, laughing without humour. 'Did you say lucky? How lucky is it to have your family torn apart? One sister sent to Lasser, the other two on the run from Lord Dorcon. You think that's lucky?'

Shanks shook his head slowly. 'Sorry, I didn't know.'

'Yeah, well, next time, think before you speak. Better yet, don't say anything at all.'

'Fine!' Shanks said angrily. 'I'm sorry I cared.'

Dane watched Shanks turn over in his bunk and pull the covers up over his head. Shaking his own head, he sank heavily down in his bunk in crushing despair. How could it have all gone so very wrong?

# CHAPTER
## ~5~

After setting out for the mountains, Kira quickly discovered that they were much farther away than she ever imagined. As a child she'd always thought the mountains were small. But after several long days of walking, she realized that they weren't small at all. In fact they were very big, just very far away.

Somewhere along the journey, Kira noticed that Elspeth was being followed. Whatever direction they walked, wherever they went, a small red fox seemed to be moving alongside her. But whenever Kira tried to approach, it would growl and yip at her and then dart off, only to return when she had moved away.

Late one night as they sat by their small fire, not only was the fox still with them, it now boldly approached Elspeth. With very few carrots and potatoes left, Kira didn't feel particularly inclined to share their meagre meal. But on more than one occasion, she caught

Elspeth tossing small pieces of potato to it.

'Shadow, you need that more than he does. Don't give him any more.'

While she spoke, Kira noticed the fox moving steadily closer to Elspeth, but he was staring directly at her. In fact, if Kira didn't know better, she could have sworn he was squinting at her, challenging her to say or do something. It wasn't a nice expression at all. Picking up a small pebble, she tossed it at the animal. 'Go home, Fox. There's nothing more for you here.'

Letting out a light yip, the fox darted out of the way and disappeared into the underbrush.

'Kira, that was mean!'

'I didn't hurt him,' she said defensively. 'Now, we've had a long day and it's getting late. I'm tired, so let's get to bed.'

Pulling out their bed covers, Kira made another small nest for her and Elspeth to sleep on. Curling up together, it wasn't long before they were both heavily asleep.

The startling sound of 'yip' woke Kira with a fright. Sitting bolt up, she discovered that not only had the fox returned, he was now sitting right beside Elspeth's head. In his mouth he held a dead pheasant.

'Onnie's back,' Elspeth said as she sat up and rubbed her eyes.

'Onnie?'

'That's his name,' Elspeth explained.

'How do you know?' Kira demanded.

'He told me,' Elspeth answered lightly. She then turned her attention back to the fox. 'Onnie, what are you doing back here? I don't have anything for you. And you look like you've got plenty there.'

In answer, the fox lowered the pheasant to the ground before her. He gave another small 'yip' then dashed off into the tall grass.

Giggling, Elspeth called after him. 'Come back here, Kira won't be mean to you any more.'

Kira could do nothing but stare in stunned silence. If she ever doubted her sister's strange charms with animals, the fox's odd behaviour removed them. Taking a final look around, she carefully reached for the dead bird. Holding it up to her nose, it smelled fresh. With her stomach growling from lack of solid food, the thought of a pheasant meal set her mouth watering.

While she built up the fire, Elspeth plucked the bird. Kira then set it up over the fire to cook. The tempting aroma of roasting pheasant filled the air, and by the time they took their first bite, both girls were feeling half starved.

Concentrating on her meal, Kira didn't notice the fox's silent return. It was only when Elspeth started to giggle that she saw him gently taking small pieces of meat right from her sister's hand.

'Shadow, be careful,' she warned.

'He won't bite,' said Elspeth confidently. 'Look how sweet he is.'

Kira watched her sister handing the fox another piece of pheasant. The small animal received it gently into his mouth and then lightly licked Elspeth's hand.

'See, I told you,' she giggled.

Kira watched in amazement as Elspeth shared her portion with the fox. Studying the animal closely, she could see that the fox showed no signs of hostility or viciousness. If anything, his big brown eyes followed Elspeth's every move with what could only be described as affection.

When they finished their meal, they felt full for the first time in ages. Settling back down to sleep, Kira expected to see the fox drift away. But she wasn't too surprised either when he settled down on the covers at Elspeth's feet.

Early the next morning, Kira awoke to the feeling of warm fur tickling the back of her neck and the sound of Elspeth's giggles. Opening her eyes, she rolled over and found the fox standing between them, playfully licking Elspeth's face.

'Stop that! Go away!' Kira tried to swat the animal. But when her hand made contact with the fox, he suddenly turned and nipped her painfully on the fingers. Crying out, she sat up and shifted further away. When she inspected her fingers, Kira saw tiny teeth marks that were just short of breaking the skin.

'Elspeth, be careful, he's a wild animal,' Kira warned. 'And he just bit me.'

'You hit him first,' Elspeth said as she protectively scooped the fox up in her arms.

'Yes, but look, he really bit me!' Kira held up her fingers to reveal the fox's teeth impressions, still showing on her skin. 'He's vicious! Put him down.'

'No, he's not,' Elspeth defended, refusing to release the fox. 'He loves me and I love him.'

Kira sat back on her haunches and eyed the fox suspiciously. He narrowed his eyes again as if to warn her away. He then lowered his head and began to lick the back of Elspeth's hand, sending her into more fits of giggles. Watching them, Kira was torn. She knew she should probably drive the fox away. Yet at the same time, his presence was making her little sister happy. After all they had suffered, all they had lost, could she really take that away from Elspeth as well?

The answer was no.

'All right,' Kira finally said. 'He can stay. But the moment he acts strange with you, he goes.'

'He won't,' Elspeth promised. 'You'll see. Soon you'll love him too.'

Kira frowned in doubt, but said nothing more.

That afternoon, however, the fox did start to act strangely. Very strangely. One moment he was walking contentedly at Elspeth's side, the next he was jumping around in front of her and yipping wildly.

'What is it, Onnie?' Elspeth asked as she bent down to the fox's level. Turning to look up at Kira, she said, 'He's is trying to tell me something important.'

In answer, the fox darted into the bushes. He then came racing back. Yipping at them again, he turned and raced back into the bushes.

'He wants us to follow him,' Elspeth said seriously. 'Something bad is going to happen.'

'No, Shadow, he just wants to play,' Kira said tiredly. She turned towards the fox. 'We don't want to play, Onnie, we're too tired.'

The fox returned to Elspeth and yipped even louder.

'Kira, you're wrong!' Elspeth said firmly, starting to rise. 'Something bad is going to happen.' Reaching for

Kira's hand, Elspeth dragged her towards the bushes. 'Come on, we've got to hurry.'

Kira stopped resisting and followed her sister.

'This way,' Elspeth ordered as she trailed behind the fox.

'All right, I'm coming.' Kira irritably shoved away the sharp branches that caught in her hair. 'This had better be good.'

The three had barely ducked into the bushes when they heard the heavy pounding of horses' hooves on the ground. Crouching down, Kira watched in shock as Lord Dorcon rode past their hiding spot. Sitting aloft his huge, black, armoured horse, he moved further along the trail then drew to a stop. Holding up his arm, the rest of his men stopped also. Lifting his visor, he inspected the ground and then the surrounding area.

'They can't be far,' he called. 'Their fire was still warm. They must be in this area somewhere. Keep searching. I want them found by nightfall!'

Kira's heart pounded fiercely in her chest as she watched Lord Dorcon and his men searching the ground for traces of their presence. Barely able to breathe, she prayed he didn't find them in the bushes.

Daring to steal a glance at her sister, Kira found Elspeth clutching the fox tightly in her arms. Her terrified eyes were glued to Lord Dorcon. The fox was baring his teeth and growling softly. But not at Elspeth – his aggression was directed at the knights.

Still holding her breath, Kira's eyes returned to Lord Dorcon. Climbing down from his horse, he bent low to the ground and seemed to search for something. After a moment, he nodded and stood up.

'This ground has not been disturbed in days. I don't think they've made it this far.' He pointed back down the trail from where they came. 'We'll back-track and see if we can't pick them up again—' Suddenly he paused.

Standing perfectly still, he tilted his head to the side. Listening. Slowly he turned. His eyes darted to their hiding spot. 'There!' he shouted, taking several long strides towards them.

This was it, Kira thought. The fox's growls had given them away. But just as Lord Dorcon entered the bushes, Onnie leaped free of Elspeth's arms. Flashing between the tall knight's legs, he turned and viciously bit into his calf.

Lord Dorcon howled in pain, lost his footing and fell heavily to the ground. As he clutched his bleeding leg, Onnie yipped and made straight for the line of mounted knights.

The effect of the fox's sudden and noisy appearance was immediate. Horses reared and whinnied in terror. Knights were thrown from their saddles and landed with heavy thumps on the hard ground. Several other horses were blinded by panic and started to bolt, taking their hapless riders with them.

Cursing loudly, Lord Dorcon climbed to his feet. He limped over to his rearing horse, reached for his sword and chased after the fox. But Onnie was too fast.

'Cursed fox!' Lord Dorcon cried as he gave up the chase. Turning back to his knights, he caught several men chuckling lightly as they watched him lose his temper.

'What's so funny?' Lord Dorcon demanded as he stormed over to his men.

Falling in line, the knights stood at attention as they answered. 'Nothing, sir.'

Still limping, Lord Dorcon walked to the end of the line. Stopping before one of the knights who'd laughed at him, he lowered his voice menacingly. 'I saw you laughing at me. Did you think this was amusing?'

'No my Lord, not at all,' the terrified knight answered.

As Kira watched from her hiding place, she saw Lord Dorcon start to walk away. But in a move faster than lightning, he suddenly turned back and ran the knight through with his sword.

When he pulled his weapon free from the dead knight, he looked over to his other men. 'Does anyone else think I am the subject of humour?'

'No, my Lord,' everyone echoed.

Drawing a scarf from inside his breastplate, Lord Dorcon started to wipe dust and twigs off his polished armour. 'Let this be a lesson to you all. I will not tolerate laughter. Do I make myself clear?'

'Yes, my Lord,' everyone agreed.

When he finished cleaning his armour, Lord Dorcon wiped the knight's blood from his sword. 'Very well,' he said. 'You men, gather your horses together. We're going back to pick up the trail. I'll be damned if I'm bested by the captain's daughters!'

Not waiting for his knights, Lord Dorcon stormed up to his horse and climbed into the saddle. Kicking his spurs viciously into the horse's flanks, he took off back down the trail from where they'd come.

Moments later his dazed knights followed.

Finally they passed into the distance. Kira let out a heavy sigh of relief. Looking over to Elspeth, she was stunned to discover the fox had somehow returned and was once again cradled in her arms. But watching Elspeth's face, Kira saw horror shining in her frightened eyes.

'He killed him,' Elspeth murmured softly. 'All he did was laugh and he killed him . . .'

'Lord Dorcon is a very bad man,' Kira said. 'We've got to be extra careful.'

Saying nothing further, Elspeth nodded.

At the fox's insistence, Kira and Elspeth remained hidden within the bushes. Finally, after a time, he jumped free of Elspeth's arms and stepped back out on to the trail. Turning to Elspeth, he gave a few short yips.

'Onnie says it's safe now,' Elspeth said quietly as she stood and followed him out.

Back on the trail, Kira's eyes couldn't help but linger on the fallen knight. His armour was exactly the same as her father used to wear, except for the medallion on his chest. Her father had his own insignia, while this knight wore Lord Dorcon's crest.

Drawing Elspeth away from the scene, she still couldn't believe that Lord Dorcon would actually kill one of his own men. When they were well away from the dead knight, Kira looked down on the fox. 'I don't know how you did it,' she admitted, 'but Onnie, you just saved our lives. Thank you.'

# CHAPTER
## ~6~

Dane woke to the harsh sounds of the dorm master storming through the dormitory. He was yelling at the boys and dragging them from their bunks. If it was possible, he smelled even worse than he had before. As he walked past Dane's bed, he kicked the frame at the bottom.

'Oy, captain's son. You waitin' for a special invitation? Get up!'

Climbing from his bunk, Dane looked up and found Shanks was already up and away from the bed.

They hadn't spoken a word to each other since the night he'd told Shanks to think before he spoke. Dane still felt bad about that. It hadn't been Shanks's fault. Now too many days had passed to clear things up.

He dressed quickly and joined the other boys on the march to the kitchen for their daily bowl of tasteless broth and a chunk of hard bread. After that, they were herded into the antechamber of the dragon stables to begin the day's lessons on dragon warfare.

Gathered in the spacious training room, Dane stood apart from the others, not talking, and not doing anything to encourage friendship. He was alone and wanted it kept that way. It was only when his father arrived, hobbling on his crutches, that Dane's face brightened.

They'd spoken little during their time together. Guards constantly surrounded his father and warned him off if he approached Dane to speak privately. This only served to anger Dane further as he ached for news of his mother and to know if they'd heard anything about his sisters.

Soon his father stood before the group of students and started to teach. As Dane struggled to listen, from the back of the group some of the older boys were making cruel comments about the captain's missing leg. They were laughing at him and calling him names for letting his own dragon attack him.

Dane tried his best to ignore their remarks and concentrate on his father. But when their comments became unbearable, he turned back and ordered them to shut up. This only caused more laughter and crude comments about his father.

Dane turned to the leader of the small gang. 'I'm

warning you, Nat, shut your mouth, or I'll shut it for you.'

Nat laughed and spoke even louder. 'Yeah, what are you going to do about it, cry to Daddy?' Nat nudged his mate. 'I'm sure the captain would punish me if he could catch me. But wait, he's only got one leg, he can't!'

The group of boys around him burst out laughing.

'Maybe not,' Dane quietly agreed as he slowly balled his hands into tight fists, 'but I can!'

Finally, all the pent-up frustrations and anger within him bubbled to the surface as Dane launched a vicious attack on Nat. Leading with his fists he punched Nat so hard in the face they both fell over. Soon they were rolling around on the ground, punching and tearing at each other with all the strength they possessed.

The other members of Nat's gang quickly joined in as they tried to haul Dane off their leader. But just as they caught hold of his arms, Shanks dashed forward and started to tear them away.

Dane soon found himself fighting side by side with Shanks against Nat and his entire gang. He heard his father and the guards shouting and ordering them to stop. But Dane couldn't. His rage wouldn't be stopped.

It took Dane's father, with the help of all the guards

in the room, to eventually break up the fight. When it was finally over, Dane and Shanks were hauled off to one side of the antechamber while the guards herded the remainder of the class to the other.

'What the hell was that all about?' The captain roared, standing no more than a hand's-breadth from Dane's face.

'Captain, it wasn't Dane's fault!' Shanks defended as he wiped blood away from his bleeding nose. 'They started it!'

The captain turned furiously to Shanks and held up a warning finger. 'Was I speaking to you?'

Shanks lowered his eyes. 'No, sir.'

The captain looked back to Dane. 'Son, you just can't go around picking fights with people who annoy you.'

'But Father,' Dane argued. 'You don't understand. They were making fun of you and what happened with Ariel! I couldn't bear what they were saying.'

Hearing this took all the anger out of his father. Calming, he shook his head. 'I do understand, Dane, I promise you,' he sighed. 'But you've got to control that temper of yours. I won't be able to teach you much longer. Soon they'll be sending you off to war. You've got to be prepared.'

'I don't want to go to war!' Dane cried furiously. 'All I ever wanted was to be a farmer, not a fighter. Kira wanted to be the dragon knight, not me.'

Heedless of the guards around him, the captain reached out and put his hands lightly on Dane's shoulders. 'I know that, son, and you were a good farmer too. But that's gone now. King Arden wants to increase the size of his kingdom, so we must attack our neighbours and take from them what he wants.'

'Even if it's wrong?' Shanks timidly asked.

The captain looked over to Shanks and nodded. 'Even if it's wrong. He's our king. We have no choice but to serve him and do whatever he orders us to.'

'How can I do that?' Dane argued. 'How can I serve a king who's put Kahrin in Lasser? I don't even know what's happened to Kira and Elspeth. Are they still alive?'

'They are,' the captain said softly. 'Dorcon hasn't found them yet and the king is furious. He's confiscated all Dorcon's lands and before long, he'll be in complete disgrace. You should be very proud of your two sisters – they have achieved more than I ever could against Lord Dorcon.'

'Enough over there!' one of the guards harshly called. 'Captain, your class is waiting.'

The captain nodded and then gave Dane's shoulders a final squeeze. 'Listen to me son,' he said, then looked over to Shanks. 'Both of you. Take these lessons I offer. Learn all you can. It's all I have left to give you. I just pray it will be enough to see you through the awful times ahead.'

Dane put his hands on his father's arms. 'I will, Father. You'll see. I'll be the best dragon knight in the palace. I'll make you proud of me.'

'I already am,' the captain said softly as he hobbled back to the front of the class.

When he was gone, Dane looked over to Shanks and nodded awkwardly. 'Thanks for backing me up.'

Shanks smiled brightly. 'Not a problem. I know you could have taken them – I just didn't want to miss out on all the fun.'

'Yeah, fun, you're right,' Dane said softly. 'So much fun, my eye should be good and black by tomorrow.'

'See what I mean?' Shanks said, laughing as he walked back towards the class. 'Fun.'

# CHAPTER
## ~7~

After countless days, Kira and Elspeth reached the base of the Rogue's Mountain. Ahead of them, they faced a thick, dense forest that climbed steadily upward. Keeping to the only trail that cut through the forest, Kira began to hope they'd seen the last of Lord Dorcon. But those hopes quickly faded when Onnie started to act strangely again.

Standing with his ears pricked, he sniffed the air. Suddenly he went mad, yipping and running around.

'He's coming!' Elspeth cried.

Moments later, Kira and Elspeth heard the heavy pounding of horses' hooves directly behind them. Lord Dorcon was bearing down on them with his sword drawn and raised in the air.

Grasping Elspeth's hand, Kira yanked her forward. 'Run, Shadow, run!'

'You girls, stop there!' Lord Dorcon roared, as he

forced more speed out of his charging horse. 'I command you to stop!'

Blinded by terror, the girls followed Onnie off the trail and smashed their way into the dark dense trees. Keeping low, they pushed steadily forward. But when the undergrowth forced them into an even tighter area, Kira glanced back over her shoulder and screamed.

Lord Dorcon was right behind her. Crawling on his hands and knees, he had thrown off his armoured gloves and breastplate and was tearing through the undergrowth faster than they were.

'Stop!' he viciously commanded. 'Stop and face your punishment!'

'Go away!' Kira screamed. 'Just leave us alone!'

'Never!'

'Faster, Elspeth!' Kira cried as she dragged her sister along. 'Move faster!'

With the forest growing denser, Kira could no longer stay beside her sister. Releasing her hand, she shoved Elspeth ahead. 'Keep moving!'

Stealing another glance back, Kira saw that in keeping his helmet on and visor down, the thorns and branches that cut into their faces and slowed them down weren't bothering Lord Dorcon at all. He was swiftly gaining on them.

'Faster,' Kira cried. She screamed again as Lord Dorcon lunged forward and caught her by the ankle.

Knocking her to the ground, he tightened his grip further as he wrenched her back. 'I've got you now. You're mine!'

'No!' Kira howled. 'No, let me go!' Struggling against the strong hand that held her fast, she kicked and tried to break free of the knight's painful grip. But the more she fought, the harder he pulled. Catching hold of branches and roots did little to stop her from being drawn back into the deadly arms of Lord Dorcon.

Desperate to escape, Kira suddenly remembered the knight's dagger resting in her waistline. Reaching down, she pulled the blade free from its sheath. Then spinning back, she stabbed it down into the hand that wrapped around her ankle.

Lord Dorcon's howls of pain and rage mixed with Kira's shouts of triumph as he instantly released her and drew back his bleeding hand.

Not waiting to see what she'd done to him, Kira moved. Keeping hidden within the trees, they heard Lord Dorcon's enraged curses fill the air behind them like a dark rumbling storm.

\* \* \*

With their third near capture behind them, Kira and Elspeth kept well hidden within the thick undergrowth as they finally started their journey up the side of the mountain.

Travelling up the Rogue's Mountain proved much harder and slower than they expected. But finally, as they made it to the halfway point, Kira let herself breathe a sigh of relief that the worst of their journey was behind them.

This relief was short lived. Rising early one morning, Kira felt that something around them had changed. The forest was silent. No bird song. No rustling of small animals. Nothing. Looking over to Onnie, she saw his eyes were bright and alert. His ears were down and the hackles at the back of his neck were raised as strange growling sounds came from deep in his throat.

Keeping her voice low, Kira crouched over her sister. 'Shadow, wake up. Something's wrong. It might be Lord Dorcon again.'

Elspeth sat up immediately and turned to the fox. 'No, it's something else.'

Kira quickly gathered their few possessions together. Taking Elspeth by the hand, she started to run. They raced up a steady incline, until they reached a small clearing and stopped to catch their breath.

Kira gazed back down the mountain. 'I don't see anything,' she panted heavily. 'No knights, no fire — there's nothing down there.'

Suddenly Onnie went mad. Racing around their feet and yipping, he tried to drive them away from the open area.

'What's wrong with him?' Kira demanded.

A ferocious roar filled the air. Instantly crouching down, they looked up fearfully. There, they saw him. The Rogue. Soaring overhead and gliding smoothly over the tops of the trees.

Kira had never see a dragon this close before. He was huge. He was terrifying. He was magnificent! Ferarchie was the colour of purple grapes at the end of the season as every one of his scales glittered like sunlight on water. Scattered along the length of his body, Kira could see remnants of the battle armour that used to cover him.

When the dragon glided smoothly over their heads, he swooped so low that Kira felt all she had to do was reach up to touch his smooth pale underside. It was only when Onnie started yipping again that she realized the danger. They were still out in the open and exposed to the dragon. Should he see either of them, there would be no chance to get away.

Catching hold of Elspeth's jumper, Kira moved them forward. They raced deeper into the wood and ducked behind a thick tree trunk. When Kira felt they were safe, she rose. Ignoring the warning yips from Onnie, she crept back to the edge of the clearing.

'Kira, no,' Elspeth warned. 'He'll see you and come back.'

'No he won't,' Kira assured her. Peering up, she couldn't see or hear the dragon any more. 'He's not here. Maybe he's gone further down the mountain.' She took another step out. Suddenly a huge shadow cut across her path. Quickly turning, she saw the Rogue bearing down on her. Mouth open and sharp teeth ready to bite.

'No!' Kira screamed as the dragon swooped down to bite. 'No—'

Suddenly Elspeth was at her side, wrenching her out of the way. They lost their balance and fell together into the protection of the trees. In that same instant, the Rogue's huge mouth snapped shut in the space where Kira had been standing. Never losing momentum, he swooped away from the clearing and roared in rage at missing her.

'Kira, are you all right?' Elspeth cried as she hovered over her.

Kira sat up and leaned against a thick tree trunk. She was panting heavily as tears of fear streamed down her cheeks. 'He tried to eat me!'

'Father always said he was bad,' Elspeth offered.

'Yes, but I thought I could tame him. I can't. Father was right; Ferarchie is dangerous. All he saw in me was food.' Suddenly the idea of spending the entire winter on the mountain didn't seem such a good one. 'Maybe I was wrong, Shadow,' she admitted. 'Maybe we should find somewhere else to live.'

Elspeth moved closer to her side. Immediately Onnie jumped on to her lap and stared up into her face. 'No, we've got to stay here,' she said in a light but serious voice. 'Lord Dorcon and all his men are looking for us down below. There is only the Rogue up here. If we listen to Onnie and all the other animals, we can stay.'

Kira didn't say anything for a long time. She couldn't erase the vision of Ferarchie's awful mouth snapping shut. 'I don't know,' she finally said.

Further down the mountain they heard another roar and a loud crashing sound. Despite her terror and the protests from Elspeth and Onnie, Kira couldn't help herself. She had to see.

Peering around the trunk, she gazed into the sky.

High over the treetops she saw him again. In his mouth he held the stag he'd just caught. Kira watched the monstrous dragon throw back his head and swallow the animal whole.

When he was gone, Kira sat back against the tree again and shook her head. 'That stag was huge but Ferarchie swallowed him in one. If he'd got me, he wouldn't have even tasted me!'

Before long the sounds of the forest started to return. The danger had passed. 'Maybe there is a way we can live on the mountain. Onnie knew the Rogue was coming. So did the rest of the forest. If we learn to pay attention, to hide whenever he's around, perhaps we can stay safe?'

'See, I told you,' Elspeth said proudly. 'Onnie really wants to help us.'

In response, the fox wagged his bushy tail and started licking her chin excitedly.

Elspeth's infectious giggles made Kira smile. 'All right, all right,' she finally surrendered. 'We'll stay.'

# CHAPTER
## ~ 8 ~

Dane spent every waking moment learning all he could about warfare. Though he never showed it, it sickened him to discover how many ways there were to kill an opponent.

Seeing the growing friendship forming between them, the captain paired Dane up with Shanks. All the other boys in the dorm were then paired up as well. The captain explained to his class that each would be the other's 'wingmate' and the bonds they formed would become the strongest of their lives.

As the class moved from instructor to instructor, they were taught sword fighting, use of bow and arrow and lance, and finally hand-to-hand combat. Long, hard days were spent on the training field until their hands bled and their bodies were covered with bruises. But soon, Dane watched his classmates changing. No longer the frightened boys crying in the dorm, these were now strong, confident young dragon knights.

Much to Dane's frustration, he hadn't had another opportunity to speak at length with his father. He now only saw him for brief periods in the morning as the students returned to the dragon stable's antechamber to learn about dragon warfare.

It was during one of these short encounters that his father was able to let Dane know that Kira and Elspeth were still eluding Lord Dorcon. In fact, the knight had been called back to the palace to explain himself to the king. Feeling no sympathy for the evil knight, Dane hoped the king would have him put to death for his failure.

'Maybe the king will have him tortured,' Shanks suggested hopefully as late one evening he and Dane walked quietly through the torch-lit corridors of the palace. 'Maybe put his eyes out.'

'I wish,' Dane said. 'But my father said if the king wanted Lord Dorcon dead, he'd have sent an assassin. I'm just hoping he makes him give up chasing my sisters and sends him into battle.'

'Now that would be great!' Shanks said. 'The way we're losing men, he wouldn't last a day out there. I heard things are getting pretty bad. I don't think King Arden expected King Casey to put up a fight. But what else could he do? What would happen if he didn't?'

'Look what's happening to our people!' Dane whispered angrily as they carefully stepped over villagers sleeping in the palace corridors. 'There's no room for all these people here at the palace, but every day, the king keeps bringing more. How are they supposed to eat? There was no harvest. We'll be out of food soon. Then what?'

'Then King Arden will have more to worry about than his attack on Casey,' Shanks offered.

'And in the meantime, a lot of good people are dying for no good reason,' Dane said bitterly.

Dane and Shanks walked tiredly back to their bunks. Around them, other young knights were also arriving from their late-night training.

'Hey, Dane, Shanks,' Tobias called excitedly as he crossed over to where Dane was undressing. 'Did you hear the news? They're assigning us our dragons tomorrow. Then it's a few days of practical training, and we're off to join our regiments in the battle.'

Both Dane and Shanks liked Tobias. Everyone in the dormitory did. Being fifteen, he was a year younger than Dane and two years younger than Shanks, He was the smallest of all the young dragon knights. But despite the teasing he received, he always had a bright smile on his face and was quick to make everyone laugh.

'Isn't that great,' he said. 'We're finally getting our dragons!'

'They going to give you the shortest dragon, right Toby?' Shanks cheerily asked as he pulled off his jerkin.

Tobias shook his head. 'Hope not. I want the biggest one in the whole stable! Then everybody'll know who I am.'

Dane looked at his young friend. 'Everyone already does, Toby. Just promise me you'll be careful around your dragon. Remember what happened to my father.'

'Yeah,' Shanks teased. 'Watch yourself. I hear dragons like their meals small and packed with flavour.'

Despite the teasing, Tobias smiled brightly. 'You'll see. I'll have the best dragon in the palace. Then King Casey will see me in the sky and surrender immediately!'

'You bet he will,' Shanks laughed as he ruffled Tobias's hair.

When Tobias walked away, his face still beaming, Dane watched him sadly. 'He shouldn't be a dragon knight. He's got the heart for it, but not the body. They should keep him as a page or stable assistant.'

'You're right,' agreed Shanks. 'He's a great kid. But he can't hold a lance with one hand. How's he supposed to support a lance while directing a dragon? It's insane.'

As he climbed into bed, Dane agreed. 'This whole thing is insane.'

Waking early the next morning, everyone was dressed long before the dorm master arrived. When he noisily barged in and saw everyone up and moving, he marched straight out again without saying a single word – but not before Shanks saw the look on his face.

'Hey Dane,' he called as he drew on his uniform. 'Did you see Stinky's face?'

Dane shook his head. Shanks laughed. 'I think the old goat is going to miss us when we're gone. That, or he's got a very bad toothache.'

'Stinky doesn't have any teeth,' Dane remarked.

'Exactly,' Shanks laughed.

Around them, the dorm was buzzing with excited dragon knights preparing to start their training on real dragons. But Dane felt none of their excitement. He hated dragons. Always had, always would. As he and Shanks walked together to the stables, he felt an increasing sense of dread.

'It won't be so bad, you'll see,' Shanks offered. 'We've learned a lot more about dragons since Ariel attacked your father. I heard they have even more armour on their mouths to keep them shut. Poor beasts can barely eat. But at least it keeps their knights safe.'

Dane inhaled deeply. 'Maybe,' he finally said. 'I just don't like them. Kira was the one who loved dragons, not me. She'd have done anything to be here and learn how to ride them.'

'With First Law?' Shanks said. 'Not very likely. She'd be put to death the moment she came within spitting distance of a dragon.'

'I don't think she'd have cared. Not if she could spend just one day with them.'

'I think I'd like to meet that sister of yours,' Shanks said. 'Maybe when the war is over.'

'Perhaps,' Dane said darkly. He didn't mention the subject they both knew was hanging in the air like thunder – the fact that Kira and Elspeth were already guilty of breaking First Law. Whether there was a war or not, they both had death warrants hanging over their heads.

Shanks quickly changed the subject. 'Well, I can understand why you hate dragons, but I don't. I'm looking forward to learning how to ride and fly with one.'

Dane looked at Shanks, but said nothing more. Instead he concentrated on the time ahead. He knew it was his father's job to assign the dragons to their riders.

He just hoped he'd picked good ones for him and Shanks.

'Good morning, knights,' the captain said as he and his guards entered the antechamber.

'Morning, Captain,' the knights all responded.

'As you know, today is the day you will all receive your mounts. The dragons you are assigned today will stay with you for the rest of your careers. You alone will feed your animals. You alone will care for them. If they are wounded in battle, you are responsible for their treatment. There is no one else to help you. Your dragon lives or dies on your actions alone.'

The captain stopped speaking as he hobbled through the group of young dragon knights. Finally he stopped before Dane and Shanks, but addressed the group. 'Just remember this. A dragon can be your closest ally, or your worst enemy. It all depends on how you treat him. If you can respect him, while at the same time remembering he is a wild, dangerous animal, there's no reason why you can't have long and successful careers together. It's all up to you.'

'What about you with Ariel?' Nat finally challenged, laughing and nudging his friends. 'What gives you the right to tell us how to treat our animals when you let your own dragon attack you?'

The hair on the back of Dane's neck rose as he turned and prepared to launch on the bully again. It was only his father's hand dropping firmly on his shoulder that stopped him.

'Nat has a very valid point,' the captain said to the group as he squeezed Dane's shoulder. 'I have the right to teach you because I *was* attacked. Many years ago, I made a terrible mistake, a mistake that anyone could make. But it cost me my leg and damn near took my life as well.'

The captain's eyes glazed over as his mind cast back into the memories of that awful time. 'We had just made it back from a particularly difficult battle. I was exhausted, but so was Ariel. I had just finished feeding him and bedding him down for the night. He seemed so calm and peaceful. No roaring. He just looked at me. Well, I thought after so long together, Ariel and I had an understanding. We didn't. I turned my back on him and he attacked me. It was only luck he didn't kill me. I just pray that none of you will ever have to face the same ordeal.'

'What happened to Ariel?' Tobias asked.

'He was destroyed,' the captain answered. 'All dragons who attack their knights are. But it wasn't what I wanted. The mistake had been mine, not his.

Ariel was only following his nature. But by the time I was well enough to speak again, it was too late and he was dead.

'So,' the captain continued as he left Dane and walked through the class, 'don't make the same error in judgement. By all means, care for your dragon. But don't for one instant think he cares for you. He doesn't. Dragons are incapable of feeling anything other than rage.'

When he finished speaking, the captain hobbled towards the doors to the main stables. 'Now, I am going to call you forward in pairs. We will go into the stables together and you will be assigned your dragons. From there, you will learn how to ride, fly and finally fight from the back of your mount.'

Dane and Shanks stood with the rest of the class as they waited to be called forward. Finally, when everyone else had gone, the captain reappeared and led them into the stable.

Dane had only been through the huge stables once before. Now as he walked slowly beside his father, he looked at the long line of enormous stalls to see the heavily armoured dragons chained within. There seemed to be beasts of every colour as he spied the scales that showed beneath the heavy armour on their long necks. At their exposed feet, long claws pawed the ground and tore into the stone floor leaving deep gashes behind them. Their eyes were wide and sharp while their thick tails lashed the walls of the stalls. Around him, the air was filled with the growling and hissing of the vicious beasts.

Walking down the centre of the aisle, Dane's stomach knotted in fear. Any one of these dragons could kill him in any number of ways. Just being struck by a whipping tail would be enough to kill a grown man. And now he was expected to actually approach one and climb on its back!

'I've spoken with the stable manager,' the captain said as he studied Dane's pale face, 'and have come to know several of the dragons myself. These two are the least aggressive animals in the stables. I've kept them aside especially for you.'

They stopped before the stalls of two very large, very angry-looking dragons.

'Dane, this one is yours,' the captain said, pointing to a large dragon that wasn't exactly black, but more a dark charcoal in colour. 'Shanks, that red one beside him is yours.'

Cautiously stepping up to the plaque hung on the outside of the stall, Dane read the name – Rexor.

'Rexor?' he repeated. 'What kind of name is that?'

'Well, it's better than Harmony,' Shanks answered, laughing as he stood before the nameplate of the bright red dragon. 'Who thinks of calling a vicious animal like this Harmony? What are some of the other names? Buttercup, Sweetpea, Lamb Chop?'

'Names aren't important,' the captain said. 'It's the dragon that counts. These two are from the same clutch. Brother and sister. They are calm-natured and haven't given the stable workers any trouble at all. Treat them with care and I promise you, they will serve you well.'

Dane gazed into the huge golden eyes of the armoured dragon he was now supposed to spend the rest of his life with. He felt for sure he was about to throw up. 'Father,' he hesitantly said. 'Forgive me, but I don't think I can do this. I'm not Kira. Dragons really scare me.'

The captain looked around the stables for any of the guards. 'Don't you dare let me catch you saying that again,' he tightly warned. 'And don't make the mistake of letting Rexor know it either. He's a dragon. If he senses your fear, you will lose control. He'll kill you, Dane. Faster than any sword ever could.'

'But they're so big. How do we control them?' Shanks quickly asked.

The captain's eyes lingered on Dane's for a moment more before turning to Shanks. 'That is what the next few days are all about. For as big and powerful as dragons are, they have a few weak spots. We know about those and use them against the animal. For example, see here.' The captain drew their eyes to the heavy bit extending out on either side of Rexor's large snout.

'It may look like a horse's bit, but it's not. There are sharp spikes all over it pressing into the dragon's sensitive tongue and roof of his mouth. From the very first day they hatch, the young dragons learn that when they misbehave, or try to fight us, one good tug on that bit and they are in terrible pain. Dragons may be vicious animals, but they are not stupid. It doesn't take them long to learn that when they behave there is no pain. But if they play up, they will spend days with a mouth full of their own blood.'

'Father, that's awful,' protested Dane. 'All they'll ever know is cruelty.'

'Can you think of a better way to control these beasts?' the captain asked. 'Dane, I once thought as you did. I let my heart rule my head with Ariel. Look where it got me.'

Dane looked at his dragon and then to his father.

Finally he turned back to Rexor again. The animal was impossibly big. How else but with fear and pain was a man supposed to control something as powerful as that?

'Now,' the captain continued. 'Dane and Shanks, I want you to join the rest of your class in the training yard. There's a dragon knight with his mount out there, ready to show you what you'll need to know. Get along now. I've got another class of recruits waiting for me.'

As Dane started to walk away, his father called after him. He turned, and saw the captain standing on his one leg with his arms outstretched.

Dashing into those arms, Dane hugged him fiercely.

'Please be careful,' the captain said tightly. 'I wish it could have been different, Dane, I really do. I know this wasn't the life you chose for yourself, and I'm sorry. But none of us gets to choose.'

'It's all right,' Dane said, squeezing his father. 'I'll be careful, I promise.'

The captain sniffed back tears. 'And remember, of all the lessons I can teach you, take this to heart. Don't ever turn your back on your mount. Please, Dane, don't let Rexor do to you what Ariel did to me.'

'I won't, Father,' he promised.

In an uncharacteristic show of affection, the captain kissed Dane on the forehead and squeezed him even tighter. 'I do love you, son. You know that, don't you? I always have, and I always will. Promise me, whatever happens, whatever you hear about me, you will always remember that I have loved you and your sisters more than anything in this world. I'll do whatever I must to protect you.'

'I'll remember,' Dane said as a knot choked his throat.

Finally the captain released him and looked over to Shanks. 'You take good care of my son, Shanks.'

'I will, Captain,' Shanks said, nodding.

Then he looked at Dane. 'And you take care of your wingmate there. Shanks is a good lad.'

'I will, Father,' Dane promised.

'Now, off you go,' said the captain as he furiously wiped away a tear that had escaped his eye. 'You don't want to miss any of your training.'

As they walked away, Dane looked back at his father a final time. Standing alone, resting heavily on his crutch, he suddenly looked very old and fragile.

Shanks also looked back at the captain. Then patted Dane lightly on the back. 'He'll be fine, Dane. He's just worried about you.'

Dane inhaled deeply and forced himself to be calm. Finally he looked over at Shanks. 'Something's wrong, Shanks. Something is terribly wrong.'

'What?'

Dane looked back in the direction of his father, but the captain was gone. He shook his head. 'I don't know. But it scares me.' Stopping, he turned again to Shanks. 'Why didn't he mention the girls? We were alone, he could have told me what's happened with Lord Dorcon. But he didn't. Shanks, why didn't he mention my sisters?'

# CHAPTER
## ~9~

Every time Kira thought she'd found the perfect place for them to spend the winter, Elspeth would protest, insisting that Onnie had a special place for them at the very top of the mountain.

Kira studied the sureness of her little sister. Elspeth was changing right before her eyes.

As another long day drew to a tiring close, the landscape around them had changed. While there were still the occasional clusters of tall pine trees, they were mainly walking on bare, open rock. Sometimes it was very steep. Other times it was flat planes of smooth rockface, which could be climbed easily.

'I don't like it here,' Elspeth said nervously. 'If the Rogue comes back, there's nowhere for us to hide.'

Kira stopped and glanced around. She looked down the side of the mountain to the dense forest beneath them. 'Well,' she said, putting her hands on her hips. 'If it's like this tomorrow, we're heading back down the mountain to where there are more trees.'

After a little searching, it was Onnie and Elspeth who found a small cave resting under a thick rock overhang. Climbing in, they settled down for the night, grateful to be out of the cold blowing wind.

Early the next morning, with the sun hanging pink and sullen in the sky, Kira and Elspeth were awakened by the sound of Onnie wildly yipping in their rocky enclosure. Behind his light yips was the much bigger, much more terrible sound of roaring dragons.

Rising quickly, Kira helped Elspeth gather their things. 'Come on, Shadow, hurry up! I want to see them. They sound really close.'

'Kira no!' Elspeth whined. 'If they see us they'll eat us. I just know they will.'

'No they won't. Now hurry up!' Quickly picking up her things, Kira excitedly raced from the small enclosure, dragging a complaining Elspeth along with her.

'Over there!' she said, pointing towards a rocky incline that ended in a sharp cliff. 'Come on, let's go and see what's happening.'

'No, Kira,' Elspeth whined, 'I don't want to.'

Ignoring her sister's protests, Kira ran in the direction of the dragon roars. Racing along the rocky incline, she thought she heard something else.

Shouting. She was hearing men's voices shouting!

It sounded as if there was some kind of fight directly beneath them.

Elspeth hung back as Kira lowered herself down to her hands and knees. She crawled up to the very edge of the cliff and peered over to the flat plateau below. Sucking in her breath, she was shocked by the sight that greeted her.

Ferarchie was standing in the middle of the plateau with three fully armoured dragons surrounding him. Two of the dragons still had their riders. The third rider was lying in a crumpled heap near the edge of the cliff. Watching him, Kira couldn't see any movement at all.

All the dragons moved with amazing agility and speed. But the three attacking dragons had armour on their heads that kept their mouths practically shut, while Ferarchie could open his deadly jaws all the way.

Kira saw the dragons lunge at Ferarchie while their riders stabbed at him with their lances. Watching them, she quickly realized the riders weren't controlling their mounts at all. Just like dogs or cocks in the farmyard, these dragons really *wanted* to fight.

'Kira, let's go,' Elspeth whined. She caught hold of Kira's left foot and started to tug. 'If they see us, there's nowhere to hide.'

Kira looked back at her sister. Then beyond. In her excitement, she'd neglected to consider the danger. Elspeth was right. If any of the dragons were to see them, there was no escape.

'You're right, I'm coming.'

As she started to back away from the edge, a roar in the distance caught her attention. Looking up, both she and Elspeth saw a riderless dragon gliding down from the sky. Like the Rogue, the dragon had the remnants of old armour covering its body and its mouth was free and able to open. But unlike the Rogue, it only had a single tail and was bright blue in colour.

As she followed the blue dragon with her eyes, Kira watched it land on the plateau to join the fight. 'Shadow, you should see this, it's amazing,' she said excitedly. 'The blue dragon just landed. It's not fighting Ferarchie. It's attacking the other dragons. I bet that's Ferarchie's mate.'

'I don't want to watch,' Elspeth whined again. 'Kira, come on. They're going to see us.'

Kira knew Elspeth was right, but she couldn't draw her eyes away from the savage fight. As she watched, she saw the blue dragon fighting side by side with the Rogue as they took on the other three dragons.

Soon the smallest of the attacking dragons caught

hold of one of the Rogue's flailing tails. But with the armour restricting its mouth, it couldn't get a good grip. Before it had the chance to do any damage, the Rogue turned and caught hold of the dragon's neck. It was quickly over as the riderless dragon fell dead to the ground.

Horrified, but still unable to draw herself away, Kira watched as the Rogue turned his back on the second dragon. When the knight made it move forward to attack, he quickly spun back. The sudden movement took the dragon's knight completely by surprise.

This was the last mistake he would ever make.

After killing the knight, the Rogue attacked his mount. Just like the first dragon, the end came quickly and horrifically. While he finished with the second dragon, Kira watched the blue dragon fighting the third. With its mouth free of restricting armour, it quickly overpowered the last dragon.

As his mount fell, the knight was knocked free. He climbed shakily to his feet and quickly picked up his sharp lance. Pointing it at the blue dragon, he started to charge. But the instant before it made contact, the Rogue raced over and caught hold of the knight.

Kira shut her eyes quickly. When she opened them again, the knight was gone.

With all the attacking dragons dead, Kira watched as both the Rogue and blue dragon threw back their heads and roared triumphantly. When they finished, they turned their attention to their dead opponents. Kira felt her stomach clench as she watched them working together to tear away the armour that covered the nearest dragon. Settling down beside each other, they started to eat.

The sights and sounds before her were too horrible to watch. She turned away and stood up slowly. 'Come on Shadow, I can't watch any more.'

'Finally!' Elspeth said, filled with relief. 'I don't like it here.'

'Me neither,' Kira agreed as visions of the terrible fight filled her head.

With Elspeth and Onnie walking closely at her side, Kira started to move away. But a few steps from the edge of the outcropping, her feet slipped on loose pebbles and she fell hard to the ground.

'Ouch!' Sitting up, she looked down to her left leg. Dane's trousers had torn on a sharp stone.

Elspeth immediately knelt at her side. 'Kira, you're bleeding!' She started to brush away the embedded grit and blood that was pooling on the surface of Kira's knee.

Gritting her teeth against the pain, Kira looked over to Onnie. He was behaving very strangely. He was spinning in tight circles and yipping madly. 'What's wrong with him?'

Elspeth sat back on her heels and looked over to the fox. 'What is it, Onnie? What's the matter?'

At the very same instant, Kira felt a warm, foul smelling breeze blow on her back. She heard heavy breathing directly behind her.

Elspeth was the first to look up. Gazing past Kira, a choked cry caught in her throat. She weakly whined, 'Kira . . .'

The Rogue's giant head peered over the top edge of the outcropping. Pulling back the skin from his teeth, he was making noises like a cat's hissing mixed with a deep growl. Along with these were the sounds of puffing as each time he took a breath he blew out his immense scaled cheeks.

Turning his massive purple head to the side, he studied them with one giant black eye. His growling increased as he started to inch forward. From beneath him, they heard loud scraping sounds. The Rogue was starting to climb the cliff face.

'He's coming for us,' Kira whimpered.

Elspeth was crying and paralysed with fear. Also

unable to move, Kira watched the Rogue's head rising higher in the air as he moved. Suddenly he lunged forward and his huge mouth snapped shut just short of where they sat.

The snap of the giant jaws broke Kira's paralysis and made her jump. She dragged Elspeth to her feet. Together they started to run. Daring to glance back, Kira saw the dragon straining to climb more urgently. From beneath him, they heard the awful sound of his claws scratching on the rock wall. But some of the rocks must have given way, for one moment Ferarchie was there, the next he wasn't. A loud crashing sound and then furious roars rose up from below.

'Faster, Shadow!' Kira cried. 'Run faster!'

Kira searched wildly for a place to hide. But this wasn't like further down the mountain with all its trees. This high up there was nothing. A few small clusters of trees were scattered here and there. But looking at them, she knew Ferarchie could easily tear through them.

Desperate for an escape, Kira stole another glance behind her, then wished she hadn't. As she feared, Ferarchie had flown off the edge of the plateau and was now circling back to get them. She looked forward again, and saw Onnie race ahead of them, yipping madly.

'Follow Onnie,' Elspeth breathlessly cried.

'Where?' Kira called. To their right, the mountain rose above them in a tall wall of sharp jagged rock. To the left, it descended down in a steep cliff. There was nowhere to go.

They were trapped.

# CHAPTER
## ~ 10 ~

The training they'd received up to this point hadn't prepared Dane or Shanks for what they now faced.

Just outside the dragon stables in the training field, stood their instructor knight with his enormous yellow dragon. Dane and his classmates formed a large circle around him. Standing beside their dragons, the young knights clutched the reins in their hands as though they expected their dragons to float away.

'All right, now we are going to mount our dragons,' shouted the instructor as he stepped up to the side of his dragon. 'Your dragons have been trained for this. They've been wearing their armour and saddles since they were young.'

Reaching forward, he caught hold of the rope ladder hanging down from the top of the saddle and demonstrated how to climb up the side and get into the saddle. Moments later, he climbed down again.

Walking from student to student, the instructor

helped each boy climb on to his dragon. When they were all seated, he returned to his own mount and climbed into the saddle. He then gave them instructions on how to use the reins to manoeuvre the large beasts.

'Remember,' he warned. 'Never yank on the reins and never pull them sharply. These aren't horses with simple bits. Those bits in your dragons' mouths hurt. When you tug the rein, it moves the bit. If you use a light touch, your dragon will respond without problem. Too much force and your dragon may bolt.'

For the balance of the afternoon, everyone in Dane's class remained in the saddle as they learned how to use the reins to direct their dragon around the large field. Finally, when the long day drew to a close, everyone started to feel a little more confident on his mount.

But then disaster struck.

As their instructor started to lead the class back towards the palace, Nat decided to show off. His plan was to get his dragon to rear up and then go racing down the field in a brilliant display of control over the huge beast.

But when he violently yanked back the reins, instead of gaining control over his dragon, he lost it. When the sharp spikes on the bit cut deeply into the dragon's soft tongue, the animal squealed in terrible pain and reared up and started to buck.

Unprepared, Nat was instantly tossed out of the saddle and landed with a heavy thud on the ground several paces away. At first the class roared with laughter as they watched Nat shaking his head and trying to get up. But their laughter quickly turned to screaming terror as they saw his dragon charging furiously forward. Rearing up, it came crashing down on him with all its weight. Because of the armour restraining its mouth, the dragon could not bite. Instead it smashed down on Nat with its head before using its sharp claws to tear into the young knight with all the fury it possessed.

It was over in an instant.

By the time the instructor reached Nat's dragon and drove it away, there was nothing left of the bully. Nat was dead.

'Do you see this?' the instructor roared while pointing a shaking finger at Nat's remains. 'This is what a dragon is. Rage and death! I warned you! I warned all of you – never abuse your mounts. Look at Nat,' he continued to rant. 'Just look at him! This was not the dragon's fault. But now it will have to be destroyed.

'I swear, if I ever catch any of you trying this with your dragons, I'll kill you myself!'

The instructor's fury ran unchecked as he continued to pace around Nat's body. Finally he ordered everyone back to the stables as he returned to the palace to arrange for the collection of Nat's remains.

Leaving the field in single file, Dane and the rest of his class stared silently at the horrible scene as they slowly directed their dragons towards the stables. Later that evening, once the dragons had been fed and settled back in their stalls, the class returned quietly to the dormitory.

There was no laughter, no loud voices and none of the usual banter between the young knights. Even the dorm master didn't shout or call any of the students the names he usually did. Instead he quietly announced that Nat had been buried.

'What happened to his dragon?' Tobias timidly asked. 'Did they kill it?'

'That evil beast should've been burned alive after what he did to one of my boys,' the dorm master said angrily. 'But with the war on, they can't afford to lose him. That monster will be assigned to some other poor bloke later in the season. Just thank the heavens above that none of you will ever be seein' him again.'

When he was gone, Shanks looked over to Dane. 'It wasn't the dragon's fault,' he said softly. 'I'm sorry Nat's dead, but I'm glad they didn't destroy his dragon. I'd have done the same thing if he'd yanked on my reins like that.'

'Yes but now he's tasted knight's blood, that dragon can't be trusted,' Dane said seriously. 'I worry for the next knight who tries to ride him.'

Shanks started to laugh. 'Dane, what dragon can be trusted? There's no such animal. Believe me, a dragon that can be trusted just doesn't exist.'

# CHAPTER
## ~ 11 ~

With the Rogue's shadow bearing down on them, neither sister dared to look back. They knew what they would see. Kira could hear the Rogue's heavy breathing just over her left shoulder. He was so close.

Onnie continued to race several paces ahead. Dashing to the right, Kira saw him disappear into a large crack in the rocky wall. An instant later he reappeared, yipping for them to follow.

Kira stole a quick glance over her shoulder. Then wished she hadn't. The Rogue was gliding smoothly above the ground behind them. His mouth was tilted to the side and wide open, ready to bite.

But it never happened. Instead, they heard a loud crash followed by an enraged roar. Looking back, they saw Ferarchie tumbling uncontrolled along the rock face. It didn't take a lot to work out that he'd clipped his wing-tip on the small cluster of trees. It hadn't been a big collision. But it was enough to bring the huge dragon down.

'Keep going, Shadow. In there!' Kira cried breathlessly as they approached the crack in the wall. Pushing Elspeth in before her, they pressed deeper into the narrow opening. Onnie was several paces ahead and calling for them to follow.

'I can't,' Elspeth cried as she stopped, gulping air. 'I can't run any more.'

Kira stole a glance back over her shoulder and saw they were deep inside the crack. 'We can rest for a bit,' she panted as she bent over and started to cough. Still trying to catch her breath, she heard Elspeth begin to cry.

'I hate him . . .' she sniffed.

Kira reached out to comfort her sister. But suddenly Elspeth started screaming and pointing. Kira turned just as the Rogue's giant snout filled the entrance. Frozen with fear, they watched as he tried to force his head deep into the crack. When that didn't work they briefly saw daylight again. Just as quickly, it was replaced by the dragon's massive claw.

The distance from the entrance was enough to keep them safe from the claws of the ferocious dragon. But his roars seemed to fill every part of the crack and make the whole mountain shake. Soon both girls were holding their hands over their ears and trying to block out the deafening sounds.

At their feet, Onnie continued to yip. But his soft voice was lost to the roars of the enraged dragon. Finally he caught hold of Elspeth's skirt and started to pull.

'He wants us to follow him,' Elspeth shouted as she split her vision between the fox and Kira.

'Go on then, let's go,' Kira called as she pressed herself deeper into the crack.

Kira glanced back to the entrance and heard the Rogue's fury growing. He was tearing large chunks out of the mountain wall as he tried to follow them. Turning away from the horrible sight, she followed Elspeth and the fox through the wall.

Onnie was still pulling Elspeth's skirt. Rounding a tight bend, they saw light coming in from the other side. Before long the walls of the crack widened. A few more steps and it was no longer a crack in the mountain wall, it was a cave.

At their feet, Onnie started to yip excitedly. He was still tugging Elspeth's skirt and trying to draw her towards the other side of the cave.

'I'm coming,' Elspeth said, following him forward.

At the entrance, both girls received a tremendous

shock. Before them lay a green meadow. The whole area was completely encircled by high rocky walls that formed the very top of the Rogue's Mountain. This wall offered the secret meadow protection from the cold winds that lashed the rest of the mountain and valley further below.

All around, they saw trees filled with fruit. Flowers continued to bloom, even though it was late autumn. Coming from the meadow were the sounds of crickets and other insects long since gone from the base of the mountain. It was as though this tiny area was somehow protected from the effects of the approaching winter.

A narrow waterfall streamed gently down the rock face. It fed a small pool at the base of the high wall and filled the air with the soft welcoming sound of trickling water.

'It's so beautiful here!' Kira cried. 'Where are we? Are we still on the mountain?'

'This is Onnie's home,' Elspeth answered proudly. 'He wanted us to come here to be safe.'

Kira looked down on her little sister. Elspeth's face was filthy, but she was smiling radiantly. 'Onnie gave us our new home.'

Bending down, Elspeth scooped the fox up in her arms and hugged him tightly. Kira watched in wonder as the small red animal yipped and licked her sister's dirty face. She doubted if she would ever understand what it was between the two of them. But whatever it was, she knew the fox had saved their lives.

# CHAPTER
## ~ 12 ~

There was little time to grieve or even think about Nat as the class spent long days training with their dragons.

Sitting on the back of Rexor, Dane listened as the instructor taught the class how to get their dragons into the sky.

Because this was such a dangerous manoeuvre, the instructor took each student on to the back of his mount and taught him how to get a dragon to take off. When it was Dane's turn, he joined the instructor on his large yellow dragon. The instructor first explained the procedure and then prepared for the real thing.

'All right, Dane, are you ready to fly?' he asked.

'Yes, sir,' Dane nervously answered.

Almost as if the instructor could feel Dane's fear, he turned in the saddle and faced him. 'Dane, your father was the best dragon knight this kingdom has ever known. I know you'll do fine. It's in your blood. Before you know it, you'll be showing your classmates how to do it.'

Dane lowered his head. 'Thank you sir, but I don't think so. My father is fearless. I don't think he'd be too proud of me right now if he knew just how frightened I really am.'

Dane expected his instructor to be angry when he admitted his fear. Instead, he laughed.

'You are so much like your father, it's scary,' the instructor said. 'I haven't told you this before, but I was in your father's class.'

Dane was speechless when he heard this. Finally all he could say was, 'Really? You knew my father when he was my age?'

The instructor nodded. 'I'll tell you something else, Dane. The first day Darious and I went up in the sky, we nearly wet ourselves with fear. I remember him telling me he couldn't do it. But he did. We both did. So I know you'll do just fine today.'

The instructor turned back in the saddle and faced forward again. 'Just let your instincts take over, Dane. You'll know what to do.'

Too shocked to say more, Dane concentrated on learning all he could from this knight. Making note of everything he did, everything he said, by the time he'd taken them up into the sky and finally brought them down again, Dane felt a bit more confident that he could do this, if only to make his father proud.

# CHAPTER
## ~13~

Settling in their new home on the mountain, Kira realized all the work they faced to get them through the approaching winter. Though it was much warmer where they were, Kira knew this wouldn't last. They had to prepare.

They spent days collecting fruit from the trees. Elspeth even found a small area where vegetables were growing wild. Calling Kira over, she said, 'I think someone used to live here. Look, there are vegetables growing.'

Kira looked at the patch and saw overgrown potato plants, carrots, marrows and an assortment of other vegetables. She then scanned the area for any traces of whoever had lived here before. 'I wonder who it was?'

Elspeth shrugged. 'Or why they left? But by the looks of this, they haven't been here in a long time.'

Kira reached down and pulled a carrot from the ground. Wiping dirt off, she took a bite. 'It's good,' she said, handing it to Elspeth. 'Well, at least we won't starve to death. Though I'm not sure how well we'll manage with the cold.'

'But it's not cold,' Elspeth said.

'Not yet, but it's coming. And we just don't have enough to keep us warm.'

'So, what do we do?' Elspeth asked.

'I'm not sure,' Kira said. 'But we are going to need more supplies. There is only one place I can think of where we can get some.'

'Where's that?'

'Back on the other side of the wall where Ferarchie and the blue dragon were fighting the knights.'

Fear filled Elspeth's eyes as she fiercely shook her head. 'We can't go back there! The Rogue and Blue will get us.'

'I know it will be dangerous,' Kira agreed, 'but Elspeth, we need the supplies in those dead dragon's packs. Father always said they have all kinds of stuff in them. Without it, I don't think we'll manage the winter.'

At their feet, the fox stood beside Elspeth and yipped once. Looking down at him, Kira watched him lead her sister to the crack. 'See? Even Onnie agrees with me. We need the supplies from the packs. Don't we?'

The fox yipped again.

Elspeth continued to complain and struggle against going back to the plateau where the terrible dragon fight had been. But when Onnie ran back to the crack in the wall again, she finally surrendered.

It took them several days to collect supplies from the dead dragons and knights. The first obstacle they faced was finding a way down to the plateau. But after a bit of searching, they found a rough trail cut into the rock. The second obstacle was having to constantly watch the sky for the two dragons.

The third obstacle was the worst of all. Halfway through the first day it started to rain. It made the trail slippery and treacherous. On more than one occasion, both girls slipped and fell to the ground. But by the end, their small cave was overflowing with supplies that would easily see them through the approaching winter.

Two of the best things they'd been able to scavenge were the round crown pieces of armour that went on the top of the dragons' heads. It had been a struggle to get them through the narrow crack in the wall, but it had been worth it. They now had two very large basins they could use to bathe in.

'But I don't want a bath,' Elspeth loudly complained.

'You may not want one,' Kira said, pouring more

boiled water into it, 'but you sure need one. So do I. We both smell worse than those dead dragons!'

Onnie sat before the basin and tilted his head to the side as Kira scrubbed Elspeth's back. She had the strange feeling that he was laughing at her.

Elspeth soon confirmed her suspicions.

'Go on and laugh, Onnie,' Elspeth playfully teased, splashing water at the fox. 'But you're next!'

After a quick yip the fox flicked his tail and dashed away to the bed to hide under the covers.

Taking the rough soap they'd found in a pack, Kira carefully washed her sister's long red hair. After all the time on the mountain without bathing or combing, it was a matted mess.

'Ouch! That hurts!' Elspeth complained as Kira tried to get the knight's comb through the thick tangles.

'I'm sorry, Shadow, but this really is a mess. Maybe we should cut it all off and let you start again?'

Elspeth shook her head. 'No, I like my hair long.'

'Me too,' Kira agreed. 'But how about we keep our hair in braids until we finally get out of this cave and into a real cottage?'

With that agreed, Kira finished clearing the tangles in her sister's hair and plaited it into two long braids, which she tied with thin leather strips. Like

Elspeth, her own hair was also a tangled mess and seemed to take all night to clear. But by the time they settled down to bed, both girls were the cleanest they'd been in ages.

Lying warmly together, Kira watched her sister gently wrestling with Onnie. She had long ago accepted that Elspeth had a very special relationship with the fox. Onnie was now providing all their meat. He was excellent at warning when the dragons were around, and his companionship was all that kept Elspeth from feeling the loss of her family as acutely as she did.

# CHAPTER
## ~14~

Early fears soon gave way to a sense of freedom Dane had never imagined possible as he and Shanks took their dragons into the sky. Dane suddenly realized what his instructor had meant. Manoeuvring Rexor quickly became instinctual. It was almost as if the dragon knew what he wanted him to do long before he told him. This was the only time when Dane didn't hate Rexor and, in fact, actually enjoyed spending time with the dragon.

Soaring with Shanks at his side, they both howled with excitement as they took their mounts higher and higher into the skies over the palace. Further below, they looked down on the rest of their classmates struggling to stay on their dragons' backs.

Long days in the sky passed as together Dane and Shanks ventured further away from the palace. But despite the joy he felt, Dane also felt a terrible sense of loss and dread when he looked down upon the snow-covered farmland and burnt out, abandoned cottages that dotted the landscape beneath them.

'Dane,' Shanks shouted. 'It's getting late, we've got to get back.'

Pulled from his thoughts, Dane looked over to Shanks and nodded. They were a long way from the palace and as he looked into the distance, he could see the sun hanging low over the horizon. It would be dark soon and, as he'd been taught, dragons hated flying at night.

Giving Rexor the gentlest tug on the reins, Dane directed the dragon to turn and head back to the palace.

When they arrived at the stables, the other members of his class were gathering in the antechamber. Joining them there, Dane and Shanks listened as their instructor read out their new orders.

'I'm sorry lads,' he was saying, 'but I can't continue your training. It seems things are going badly with the war and they need you at the front sooner than expected. Regardless of how I feel, ready or not, you are all being sent off to war tomorrow.'

That news shocked everyone into silence as they milled around the antechamber, uncertain of what to do next.

Later that night, Dane lay awake picking at the wood slats of Shanks's bunk above him. His heart was filled with dread at the approaching dawn. Most of the others in the dorm were also awake.

When the dawn arrived, the dorm master entered. He did not shout, didn't swear. Instead he walked down the aisle between the rows of beds with his head hanging low.

'Come on, lads. Get moving. We've a war to win,' he said without enthusiasm. 'I need this chamber cleared for the next lot of boy fighters.'

As Dane watched the dorm master moving slowly between the beds, he realized the man genuinely cared for everyone assigned to him. All the shouting, all the name-calling was just his way of hiding what he really felt. But looking at his sad face, Dane realized it hadn't worked. He was suffering at the loss of 'his boys'.

'Well, this is it,' Shanks said as he hopped down from the top bunk. 'This is what we've been trained for.'

Dane looked at his friend. 'Do you feel ready for it?'

'Not really,' Shanks answered truthfully. 'You?'

'No,' Dane admitted.

'We'd better try,' Shanks said, 'because like it or not, we're on our way to war.'

The journey to the battlefield took two days.

Following behind a guide who had come to the palace to collect them, Dane looked down on parts of the kingdom he'd only ever heard of before from his father.

They passed over a large lake, mostly frozen over with ice. But the very centre was still open as a light current brushed small waves over the ice. Ahead were dense forests that looked like no one had ever been in them before. As he passed over the tall pine trees, Dane wondered if he and Shanks could drop out of formation and find a safe place to hide for the balance of the war. But that thought passed just as quickly. His parents were still at the palace and Kahrin at Lasser. What would happen to them if he should run away?

It was almost dark when they finally stopped for the night. Everyone was exhausted and too tired to speak. After feeding their dragons, the knights all went to bed feeling sick and unable to eat.

Dawn brought little relief from fatigue as they woke up to a heavy snowstorm. But despite the bad weather, the scout had everyone up in the sky again, heading on a southern course.

By late afternoon the snow let up and they could all

see the ground beneath them again. A sight more horrifying than any could have imagined met their eyes as the young dragon knights looked down on the snow-covered bodies of knights, foot soldiers, horses and dragons, littering the countryside.

They had reached the edge of the battleground.

Flying deeper into the war zone, Dane saw areas where the freshly fallen snow was stained bright red from the battle fought earlier that day. Looking at the haunted and shocked faces of the other knights around him, he realized how unprepared they all were.

'We're going down over there!' shouted the scout as he directed his dragon out of the sky.

As Dane surveyed the area, he saw what looked like a huge encampment. Campfires burned brightly and there were fighters milling around the hastily erected shelters. Everywhere he looked, he saw the red stains of blood in the snow.

Soon everyone was taking their mounts down into a huge field filled with other dragons. Most of the dragons on the ground raised their heads and started to growl at the new arrivals. But others seemed either too tired or wounded to care.

As Dane had Rexor touch down, he saw a sight that chilled him to the bone. Not far from where they landed, he saw a wounded dragon knight with his mount. The short, stocky knight looked to be his father's age. His left arm was hanging limply at his side and the tip of a lance poked through the back of his shoulder armour. But instead of taking care of himself, the knight was doing what he could to tend his fatally wounded dragon.

Dane climbed down from Rexor and secured him to the ground. He and Shanks crossed over to the knight. They could see the thicker, broken end of the same lance cutting through the throat of his mount. The dragon had collapsed to the ground and was making terrible gurgling sounds as it struggled to breathe.

'Can we help you with your dragon?' Dane asked.

When the knight turned to him, Dane saw his face was filled with misery. He sadly shook his head. 'Thanks lads, but it's too late for my girl. Her wounds are more than I can treat. It's only a matter of time. She's in so much pain. For her sake, I know what I should do. I just can't seem to do it . . .'

The knight's heart was breaking as he stood beside his dying dragon. 'Beauty has been with me since I was your age,' he said and tears welled in his eyes. 'I know some dragons can be monsters. But Beauty has never given me a day's grief. I just don't know what I'll do without her.'

Finally the knight drew his sword. Sighing heavily, he stepped up to the dragon's head. 'Goodbye my sweet Beauty.'

The end was quick for the suffering dragon as the knight plunged his sword through the armour at the base of her skull. With one final grunt, she was dead.

'You're bleeding,' Shanks said gently. 'We've got to get that lance out of your shoulder.'

With tears openly flowing down his cheeks, the knight turned to Shanks. 'I don't think I care. What's a knight without his mount? With Beauty gone, how am I supposed to fight?'

'There are other dragons,' Dane offered. 'The palace stables are full of them. You could get another one.'

'Aye, lad,' the knight agreed. 'But it wouldn't be my Beauty, now would it?' Dropping his head, the knight patted his dead dragon a final time then slowly wandered away.

As Dane watched him go, he simply couldn't understand why the knight grieved so badly for an animal that would have eaten him if ever given the chance. Walking beside Shanks to where their new commander was waiting, he doubted he would.

'There's another storm moving in,' their commander was saying. 'We can't fight if we can't see so we'll have to wait it out. I want all of you to take some time to wander around the camp. We have a lot of wounded knights here needing help. I want you to do what you can for them. Then when the storm breaks, I want you ready to fight. Understood?'

When everyone nodded, he strode away.

Left on their own, Dane and Shanks returned to Rexor and Harmony to see to their needs. After that, they started to explore the camp. They had no sooner entered the first shelter than they saw what the commander had meant. There seemed to be more wounded knights than healthy ones.

The moment the physician saw them standing at the entrance, he immediately called them forward. Taking a moment to show them how to sew up and bandage wounds, he set them to work on the steady flow of knights who were being brought in.

The sight of blood had never bothered Dane before. But it did now. Spending a long and exhausting afternoon working with Shanks, he closed wounds he never imagined possible. Many times Dane found himself needing to run outside to empty his stomach.

'This is awful,' he commented as Shanks joined him in the cold fresh air.

'None of us are ready for that!' Shanks said, pointing back to the shelter. 'If King Arden could only see it, he'd stop the war.'

'King Arden doesn't care,' Dane said harshly. 'We could all die out here and he wouldn't shed a tear for any of us.'

As they talked, the knight who'd lost his dragon crawled up to the shelter. His face was pale from loss of blood and he could no longer stand. Instantly running to him, Dane and Shanks helped him to his feet. 'Come inside,' Dane ordered. 'We've got to get that treated.'

The knight said nothing as they led him into the shelter. But when they helped him to lie down on a bench, he reached up and caught hold of Dane. 'I wanted to die,' he insisted. 'I went out into the cold to die. But Beauty wouldn't let me.'

Dane looked at Shanks, then back to the knight. 'I'm sorry, sir, but your dragon is dead.'

'I know that,' the knight said. 'I'm wounded, not daft. Believe me, Beauty came to me. She wouldn't let me die. Said I had something important to do before I could join her.'

Again Dane and Shanks exchanged looks. Finally Shanks whispered, 'It's got to be the fever. That beast couldn't come back. He's sick, that's all.'

'Sick or not, he's going to die unless we get that lance out of him,' Dane responded. Then he turned to the knight. 'What's your name?'

'Marcus,' he answered.

'Well, Marcus,' Dane said, 'this is going to hurt, but we're going to pull the lance out of your shoulder and then sew you up. Is that all right?'

When Marcus nodded, Dane looked to Shanks. 'Let's get his armour off. This is going to be a long night.'

# CHAPTER
## ~15~

Winter finally arrived in their private meadow. The days grew cold and short, while the nights were long and dark. Around them, the fruit and leaves on the trees had all fallen to the ground and the flowers were gone. A light dusting of snow now covered the grass.

Early on, Kira discovered that not only would Ferarchie and Blue regularly pass over their heads, but they actually lived just opposite their cave. High on the rim overlooking the meadow, it was right at the top of a sheer rock face that climbed to the tallest part of the mountain.

Often – once Onnie said it was safe – Kira and Elspeth would hike over to where the dragons threw the leavings from their meals. With a bit of searching, they would find fresh meat that Onnie could never have hunted for them. As well as meat, they sometimes found large pieces of deerskins. These they would tan and make into winter clothes and covers for the entrance of their cave.

As winter deepened and heavy snow fell, they found themselves relying more and more on the dragons for food. Rising early in the morning, Kira put on several layers of clothing as she prepared to make the journey to the waste pile.

'I wish you didn't have to go,' Elspeth said as she helped her sister draw on the layers of skins.

'Me too,' Kira agreed. 'But with this snow, Onnie isn't having much luck with rabbits. We need the meat from the dragons.'

'I know,' Elspeth agreed. 'Just be careful. We haven't seen Blue for ages and the Rogue is getting even meaner if that's possible.'

Kira nodded. Elspeth was right. Blue had been missing for ages and Ferarchie was getting nastier. He had chased her across the meadow on more than one occasion, but she had been lucky and was able to duck back to the cave before he caught her. The strange thing was, he never really stayed very long once he realized he'd missed her. Something was definitely wrong with the dragons. But with their survival in question, suddenly Kira didn't have time to worry about it.

Picking up an empty deerskin bag, she prepared to leave.

'Please be extra careful,' Elspeth begged. 'I have a bad feeling about today.'

'I will,' Kira promised. Pushing back the covering on the entrance of their cave, Kira stepped out into the cold crisp morning air and gazed out over the silent stillness of the snow-covered meadow. Above her, the sky was filled with white flakes falling steadily. Studying the solid mass of grey leaden clouds, it looked like the snowstorm was going to last.

Staring up at the rim where she knew the dragons lived, she waited and listened for sounds of Ferarchie. She heard nothing. Adjusting her clothing a final time, she took a deep breath and stepped further out into the snow.

Kira stuck close to the wall as she slowly made her way around the meadow. It would have been much faster to cut across it. But with the deep snow on the ground, walking out in the open she would be too easy a target for the Rogue.

Passing the small pond, Kira saw a thin layer of ice covering the surface. Long heavy icicles hung from where the water trickled off the mountain. Very soon she and Elspeth would need to melt snow in order to have fresh water. Winter may well have been delayed in the meadow, but as a cold icy wind bit into her forehead, she knew it had finally arrived.

After a long walk, Kira eventually made it over to the dragons' waste pile. All around she saw snow-covered bones. She soon found traces of fresh kills. Glancing back up the grey cliff face, she ached to know if Blue was up there. Was the dragon still alive or had Lord Dorcon's men killed her?

Starting to collect bones and pieces of meat, Kira kept her eyes and ears open. Knowing this area could be treacherous, she trod carefully. The snow hid sharp rocks and logs that she could easily miss and trip over.

As she bent to reach for a large bone, terrible roars suddenly cut through the meadow's wintry silence. They seemed to come from all around – but were strongest from above. Looking up, Kira gasped.

Clear amongst the blazing white of the snow, she saw Blue. The dragon was leaning her head over the rim and staring directly at her.

'Blue . . .' Kira whispered. Staring up into the face of the dragon, she saw Blue pulling the skin back from her teeth. A deep rumbling growl filled the still air around her and Kira could actually feel the dragon's rage like a cold wind whipping her face.

Stumbling backward through the waste pile, Kira couldn't take her eyes off the dragon. Blue's head rose higher and higher, as though she was tensing to fly off the edge of the cliff.

Kira glanced around wildly. There was no escape. With the rocky wall beside her and the open meadow spreading out before her, she was trapped. She knew it. And she sensed the dragon knew it too.

Then Blue roared again and leaped off the edge of the rim. The dragon didn't take her dark eyes off Kira as she plunged towards the ground.

'No!' Kira howled. 'No, Blue, please!'

Stepping backwards, Kira's foot slipped in the snow. Losing her balance she stumbled and fell to the side. But instead of hitting the hard ground, she felt herself crashing through snow-covered bones and falling into a hidden crevasse.

She tumbled down a steep trail as rough stones cut viciously into her legs and back. The fall seemed endless. But finally she felt herself land with a painful thud.

Lying at the bottom, Kira was grateful to be alive. Lifting her arm over her head, she angrily shoved away a stick that was poking into her scalp. She moaned, feeling sick and dizzy. Weakly raising her head, she looked around but in the darkness she couldn't see anything. Moaning, she tried to sit up. Then stopped. There was a sound – a very strange and frightening sound. And it was close.

'Who's there?' she called, suddenly so frightened she couldn't move.

At first there was silence. Then she heard it again. *'Ji-ji, ji-ji, ji-ji, ji-jin . . .'*

Along with the sounds, Kira heard heavy movement. She wasn't alone in the hole! Whoever or whatever else was down there was coming closer.

'Please,' Kira begged, 'please leave me alone.'

Waiting for her eyes to adjust to the darkness, Kira heard the strange sound but the movement had stopped. After a time, the sounds stopped too.

The ground beneath her was cold and painfully lumpy. Finally rising to an elbow, she brushed aside the stones that had been digging into her back. But the moment she moved, the sounds started again. *'Ji-ji, ji-ji, ji-ji, ji-jin . . .'*

'No!' Kira cried. 'Stay away!'

The sounds returned for a bit then, as before, died away. She soon realized that whatever caused the sounds stopped the moment she stopped moving or speaking. But in the surrounding darkness, she still couldn't see anything. Lying very still, she closed her eyes and tried very hard not to be afraid. But she was afraid.

Opening her eyes again, Kira looked up and saw weak daylight filtering down from the opening in the ceiling. Large snowflakes drifted down and settled lightly on her face and all around. Slowly sitting up, she heard the sound again.

'Ji-ji, ji-ji, ji-ji, ji-jin . . .'

Kira screamed. A monster was drawing near. When it entered the small circle of daylight from above, she kicked out her sore legs to drive the thing away. But it was too heavy to move. Quickly gaining her feet, she stood up and smashed her head on a rock sticking out from the wall behind her. She fell to her knees, grasping her head.

'Ji-ji, ji-ji, ji-ji, ji-jin . . .' it called again.

'Get away!'

Still clutching her sore head, Kira backed away until she saw the monster wasn't trying to follow her. Moving just a bit further back she felt the ground behind her fall off. Screaming again, she caught herself just before she fell. Turning, she peered over the ledge and dimly saw the cave floor, a short distance below.

'*Ji-ji, ji-ji, ji-ji, ji-jin* . . .'

Glancing back to the monster, Kira sat on her heels and stared at it. Snow continued to drift down from the hole and land on its pale blue head. Along its back she saw two tiny wings pressed closely to the thin body. Further still, she saw where its back ended and split into two long, thin tails.

This wasn't a monster at all. Lying before her, Kira was watching a baby dragon.

Inhaling in surprise, she watched the baby turn its head towards her and make the same call. '*Ji-ji, ji-ji, ji-ji, ji-jin* . . .'

In the dim light, Kira saw that it had no teeth. Its eyes were still closed, not unlike the kittens on the farm whose eyes stayed shut for the first few days.

'Don't be afraid, I won't hurt you,' Kira gently said as she crawled up to the side of the baby. When she stopped, it raised its head and weakly nuzzled closer to her. Reaching out, she forgot all about her fear and stroked the baby's thick neck.

'You're so cold!' she cried. As she spoke, the small dragon struggled to move closer. 'I'll bet you're hungry too.'

'Kira?'

Looking up, Kira searched for the source of the

sound. 'Shadow!' she called.

'Kira, where are you?'

'I'm down here! I fell down the hole. Be careful up there, I don't want you to fall too.'

At her side, Kira heard a light growl. Looking down, she saw Onnie nearing the baby dragon with his hackles raised and his teeth bared.

'Onnie, no!' Kira shouted.

Drawing her eyes away from Onnie and the dragon, Kira looked up. For the first time, she noticed the steep trail leading up to the entrance of the crevasse. It was littered with large rocks and broken bones from the trash pile.

'I'm down here, Shadow. Can you see the hole?'

A moment later, Elspeth was standing at the entrance. As she climbed down, Kira met her halfway and gave her a fierce hug.

'We saw Blue diving off the mountain!' she cried. 'We thought she got you.'

'Not quite,' Kira said. 'But it was close. Where is she now?'

'Onnie says she's back at the top. He says he thinks she might have eggs up there.'

'Not eggs,' Kira corrected. 'Baby dragons.'

'How do you know?'

'Because I found one down here.'

'Is he alive?' Fear appeared on Elspeth's face.

Kira nodded. 'But I don't know for how long. He's so cold. Come on, I'll show you. He's over here.'

Elspeth hesitated for a moment.

'It's all right, Shadow. He's harmless. You'll see.'

When they made it back to the baby dragon, its head was lifted and it was making the strange noises again. Kneeling down at its side, Kira stroked its cold head.

Taking off her outer layer of clothing, Kira draped it over the baby dragon. 'That's a start, but it won't do much good if he's chilled right through.'

'Then we've got to build a fire to warm him up.'

Kira smiled. 'But I thought you didn't like dragons?'

Elspeth shrugged, clinging to the fox. 'I don't. But he's just a baby. That's different.'

Kira looked at her sister. She knew the situation was grim. The dragon was dangerously cold. He might also have been hurt in the fall. Looking at him, she realized there was no way that they could get him back to their cave. He was tiny in comparison to his parents, but in truth, lying on the ground, he was almost as big as a cow. If they were to try to save him, it would have to be down here.

Leaving the dragon, Kira explored the chamber. She

soon came upon a terrible sight. Not far from the trail leading up and out of the crevasse she saw a second baby dragon lying broken and dead in a heap.

'Oh no . . .' she softly said. Stepping over to the dead body, she crouched at its side and gently touched it. 'There were two of you.'

'Kira?' Elspeth called. 'What have you found?'

'There's another dragon over here, but it's dead.'

Crossing back to the living dragon, Kira petted its cold head again. 'You poor thing.' Kneeling beside him, she peeled off another layer of her clothing and started to draw the skins over its back.

As she worked, the baby kept nuzzling her and weakly lifting his head. 'I know you're hungry, baby,' she said, 'but I don't know what to feed you.'

'He's more cold than hungry,' Elspeth said. 'And he's frightened too.'

Kira was about to ask how she knew this, then decided against it. She already knew the answer.

'Well,' she said. 'I don't know about food, but I do know how to warm him up. Shadow, why don't you and Onnie stay here? I'll go back to our cave and grab some extra covers and supplies to make a fire.'

Elspeth nodded and returned her full attention to the dragon.

Ignoring the pain in her protesting body, Kira slowly climbed back up the trail. At the entrance, she was surprised that they'd never seen it before. Stepping out on to the ground, she immediately looked up. There was no sign of Blue or Ferarchie. Turning back, she called down to her sister, 'Shadow, would you ask Onnie if it's safe for me to go out there?'

A moment later the fox appeared at Kira's side. Soon Elspeth called up, 'He said he's going to go with you to make sure. But he says it's safe.'

Kira looked at the small fox and smiled. 'Don't worry, Onnie. Shadow will always love you the very best. She's just frightened for the dragon, that's all.'

Expecting him to do his usual trick of squinting angrily at her, Kira was surprised when Onnie seemed to consider her words and then nod his head. A moment later he raced ahead and yipped back to her.

'I'm coming,' Kira said as she painfully followed him.

After several trips to their cave, Kira was back in the crevasse and building a fire. Onnie was cradled in Elspeth's arms and making things difficult for her as she awkwardly drew more covers over the dragon.

'How do you think he got here?' she asked.

As Kira fed small pieces of dried wood into the fire,

she sat back on her heels and turned to her sister. 'Well, Father once told me that in the dragon stables, when a female lays her eggs, they are always laid several days apart. Just like some birds. So when the oldest baby is strong enough, he pushes the younger ones out of the nest so he can have all the food.'

'So you think the baby up in the nest pushed this baby and the other one off the cliff?'

Drawing her eyes away from her sister and back over to the dead dragon, Kira nodded. 'Probably.'

With the fire burning at his side, the dragon seemed to settle down into a peaceful sleep. Feeling confident that he was starting to warm up, Kira and Elspeth gazed around the area and considered what to do next.

'Maybe we could take him back to our cave?' Elspeth suggested.

Kira looked at her sister and chuckled lightly. 'Shadow, look at the size of him. I know we are strong, but I don't think either of us is strong enough to carry him up the trail, let alone across the meadow to our cave.'

'Then we'll just have to move in here.'

Kira opened her mouth to protest then closed it again. Were they really considering taking on the care of a dragon? It was insane.

*Father says dragons are evil*, a little voice in her head said. All her experiences with Ferarchie and then Blue seemed to confirm this. Yet Kira knew she just couldn't let him die.

Gazing around the chamber again, Kira considered. 'Well, it does look safe enough from the bigger dragons. It's close to the pond . . .'

'And we're right under where the dragons throw their old food, so we don't have to go out as much,' Elspeth offered helpfully.

'But what a mess,' Kira said. 'Shadow, it will take a lot of work to make it liveable.'

'I'll do it,' Elspeth offered. 'Please, Kira, say we can stay.'

Kira's eyes trailed from her sister to their very own dragon. This was a dream come true. And much to her private satisfaction, the ultimate betrayal of the king's First Law. She smugly wondered what Lord Dorcon would think of that!

Kira reached into the fire for a burning branch. Using it like a torch, she and Elspeth explored their new home. They quickly discovered that it wasn't really a small pit at all but part of a bigger cave that went on further below the ledge she'd nearly fallen off. And though she hadn't seen it before, just past the body of the dead baby, they found an area where the ground sloped down into the lower part naturally. They wouldn't have to climb down to get to the bottom.

Walking down into the lower cave, they discovered, at the very back, the entrance to a dark tunnel that ran deeper into the heart of the mountain. Taking a few steps in, Kira held up the torch. Heavy winds came from the darkness and were almost strong enough to blow out the flames. Part of her wondered what monsters lived in that darkness. But then she considered that some would consider the baby dragon more of a monster.

It took them the full day to complete the move. Kira was surprised to discover just how much they had managed to amass, most of which she knew they would probably never use.

While they worked, they split their time with the dragon. They quickly discovered that he would take tiny pieces of meat, but only when Kira put it on his tongue at the very back of his mouth.

Once they were settled in the lower part of the cave with a blazing fire to warm it up, it was time to try to bring the baby down into their living area. Working with Elspeth and several skins, they actually managed to half drag, half walk the baby dragon down to the lower level. It was an exhausting job, but finally they settled him near the fire and covered him with skins.

Some time later, as Kira sat down, leaning against the sleeping baby dragon, she sighed contentedly. 'You know, Shadow,' she said softly, 'we just can't keep calling him Baby. This dragon needs a real name.'

'What do you think we should call him?' Elspeth asked, as she played with Onnie on her lap while she was supposed to be cutting up pieces of meat for the stew.

'I'm not sure,' Kira admitted. 'I'm not good with names. Come on, you're the one who always named the animals on the farm. What should we call him?'

Elspeth took the job of naming the dragon very seriously. Rubbing her chin, she put Onnie down and stepped over to the baby. Patting him on the head affectionately, she mused, 'Now, what shall we call you?'

In response, the dragon lifted his head and pressed close to her.

Elspeth slowly nodded, as if she'd been spoken to. A smile played across her lips and her eyes sparkled. 'Yes, that's it.'

'What is it?' Kira asked. 'What's his name?'

Elspeth turned back to her and smiled. 'Jinx. His name is Jinx.'

Kira repeated the name several times and considered. It sounded very close to the noises he made every time he wanted to be fed. Finally she smiled too. 'Perfect.'

Bending over, Elspeth leaned forward and kissed the dragon on the head. 'From now on, your name is Jinx,' she said proudly.

# CHAPTER
## ~16~

As their commander had predicted, the blizzard arrived with a fury. The only good thing about the heavy snow was that it kept everyone from fighting. After working through another long day caring for the wounded, Dane and Shanks stepped out of the medical shelter and looked up to see the large flakes falling lightly from the sky.

'I hope it never stops,' said Dane tiredly, 'if it means keeping all of us on the ground and from doing that to each other.'

'Me too,' Shanks agreed. 'I don't think I'll ever get over what I've seen.'

Dane nodded. 'We're losing so many men. I've never seen so many people die before. It's awful.'

'At least Marcus will live,' Shanks said brightly. 'Though I don't know how. He lost so much blood; by rights he should be dead. Yet his fever is down and he's asked for something to eat.'

Dane looked over to Shanks. 'But he's still talking about Beauty coming to him and saying he's got something important to do.'

'Dane,' Shanks said, 'Marcus was hurt and he was grieving. His mind played a trick on him to keep him alive. He's probably just missing his dragon.'

'I hope you're right,' Dane agreed.

As they both turned to walk back into the medical shelter, they heard a commotion in the dragon field. Looking over, they saw two dragons landing.

'They're mad to be flying in this,' Shanks commented.

'But they sure look like they're in a hurry,' Dane said as he watched the two knights jumping down from their mounts and running up to the camp commander. The commander then turned and pointed in their direction.

'They're coming this way,' Shanks said. 'Maybe they know someone who's been hurt.'

As the knights moved closer, they didn't seem to be interested in going to the medical shelter. Instead, they walked straight up to Dane and Shanks.

'Dane, son of Captain Darious?' the taller of the two knights demanded.

'That's me,' Dane said nervously.

The second knight produced a set of shackles. Stepping forward he ordered Dane to hold out his hands while he started to put them on.

'What's this about?' Shanks demanded as he pushed the chains away.

'No, Shanks,' the commander ordered. 'They've come to take Dane back to the palace.'

'The palace?' Dane finally said. 'Why? I don't understand.'

'You are to be punished for attempted murder,' said the first knight.

'What?' Dane cried. 'I haven't tried to kill anybody. I've been here. I swear. I've done nothing wrong!'

'Not you,' said the knight harshly. 'Your father, Captain Darious. And by the king's law, the crimes of your father become your crimes when he can't be punished.'

'I— I don't understand,' Dane stuttered. 'What crime? What has my father done?'

'He tried to kill Lord Dorcon,' the knight answered. 'Three days ago while he was at the palace reporting to the king.'

Dane could hardly believe his ears. 'He wouldn't do that,' he finally said. 'My father is a good knight and loyal to the king.'

'*Was*,' the knight corrected. 'Now he's a dead traitor.'

'What?' Dane cried, unable to believe what he'd just heard. 'You're lying! My father isn't a traitor and he's not dead!'

'He is,' the knight said. 'Lord Dorcon killed him during the attack. Now we're here to take you back to the palace to face his punishment.'

'That's not fair!' Shanks yelled. 'The captain did it, not Dane. Why should he be punished for something his father did?'

'It's the law,' the knight said. 'Now come along, we've got to get back to the palace before the storm worsens.'

Dane was hardly aware of his surroundings or Shanks yelling at the knights. He was in shock. Unable to feel, hear or think any more. He was losing himself in his grief. His father was dead and branded a traitor. Stolen away from him by Lord Dorcon.

Unmoving, Dane didn't fight the knights as they roughly put the shackles on his wrists. He was then dragged over to the dragon field where he was hoisted on to the back of a dragon and taken back to the palace. When they arrived, he was immediately delivered into the cold, dark dungeons and thrown into a tiny cell.

Left on his own, he sat on the damp stone floor and

wrapped his arms around his knees. Though they insisted it was true, he could hardly believe that his father was really dead.

'Dane,' came a hushed voice from the other side of his cell door.

Through tear-filled eyes, Dane looked up to the small barred window in the door. There he saw the worried face of his dragon-knight instructor. Quickly gaining his feet, he ran to the door.

'Is it true?' he demanded. 'Did Lord Dorcon really kill my father?'

'Aye, lad, it's true,' the instructor said. 'But don't listen to the stories they're telling about him. Darious was a good man. He died trying to protect his family. Dorcon is still after your sisters. It was the only thing he could do to stop him.'

'But he failed,' Dane moaned.

'Not entirely,' the instructor said. 'Because of his leg, your father couldn't move as well as Dorcon. But he was still the better fighter. Dane, you should be very proud of him. He fought like a hero for you and your sisters. With only one leg, he showed more courage going after Dorcon like he did than most knights do in their entire lives. And know this, before your father went down, he managed to stab Dorcon in the chest.'

This was the best news Dane had heard since the nightmare started. 'Is he dead?'

'Not yet. The physicians are with him. They don't know if he'll live or die.'

'I hope he dies screaming in agony!' Dane spat.

'A lot of us do,' the instructor agreed. 'But until we know the outcome, I'm afraid you're going to have to stay in here.'

'I don't care,' Dane said miserably. 'Whether in here or on the battlefield, I'm dead just the same.'

'Stop that!' the instructor barked. 'Your father didn't surrender his life just so you could give up on yours. He died doing what he could for his family. He'd be ashamed if he heard you saying that. You've got to fight Dane, any way you can. Your mother is still here at the palace. You've got to think of her.'

Dane was ashamed, for he hadn't thought of his mother once. 'How is she?' he finally asked.

'Grieving,' the instructor answered. 'But at least they didn't lock her away, though they're working her like a dog making uniforms for the war.'

Dane's emotions were running wild. He was still reeling from the shock of losing his father. Yet he was grateful to hear that his mother was unharmed. But what of his sisters? If Lord Dorcon lived, would he continue to hunt Kira and Elspeth? Would he kill them? If the evil knight did manage to survive, Dane promised himself that one day, he would kill him for what he'd done to his family.

Finally looking back to the instructor, he asked, 'Will I be able to see my mother? Can you bring her down here?'

The instructor shook his head. '*I'm* not even allowed down here. I had to bribe the guard just for this visit. I don't think they'll let me bring a woman down here for any sum. But I will pass along a message for you.'

Dane tried to think of all the things he wanted to say to his mother. Finally he said, 'Would you tell her that I love her and that some day Lord Dorcon will pay for everything he's done. Will you tell her that for me?'

'Aye, lad, I will. Now I'd best get back before I'm missed. I'll do what I can to get down here again.' Pausing before he left, he turned back to the window. 'This isn't over, Dane. You just hold on and do what you can to survive. A change is coming. I know Darious would want you here for it.'

'I will be,' Dane said. 'For my father, I will.'

With a quick nod, the instructor moved away.

\* \* \*

Without a window to mark time, Dane was unaware of how long he was in the palace dungeon, though it had to be long enough for the cold and stink of the foul cell to stop bothering him and for him to become used to his one meagre meal a day.

Left alone with his thoughts, Dane realized how much his life had changed. Was it really so long ago that he had been working happily on the farm with his father? He'd been an innocent boy back then. That time was over. Finished. After what he'd seen in battle, his innocence was gone. After losing his father, he was no longer a boy. He was the only man left in his family and it was his responsibility to protect them.

But sitting in his cell, all he could do was worry and pray for his mother, sisters and Shanks. Mixed in with the prayers for his family and friend, he also prayed for the death of Lord Dorcon. But the arrival of a visitor proved that at least one of his prayers had gone unanswered.

'Open it,' he heard a familiar deep voice say.

When the door to his cell was opened, Dane looked into the corridor and saw a sight that chilled his blood.

'Bring him out here,' Lord Dorcon ordered.

Guards filed into Dane's cell and roughly hauled him into the corridor. Dragged before the tall knight, Dane couldn't see any traces of the wound left by his father.

'I assume you know why you are here?' Lord Dorcon said. When Dane refused to answer, he smiled. 'Of course you do. You know your father was a traitor and tried to kill me.'

'My father was no traitor!' Dane spat. 'You're the traitor—'

'He was a traitor who deserved to die!' Lord Dorcon shouted back. Then he lowered his voice to a deadly tone. 'I'm sure you know the king's law says that without your father here to punish, you will stand in his stead.'

'Go ahead and kill me,' Dane challenged. 'It won't change anything. You're a failure, Lord Dorcon. My sisters are free and making a fool of you!'

Lord Dorcon's face turned red with rage as he whipped Dane violently across the cheek. But as he did, he grunted in pain and brought his hand protectively up to his chest. 'Silence, boy,' he warned through gritted teeth, 'or I swear I'll have the skin flayed off your body.'

'Do it. See if I care. You can't hurt me any more than you already have.'

Lord Dorcon instantly calmed and stood erect again. He smiled. But it was a smile filled with poison. 'You foolish pup. I can hurt you in ways you never imagined possible. Ways that will make your father turn in his grave – if the filthy traitor had a grave.'

'Stop calling my father a traitor!' Dane shouted as he lunged at Lord Dorcon. It was only the guard's quick reactions that stopped him from reaching the knight.

'I can and will do anything I please,' Lord Dorcon replied. 'You see, Dane, I own you now. For your punishment, the king has given you to me. I could kill you, but I won't. Not until you have witnessed the destruction of your runaway sisters.'

'You monster!' Dane cried as he strained against the grip of the guards. 'You'll never catch my sisters. The king will see your failure and have you executed! I'll watch you die, Lord Dorcon, I swear I will!'

Lord Dorcon laughed. 'That will never happen. Your father is dead and before long, the rest of his family will join him.' He then motioned to the guards. 'Take him away. You know what to do.'

# CHAPTER
## ~ 17 ~

As Kira looked over the meadow, she saw the snow melting and first traces of spring starting to appear. But further down the mountain, heavy snows continued to fall. It left her with a strange feeling that their secret meadow was indeed a very special place.

Every day that passed, Jinx seemed to grow so much bigger. He now stood more than twice her height. If he wanted her or Elspeth to scratch behind his ears – which he always did – he had to lower his head for them to do it.

Though he was not yet an adult, he had grown a full set of very sharp adult dragon teeth, but remained as gentle as a kitten whenever Kira fed him chunks of meat. He was also moving around a lot more. Much to Kira's joy and sometimes annoyance, he constantly followed her everywhere she went.

'Now you stay here, Jinx.' Patting his neck, Kira reached for her empty leather pouch to collect water.

But when she'd taken a few steps, she heard the sound of the dragon's claws clicking on the rocks behind her.

'He's right behind you,' Elspeth giggled. Onnie was on her lap, wrestling with her and demanding that his tummy be rubbed.

Turning back, Kira saw the dragon awkwardly starting up the trail. 'Jinx, this is silly. You know you can't go out yet, you're still too young.' Walking over to him, she reached up and stroked the dragon's thick neck. 'You have to stay here with Elspeth and Onnie to keep them company. I'll be right back, don't worry.'

'It won't work,' Elspeth teased.

'It's going to have to,' Kira answered. 'He's got to learn to stay.'

Turning her attention back to the dragon, Kira held up her hands the way her father had when he'd been teaching his hunting dogs. 'Stay, Jinx. Stay!'

When the dragon took a step forward, Kira gently pushed him back. 'I said stay. Now, stay!' She tried to be firm, but a smile stole up to her lips when he lowered his head and nudged her. Unaware of his own strength, he nearly knocked her over.

'Good boy!' Elspeth cried, rolling back in fits of laughter. 'Do it again!'

'Shadow, you're not helping very much,' Kira said,

though she was laughing too. Turning back to the dragon, she sighed heavily and hugged his head. 'What am I going to do with you?'

When she released him, Jinx raised himself as high as he could on his legs and started to flap his large wings.

Watching him, Kira shook her head in wonder. 'Look how big his wings have grown!'

'He's so beautiful!' Elspeth cried. 'I bet he can fly too.'

Kira stepped forward and started to scratch the dragon behind his ears. 'You're probably right,' she said, looking at Elspeth. 'But we're not going to let him. Not with Ferarchie and Blue nesting right above us. I hate to think what might happen if they ever saw him.'

'Do you think they'd want to take him back?'

Kira shook her head. 'No. I think they might actually try to kill him.'

'What?' Elspeth cried. 'They wouldn't!'

'They would,' Kira said seriously. 'Shadow, Jinx has been with us a very long time. If they were to see him now, Ferarchie would think he's an invading dragon and attack him. Which is why I've tried so hard to keep him from going near the trail to the entrance.'

'But he's going to have to go out some time,' Elspeth

149

said. Crossing to the dragon, she straddled his neck so she was riding him. When Jinx raised his head, she was lightly lifted off the ground. Finally she looked back to Kira. 'We can't keep him down here for ever. He's a dragon. He needs to fly.'

'And he will,' Kira agreed. 'But only when he's older. For now, we've got to get him to stretch and flap his wings in here, but we can't let him leave.'

Elspeth nodded. 'We'd better tell him then.'

A gentle smile rose on Kira's face. 'You do that, Shadow. I think he will understand it better coming from you.'

Leaning forward on his neck, Elspeth called up to the dragon's head. 'Jinx, you mustn't go anywhere near the trail going out of the cave. Do you understand? You've got to stay here with Kira, Onnie and me. Will you do that?'

Kira watched Jinx turn his large head and look back at Elspeth. He reached round to nudge her gently with his snout.

'That's a good boy,' Elspeth cooed, as she stroked the dragon's head and neck. She looked back to Kira. 'He won't go out.'

# CHAPTER
## ~ 18 ~

Dane woke in agony.

He was back in his cell and lying on the cold stone floor where the guards had dumped him. His left cheek was on fire and his eye was swollen shut.

Gingerly touching his face, he could feel the angry, weeping wound where the branding iron had burned the mark of Lord Dorcon into his cheek. He tried to sit up, but the pain from his face drove him back down again. Too weak and tired to do anything, he rolled on his right side and drifted back into a pain-filled sleep.

'Dane,' the instructor called. 'Dane, wake up!'

Slowly waking, Dane rolled over and through bleary eyes, looked to the cell door.

'Quickly, I don't have a lot of time before the guards come back. I heard Lord Dorcon had you branded like an animal.' He stared in shock when he saw the damage done to Dane's face.

'My God. If I could only get at him, I swear I'd finish what your father started!'

Dane opened his mouth to speak, but even moving his lips caused searing pain in his face.

'Don't try to talk,' the instructor warned. 'It will make it worse. Here, take this.' The instructor forced a small leather pouch through the bars. It landed on the floor near Dane's feet. 'Rub this cream into your burns as quickly as you can. It will reduce the swelling and stop it from hurting so badly.'

Dane's face was throbbing as he forced himself up on to his hands and knees and slowly crawled over to the bag of medicine. When he caught hold of it, he looked up to his instructor and nodded.

'Remember, Dane, put a little on your burns three times a day. It will help, I promise.'

Sounds from the corridor made the instructor turn away. When he looked back he hastily said, 'They're coming back, I've got to go. Use the medicine, Dane, get well. Darious must be avenged and you're the only one who can do it.'

Then he was gone.

Clutching the bag in his hand, Dane weakly crawled back to the corner. Turning his back to the door, he opened the bag and reached in for a finger full of thick, smelly cream. Starting at the bottom of his chin, Dane almost cried out as his trembling fingers smoothed the cool cream into the deep burns on his cheek. But after a moment, wherever the cream went, the pain was greatly reduced.

When he finished, Dane resealed the bag and stored it inside his shirt. He lay down on the hard stone floor again and slipped back into a restless sleep.

Days passed as Dane slowly healed. The instructor's medicine had done what he'd promised. Though his face still throbbed, the worst of the pain was behind him.

'Oy, you there, wake up,' said a harsh voice.

'Leave me alone,' Dane mumbled.

'Can't do that,' said a second voice. 'You're getting out of here today.'

As the guards hauled Dane to his feet, the first guard looked at his face and laughed. 'Ain't you the pretty one? Lord Dorcon's brand suits you. Now everyone will see the great captain's son is a slave.'

'I'm no slave,' Dane challenged. He knew how badly the unfortunate slaves of the kingdom were treated. It had been something his father had fought against for many years. There was no way he would ever allow anyone to call him that. 'Lord Dorcon can brand me all he wants, I'll never be his slave.'

'I wouldn't be too sure of that,' said Lord Dorcon casually as he entered the cell. Stepping closer, he held up his torch to inspect Dane's face. 'It's healed better than I wanted.' He turned to the first guard. 'I think your men went a little easy on him with their irons.'

'No sir,' the guard defended. 'I saw what they done to him. They was brutal. His face should be ruined.'

'Ruined or not,' Lord Dorcon continued, 'no one can mistake my mark.' He then said to Dane, 'Anyone who sees you will know you are mine. There is no escape for you, Dane, so I suggest you don't try.'

'I'm not your slave,' Dane repeated.

'King Arden and that brand on your face beg to differ,' Lord Dorcon said. 'But don't worry, you'll be dead soon. Right after I take care of those two sisters of yours.'

'You'll never find them,' Dane challenged.

'On the contrary, I already have. They are living at the top of the Rogue's Mountain. How that monster dragon hasn't eaten them is beyond me. But now that I know where they are, there is no escape for them. Or for you.'

As Dane started to protest, Lord Dorcon held up his

hand. 'Enough chatter. Guards, put the chains on him. We'll be leaving shortly.'

Dane was roughly hauled from his cell and put in chains. He was then dragged out into the palace courtyard and hoisted up on to the back of a dragon behind a knight.

'Is it true?' Dane asked. 'Are we really going to the Rogue's Mountain?'

The knight turned in his seat and looked at Dane. Then his eyes came to rest on the brand on his cheek. 'It is,' he answered. Saying nothing more, the knight faced forward and waited for Lord Dorcon to climb behind the knight on the lead dragon.

Moments later, they were taking off. Flying over the training field, Dane sucked in his breath as he saw eight other dragon knights taking their mounts into the air. There were ten altogether going after his sisters. Heartsick, he couldn't see any way out of the impending disaster.

The journey to the Rogue's Mountain was long and grim for Dane. Rising early on the final morning, Lord Dorcon called his men together for a last briefing before the assault on the mountain. He quickly reviewed the plan. As Dane listened, he realized that Lord Dorcon was a coward. He was ordering his men to go after Kira and Elspeth while he planned to stand back and watch.

'All right,' Lord Dorcon finished. 'I will wait at the upper rim while you men go down and secure the meadow. Once you have the girls, bring them to me.'

Around him, the knights nodded, but the knight escorting Dane asked, 'What about the Rogue?'

'If you see him,' Lord Dorcon replied, 'kill him. He's just one dragon. What is he against the might of the king's best fighters? Now, if there's nothing more, let's get moving. Those girls have been a thorn in my side long enough.' He then looked at Dane. 'That ends today.'

# CHAPTER
## ~19~

Elspeth's eighth and Kira's thirteenth birthdays both came and went without notice on the mountain. Struggling to survive and raise a very hungry, growing dragon meant there was little time left to celebrate.

But making her way over to the water pool, Kira realized that if the king and Lord Dorcon hadn't destroyed her life, she would have celebrated her birthday with her family. There would have been sweets and her mother would have made a special meal. Dane, Kahrin and Elspeth would have done all her chores and her father would have taken her into the village to pick out a special gift.

Instead, the last words she ever said to her parents were words of anger. How she ached to take them back. But she couldn't, and now it was too late. Lord Dorcon had stolen her family away.

Silent tears of hurt and rage came to her eyes as Kira remembered all the things she had lost. She promised herself that somehow she would get back the life that had been taken. She and Elspeth would rescue Kahrin from Lasser and find their family. Then they would all go someplace safe to live, far away from King Arden and First Law.

Lost deep within her thoughts, Kira failed to notice the many eyes watching her from the top rim of the mountain. As she finished filling the deerskin bag, she sealed the top and stood again. Turning to walk back to the cave, she suddenly heard the sound of a voice shouting her name and warning her to run.

Following the voice, Kira looked up and saw a terrifying sight. At least ten dragon knights were soaring over the rim of the mountain. Lord Dorcon had finally found them.

As she tensed to run, Kira suddenly heard deep and ferocious roars from the opposite side of the rim. The Rogue.

Looking up, she saw both Ferarchie and Blue throwing back their heads in rage at the invading dragon knights. Without hesitation, both dragons launched themselves into the air.

Stunned, Kira couldn't move. But when an arrow struck the ground at her feet and she realized the knights intended to kill her, she forced her legs to work.

'Run, Kira!' Elspeth cried. Having heard the roars, she had climbed to the entrance to see her sister trying to escape. 'Run!'

Kira tried to make it to safety. But as she ran for the cave's entrance, the Rogue suddenly landed on the ground before her. Ignoring her, he kept his massive wings held wide as he charged the first of the dragon knights to touch down on the ground.

As the deafening sounds of roaring dragons filled the air, the memories of the first dragon fight flooded back. But when a knight's sharp arrow grazed her left shoulder, they quickly vanished. Clutching her bleeding wound, Kira struggled to find a way around the charging dragons.

Arrows flew at her as she tried to dart away from the fight between the Rogue and a large green dragon. But even though neither dragon took any notice of her, they managed to keep her trapped within the boundaries of their vicious fight.

She tried to escape. But each attempt was blocked by dragons' whipping tails. Surrendering any hope of running from the fight, she went down on her hands and knees and tried to crawl. But as she neared Ferarchie's outstretched wing, she saw him catch hold of the green dragon's throat. Moments later, he was driven to the ground.

Quickly gaining her feet, Kira dashed forward. But just as she was racing past the Rogue's wing, he caught sight of her and turned. He snapped the air, missing her by just a short reach. But then the enraged Rogue left the dying green dragon and took several strides towards her. Standing before the huge dragon, Kira knew she had lost. The Rogue knew it too. As Ferarchie reared up to attack, she closed her eyes and waited for his final fatal bite.

# CHAPTER
## ~20~

Dane lay chained on the ground at Lord Dorcon's feet, overlooking the gory battle in the meadow. His shouted warning hadn't been enough. Kira had been caught off guard, as had the two dragons nesting on the opposite side of the rim.

Seeing Kira for the first time since the farm, his heart swelled with joy. But that quickly vanished as he watched her bravely struggling to escape the fighting dragons. Then when the green dragon and its rider fell, he was terror filled as he watched the mighty Rogue rearing up to kill her. But what he and Lord Dorcon could see, and the Rogue and Kira could not, was two other dragons moving in to attack.

As the Rogue's massive mouth started to descend on Kira, the two dragons struck. With their riders no longer in control, the nearest dragon rose and leaped on to the Rogue's back. Opening its mouth as wide as the restricting armour would allow, it bit into the scales at the back of the Rogue's neck. The second dragon quickly caught hold of the Rogue's back leg and started to pull.

The sudden attack caused the massive dragon to turn away from Kira. With the Rogue's attention off her, Dane rejoiced as he watched her springing forward to finally make it to the safety of her cave.

'Thank you,' Dane silently prayed as he watched Kira and Elspeth embracing. It filled him with joy to see Elspeth had also survived on the mountain and that both his sisters were together.

'No!' Lord Dorcon howled at the sight of the two girls. 'Kill them,' he shouted at his men. 'Forget the Rogue, just kill the girls.'

As Dane watched the fight in the meadow, he knew the knights couldn't hear Lord Dorcon's orders, let alone follow them. They had lost control of their dragons and were struggling just to hang on. Turning his gaze from the Rogue, Dane watched a large red dragon fighting with the Rogue's mate. Suddenly the armour on its head broke free, allowing the dragon to fully open its vicious mouth.

Larger and much stronger than the blue female, the red dragon caught hold of her wing and tore into the soft flesh. From the wing, it turned its attention to the blue dragon's throat. Catching hold at the base, it started to tear. Unable to defend herself, the blue dragon howled in agony and then went down.

Reacting to the desperate cries of his wounded mate, the Rogue quickly finished his fight. He crossed to his mate and attacked the red dragon with unequalled fury. The fight was brief, but one of the most violent of the day. When it was over, the red dragon fell, headless, to the ground.

Looking around at the scene in the meadow, Dane could hardly believe one dragon could do so much damage to so many others. None of the king's dragons had survived the fight. If there were any knights still alive, Dane couldn't see them from where he lay.

'That dragon is a demon from hell,' Lord Dorcon muttered as he too stared in shock at the carnage in the meadow.

From above, they both heard the sound of another dragon. Searching the sky, they watched as a smaller, twin-tailed dragon flew down and landed beside the Rogue. They were identical in every way except size.

'Offspring?' Lord Dorcon uttered. 'The Rogue has bred? I must warn the king. If the Rogue is breeding, then this kingdom faces a much bigger problem than the war!'

It was only then that Lord Dorcon seemed to remember Dane on the ground.

'On your feet, boy,' he ordered harshly. 'We've got to get back to the palace. The king must be told of this new development.'

# CHAPTER
## ~ 21 ~

When the fight worsened, Kira ordered Elspeth back down into their cave so she wouldn't see the horrors in the meadow. But standing alone in the waste pile, Kira had watched it all.

When it was over, of all the terrible things she'd witnessed, the most heartbreaking of all was watching the Rogue with Blue. Creeping up to his mate, Ferarchie made strange clicking sounds Kira had never heard before. Lowering his head, he gently nudged her. But she remained still.

Sadly, Kira realized Blue was dead.

Tears sprang to her eyes. The dragon was dead because of her. If she and Elspeth hadn't come up the Rogue's Mountain, Lord Dorcon's men wouldn't have followed. Then Blue could have lived a long life with the Rogue.

Instead, everything was ruined. Blue was dead and Lord Dorcon knew exactly where they were. How long did they have before he sent more dragon knights up the mountain to finish the fight with Ferarchie?

From over her head, Kira heard another roar. Quickly looking up, she got her first glimpse of the Rogue's other offspring. This dragon was as purple as Ferarchie and about the same size as Jinx. Like Jinx and the Rogue, it also had twin tails. Landing on the meadow floor, it made soft whining sounds as it approached its dead mother.

A moan escaped Kira's lips at the sight of the young dragon nudging its dead mother. Beside him, Ferarchie did the same, while making the same soft clicking sounds.

Unable to watch the scene any longer, Kira turned and walked slowly down into the cave.

'Is it over?' Elspeth asked as she left Jinx and crossed to meet her on the trail.

When Kira sniffed and nodded, Elspeth frowned. 'What is it?'

Sniffing again, Kira wiped away fresh tears. 'Blue is dead. That big red dragon got her before Ferarchie could stop him.'

'Blue is dead?' Elspeth repeated in a hushed voice.

Again Kira nodded. Stepping over to Jinx, she pressed her face against the smooth blue scales of his neck. 'It was awful. Ferarchie can't understand she's gone and keeps nudging her to get up. Then the young one came down from the nest and started doing the same.'

'You saw Jinx's brother?'

'Yes.' Kira sniffed as she looked back to Elspeth. 'He looks just like Ferarchie.' Putting her arms around Jinx's thick neck, she moaned, 'Oh Shadow, it's all gone wrong.'

Though not fully grown yet, Jinx was no baby and seemed to understand that something was very wrong. As Kira stood with her arms around him, he leaned his head back and gently nudged her as he softly whined.

Comforted by him, she sniffed and kissed his smooth blue scales. 'I'm sorry Jinx, your mother is dead.'

'*You're* his mother,' Elspeth offered gently as she stood with Onnie in her arms. 'Look at him, Kira. Look how big and strong he is. You did this for him. Not Blue. I'm sorry she's dead, but you are Jinx's mother and he knows it.'

'He is big, isn't he?' Kira said. 'He's almost as big as the fighting dragons out there.'

Elspeth nodded and then added, 'Onnie says we have to leave here. He says the knights will be back. Now they know where we are, they'll never leave us alone.'

'I know,' Kira agreed as she reached up and scratched behind Jinx's ears. 'But wherever we go, you're coming with us.'

Resting in Elspeth's arms, Onnie started to yip wildly. Leaping free of Elspeth, he raced up the trail and started to growl and bark. Immediately both girls looked up as a shadow blocked the light from the entrance of the cave.

'By order of Lord Dorcon, I command you girls to come out of there!'

Kira's scream caught in her throat as she looked up into the armoured face of the knight who'd been riding the red dragon. Onnie was at his feet and continued to yip and then nip at the knight's legs.

'Get away from me, you filthy animal!' Kicking out his foot, he caught Onnie on the side and sent him tumbling back down the trail.

'Onnie!' Elspeth howled. Quickly racing up the trail to where he fell, she scooped him up in her arms. 'Leave him alone, you monster!'

'What did you just call me?' the knight cried in surprise. 'Why you insolent child, how dare you!' Drawing his sword, the knight started down the trail towards her.

'No!' Kira shouted. Leaving Jinx, she raced to the

upper level of the cave and placed herself between Elspeth and the knight. Quickly drawing her dagger, she stood defiantly before him.

'Don't you dare touch her, do you hear me?' Taking a step forward, Kira bravely advanced on the knight. 'I'm warning you, leave us alone. We're not hurting anyone by being here. So go and tell Lord Dorcon to leave us alone!'

'*You* are warning *me*?' the knight said incredulously. 'Just who do you think you are?' Taking several more steps down the trail, he raised his sword higher. 'You and your sister are guilty of breaking First Law. It is my duty to see that you are punished. Drop that weapon and surrender!'

Kira had been unaware of the soft, deep growls rising from below. But when the knight advanced on her, the growls turned into ferocious roars. Turning back to the lower level, both Kira and Elspeth were shocked to see Jinx rearing on his hind legs and bearing his sharp teeth, his twin tails thrashing in the air.

Though to her and Elspeth Jinx would always be their baby, Kira suddenly realized just how big and dangerous he truly was.

'Jinx, no! Get down!' Kira ordered. Looking back to the knight, she quickly cried, 'Get out of here,

I don't know what he'll do!'

'You've got a dragon down there?' the knight cried. 'It's not possible!'

Suddenly springing forward, Jinx sent both girls tumbling as he rushed past them and started up the trail towards the stunned knight.

Seeing the enraged dragon charging him, the knight dropped his sword and started to run. Barely making it to the top of the trail, he raced out into the daylight – and straight into the waiting mouth of the Rogue.

Kira and Elspeth didn't see the knight's death. But as they climbed to their feet, they heard it. Immediately after, they heard a terrible roar coming from the entrance of their cave. Looking up, they watched the Rogue forcing his snout into the entrance.

Both girls screamed and leaped back. But Jinx did not retreat. Instead, he reared up on his hind legs and let out another roar equal to that of his father. Jinx was no longer their tame baby dragon. He was as rage filled and ferocious as Ferarchie. Suddenly his twin tails whipped wildly around the cave as he started to move.

'Jinx, no—' Kira and Elspeth cried together as they watched him climbing further up the trail.

'He'll kill you!' Kira finished. Quickly scrambling

forward, she tried to call the dragon back. But her cries were lost to the deafening roars echoing through the chamber.

'Onnie, no!' Elspeth suddenly screamed.

Kira turned in time to see the fox leaping from Elspeth's arms. In a flash of red, he was racing forward beside Jinx, while at the cave's entrance, Ferarchie was trying to force more of his snout down into their cave.

'No, Jinx, no!' Kira cried again as their dragon made it to the entrance. But Jinx wasn't listening. Like his father, he wanted to fight.

With fury burning in his eyes, Ferarchie suddenly pulled his wounded and bleeding snout out of the cave entrance and started to dig at it with his sharp claws. Tearing into the rock, huge chunks of stone and dirt rained down on Kira and Elspeth's heads.

Still roaring in rage, Jinx lunged forward and caught hold of the Rogue's largest toe. Violently shaking his head, his sharp teeth tore into the flesh and filled the air with a spray of dragon's blood.

Kira and Elspeth cringed at the howls of rage and pain coming from Ferarchie. But it was the ferocious growls coming from Jinx that scared them the most. He was as wild and savage as his father.

'Please Jinx, stop!' Kira begged. Ignoring the danger

to herself, she raced up the trail and caught hold of the leather reins they had tied around Jinx's neck. Using all her strength she tried to pull Jinx off Ferarchie. But it wasn't working. Jinx was concentrating only on his father.

'Stop it, Jinx. Please, stop!'

Elspeth quickly joined Kira. But after several more tugs, the leather reins snapped and cast them both down the trail again.

'What are we going to do?' Elspeth cried as she sat up and watched in horror while Jinx tore into Ferarchie's big toe.

'I don't know!' Kira shouted back. 'But if Ferarchie gets hold of Jinx, he'll kill him!' When she finished speaking, Kira's eyes darted around the area. 'Where's Onnie?'

Tears were streaming down Elspeth's flushed cheeks as she pointed. 'He's still up there fighting the Rogue!'

Kira saw a tiny red blur darting around the ground at Jinx's feet. Several times he was nearly stepped on as the two dragons fought. 'Call him back. He'll be killed!'

'I've tried. He just won't come!'

Quickly gaining their feet again, they raced up the trail. Approaching Jinx, they heard his terrible roars as he shook his head a final time and violently tore the Rogue's toe away from his foot. Casting it aside, Jinx snapped again at his father's retreating claws. But Ferarchie was faster and managed to get his foot free of the cave.

Moments later, both girls screamed as they watched his massive head filling the entrance again. With terrifying speed, it came lunging down to snap at their young dragon.

'Please, Jinx,' cried Kira. 'Please, stop. He'll kill you!'

'Stop, Jinx!' Elspeth ordered, but to not avail. 'Onnie, get away from there!'

Like Jinx, Onnie was ignoring their shouts. He wanted to fight.

Standing together, both girls watched Ferarchie press his head deeper into the cave. Rising on his hind legs, Jinx snapped and tried to bite Ferarchie's snout. But he was young and inexperienced. When he took a step further up the trail, the Rogue opened his huge mouth and snapped it shut on Jinx's snout.

'No!' Kira howled.

Both girls screamed as Ferarchie viciously shook his head and sank his teeth deeper into Jinx's snout. Once his grip was secure, he started to back up, dragging the crying and howling Jinx along with him.

Crippled with fear, Kira followed Jinx as he was drawn further and further up the trail. She could hear the sickening sounds of his claws on the rocks as he fought all the way up. His cries of pain and fear tore at her heart like a dagger.

Jinx was going to die!

Suddenly furious, Kira snapped out of her shock and started to move. 'Shadow, stay here!'

Racing down into the lower cave, she grabbed one of the knights' heavy lances that they'd collected after the first dragon fight. Carrying it back up the trail, she prepared to stab it into the Rogue's mouth when her heart stopped with terror. Elspeth was running up the trail towards the massive dragon. Dodging around Jinx, she approached Ferarchie's mouth.

'No,' Kira shouted. 'Elspeth, stop!'

Ignoring her, Elspeth moved closer to the deadly dragon. 'Let him go!' she ordered, her voice becoming shrill. 'I said let him go!'

As though he'd been struck by lightning, Ferarchie suddenly stopped. Opening his mouth, he released his grip on the young dragon and became strangely silent.

Free of the terrible mouth, Kira watched Jinx start tumbling down the trail. Stepping aside, the young dragon somersaulted past her and right off the upper ledge in the cave. A moment later, she heard the heavy thump as he landed in the lower living area.

Turning her attention back to Elspeth, Kira watched her sister giving the monstrous dragon a punch that she knew he could never have felt.

'Now get out of here, Rogue!' Elspeth ordered. 'Go back to your own baby and leave ours alone!'

But Ferarchie did feel it. Closing his mouth, he regarded Elspeth with the one eye he could squeeze into the cave entrance. Blinking, he seemed shocked and uncertain what to do next.

Kira held her breath. Taking cautious steps up the trail, she was certain she was about to witness her sister being eaten by the huge dragon.

'I said go!' Elspeth cried. 'You heard me, Rogue, go!'

Mesmerized, Kira watched the deadliest dragon in the world blink a final time then slowly withdraw from the entrance. Hesitant and confused, he paused. Pointing her finger at him, Elspeth took another step forward. 'Go on, get out of here!'

A moment later, Ferarchie was gone.

With the spell broken, insanity erupted in the cave. Onnie started yipping loudly as he raced around Elspeth's feet. From the lower cave, Kira heard the painful cries of Jinx as he called to them.

Still unable to believe what she had just witnessed, Kira watched Elspeth come striding confidently down the trail to stand before her. 'It's safe now. He won't bother us again.'

'Shadow?' she said hesitantly. 'Shadow, what just happened?'

Elspeth shrugged. 'I'm not really sure. I knew the Rogue was going to kill Jinx. Then, suddenly I knew I could stop him.'

'How?'

'I don't know.'

Kira was too shocked to be angry at the foolish risk her sister had taken. Instead she pulled her into a tight embrace. She could feel herself shaking, but in her arms, Elspeth remained calm.

At their feet, Onnie continued to yip loudly and race in circles. Looking down on him, Kira asked, 'What's he saying?'

'Onnie is yelling at me. He's mad at what I did.'

'I would be too if I weren't so grateful you're alive! Remind me later to get mad at you.'

Elspeth smiled. 'I will. Come on, let's see what the Rogue did to our baby.'

Kira let Elspeth lead her by the hand down the trail into the lower cave. They found Jinx lying where he had fallen from the top level.

'Jinx?' Kira said hesitantly as she approached. 'Jinx, it's us. Are you all right?'

Lying on his side, he weakly raised his bleeding head to her and whined.

'I know it hurts,' Kira said softly as she inspected the deep angry wounds that ran across and down his snout.

'It's all right, Jinx,' Elspeth said as she lightly stroked the dragon's heaving side. 'We'll make you something that will take the pain away.' Elspeth then turned to Kira. 'And I'll make something to help with your shoulder.'

Kira looked at Elspeth and frowned. Then she looked back to her bleeding shoulder. In all the excitement, she'd forgotten about her own wound. 'What can you do? We don't have any medicines.'

'Yes we do,' Elspeth said confidently. 'In the knights' packs that we got from the dead dragons there are some herbs. Onnie always promised to show me how to make medicine. Now we will. If you go and get us some fresh mud, we can get started.'

# CHAPTER
## ~22~

With no dragons left alive to fly them back to the palace, Lord Dorcon and Dane had to walk. Each step of the long journey seemed to anger Lord Dorcon even more. The only time he spoke to Dane was to tell him all the things he planned to do to his sisters once they were captured.

Dane had to hold himself back from attacking the knight. It was only the chains on his wrist and ankles that stopped him. Keeping silent, he knew that one day there would be an opportunity to kill Lord Dorcon. Like his father, he could wait.

When they finally arrived at the palace, Dane was immediately taken back down to the dungeons and returned to his cell. Not long after, his instructor arrived at his door.

'Dane,' he softly called.

Climbing to his feet, Dane crossed to the barred window in the door.

The instructor slipped some bread and a large chunk of cheese through the bars. 'I thought you might be hungry. I can't imagine Dorcon would have fed you on the way back to the palace.'

Gratefully accepting the food, Dane bit hungrily into the soft bread. Speaking with his mouth full, he said, 'Not really.' Then he asked, 'Has the king punished Lord Dorcon for getting all his men and their dragons killed?'

'No,' the instructor said. 'Dane, what happened out there? The king is in an uproar and has called all of his advisors together. Dorcon is in the thick of it.'

'I'm not really sure,' Dane said as he took a bite of the cheese. 'When we arrived at the top of the mountain, I was so glad to see Kira alive. But then Lord Dorcon's men flew down into her meadow to get her. Right after that, the Rogue appeared with his mate—'

'The Rogue has a mate?' the instructor interrupted. 'You saw her? You're sure it was his mate?'

Dane nodded. 'She was killed during the fight. But right after, I saw their offspring. He looks just like his father. Same colour, same twin tails.' Dane paused and frowned. 'I've never seen a twin-tailed dragon before.'

'I have prayed to God none of us ever would again. A lot of us hoped when he escaped to the mountains that that would be the end of it. Now you say he's breeding up there? This is terrible news. No wonder the king is in an uproar.'

'I don't understand,' Dane said.

Taking a deep breath, the instructor started. 'Back when your father and I were lads, there was a wizard here at the palace. Paradon was his name. We all thought he was just a harmless old man. None of his spells ever worked right.' He paused.

'And,' Dane prodded.

'And one day, Paradon had an idea. He wanted to create a new breed of dragon. One that could be tamed and wouldn't be so dangerous to its rider. So without telling anyone, he went into the dragon stables, to a clutch of freshly laid dragon eggs. He cast a spell. Later on, he told everyone he was just trying to help. But what he did was create monsters.'

'I still don't understand,' Dane said. 'You're saying the Rogue is one of Paradon's dragons?'

'He is,' the instructor confirmed. 'There were three in the clutch. When they first hatched, everyone could see how different they were. Unlike normal dragons, these ones had twin tails. But soon, we realized there was more than just their appearance that made them different. These dragons were sweet and would let anyone play with them. No one had ever played with dragons before. But more than that, they grew incredibly fast. They were much bigger than normal dragons. And they were clever.'

'That doesn't sound like such a bad thing,' Dane said.

'Not in the beginning. But before long we discovered these dragons had formed tight bonds with the people who raised them. In this case, it was their knights. No one had ever seen dragons so fiercely loyal and protective of their riders. In fact, one of the dragons attacked several pages when they got into an argument with her rider. Fergain killed two pages and wounded a third.'

'Was she killed?' Dane asked.

'She was,' the instructor said. 'Then the king ordered the other two to be destroyed as well. But the night of the order, one of the other riders broke into the stables and stole his dragon away. We've not seen Fereric since. As for Ferarchie . . .'

'I remember this,' Dane said. 'My father told Kira and me that Ferarchie's rider was killed in battle and that he escaped to the mountains. That's when they started calling him the Rogue.'

'That's right,' the instructor said. 'But if the Rogue is

up that mountain breeding, we're all in a grave danger.'

'I still don't understand,' Dane said. 'What's so dangerous about the Rogue breeding?'

'Those dragons shouldn't exist. They're an abomination to nature. They *think*, Dane. Can you imagine how dangerous intelligent dragons can be? Especially if they don't have riders to control them. We don't even know how big they'll grow or how long they will live. They were created by the magic of a wizard who couldn't cast a proper spell to save his life.

'Believe me, hearing about the Rogue's offspring could stop this war and have the king sending more men up that mountain to kill him.'

'I was there,' said Dane. 'The Rogue is huge. I saw what he could do. I don't think an entire legion could stop him. He fought ten dragons without any effort at all. His offspring isn't nearly as big as he is, but he's still a good size. *He* won't be easy to kill either.'

The instructor rubbed his chin. 'If that's the case, then, my boy, we are all in terrible danger.'

# CHAPTER
## ~23~

Kira and Elspeth stayed at Jinx's side while he healed. As the days passed, constant trips to the entrance of the cave confirmed Kira's worst fears. Ferarchie and the young dragon were now living in the meadow.

As she watched Ferarchie resting beside Blue's body, she saw his offspring starting to explore the meadow. Knowing that he was the same size as Jinx, Kira felt a growing fear that very soon the young dragon would find his way to their cave. And unlike Ferarchie, he would fit through the entrance and make it down to their living area.

Stepping back down into the lower level, Kira checked on Jinx before walking over to her sister. 'Shadow, we've got to get him moving soon. Jinx's brother is starting to wander around the meadow. If he finds us down here, I don't know what will happen.'

Sitting beside the fire with Onnie in her lap, Elspeth sighed. 'I know. But where can we go? Jinx is just too big to hide. And with Lord Dorcon looking for us, we can't go where other people are.'

Taking a seat beside her sister, Kira nodded. 'I'm hoping we can find another mountain to live on. With Blue gone, Ferarchie is the only one who can care for the young one. Maybe he won't try to chase us.'

'Maybe,' Elspeth agreed, as she turned her attention back to scratching Onnie's tummy. 'But we still have an even bigger problem.'

When Kira looked at her, she continued. 'How do we get out of here? With Ferarchie staying in the meadow, we can't leave the cave.'

'We don't even know if Jinx can fly,' Kira added. 'That's the only way we are going to get off this mountain. He won't fit through the crack in the wall.'

In her lap, Onnie stopped playing and looked intently into Elspeth's face. A moment later, he let out several soft yips.

'What's he saying?' Kira asked.

'Onnie says he knows another way for us to leave.'

Kira looked down on the fox, then back to Elspeth. 'Go on,' she coaxed.

'He says we should go through the tunnels at the back of our cave. He says they lead deeper into the mountain and come out the other side. Onnie thinks we could walk Jinx through there and get out.'

Kira's eyes were drawn to the black hole in the wall at the rear of the cave. It gave her the shivers to think of actually going down there. But things had changed. They had no choice, not if they wanted to keep Jinx safe.

Looking back to Elspeth, Kira nodded. 'For once, I think Onnie's right. That's the only real way out of here. Just as soon as Jinx is ready, we'll go.'

It took two more days before Jinx showed any signs of recovery. But soon, he was eating again and starting to follow Kira around the cave. His clinging to her and seeking constant affection made packing the things they needed very difficult.

'Are we going to take Jinx out of here at night?' Elspeth asked as she carefully helped her sister prepare torches for the journey.

Kira looked over to her. 'I don't know. But it's probably best if we leave early in the morning. That way, when we come out the other side, it should still be light.'

Elspeth shook her head. 'We won't be coming out the same day. Onnie says it will take a few days to go through the mountain.'

Looking from her sister to the dark caves at the back of their living area, Kira shivered again. The thought of spending a moment in there terrified her. Hearing that it might be a few days made it even worse.

That night as the preparations for the journey drew to a close, with Jinx lying at her side, Kira looked over to Elspeth. 'With a little luck, I think we'll be ready to go in a couple of days.'

'I'd like to stay here as long as we can,' Elspeth offered. 'Just to be sure Jinx is all right.'

'Me too,' Kira agreed. 'I just hope Ferarchie doesn't have other ideas.'

Rising early the next morning, Kira stepped up to the entrance of the cave and discovered the Rogue's baby wandering around the waste pile, searching through the discarded bones.

Quickly ducking down, she followed his progress. He didn't seem so much interested in the bones as he was with sniffing the air. Was he picking up her scent? Or maybe Jinx's?

Suddenly she felt fear constrict her throat. They had to get moving.

Racing back down into the cave, Kira knelt beside her sleeping sister. 'Elspeth, wake up!' she whispered urgently. 'Get up and don't make a sound. The purple baby is right outside the cave. I think he can smell us down here. Ready or not, we've got to go now.'

Instantly awake, Elspeth sat up and nodded.

Moving in silence, they woke Jinx up and quickly fed him all he would take. After that they raced to put blankets on his back and then tied the dragon packs on either side of him. When they were in position, Kira filled one with supplies while Elspeth packed the other.

Suddenly from above, they heard the sound of pebbles falling down into the cave. Looking up the trail, they saw the purple head of the baby as he investigated the upper entrance.

Jinx turned and also glanced up. Exposing his sharp teeth, he started a deep rumbling growl.

'Stop it, Jinx,' Kira ordered, stepping up to the young dragon's head. 'Don't even think of going up there, do you hear me?' After a weaker growl, Jinx settled. Kira then turned to Elspeth. 'Leave everything that's not packed. We've got to go now.'

Elspeth finished tying closed her pack. Kira came up to her side. 'All right, I want you and Onnie to climb up on Jinx's back and get settled. I'll walk beside his head to lead him into the tunnel.'

Without arguing, Elspeth did as she was told and climbed up on to the dragon's back. With Onnie settled in his pouch on her back, she looked over her shoulder. 'Are you ready to go, Onnie?' she softly asked. When the fox yipped, she looked down on Kira. 'We're both ready.'

Kira nodded. Taking a final look back up the trail, the baby dragon was gone. But it wouldn't be long before he came back. Her eyes travelled around the cave that they'd called home for so long. Leaving it now, she felt pangs of sadness and regret. She always knew they would leave it one day. She just hated that it had been Lord Dorcon who drove them out. Holding the new leather reins that went around Jinx's neck in one hand, Kira reached for a burning torch with the other. 'Well, here we go.'

Giving the reins a light tug, Kira directed Jinx forward. 'All right, there's a good boy. Just like we taught you, let's go for a little walk.'

In response to her coaxing, the dragon lifted his head and moved alongside her. Walking towards the back of the cave, Kira felt the winds coming from the tunnels deep inside the mountain.

As they approached the dark cave, she felt Jinx start to hesitate. 'Good boy, Jinx,' she coaxed. 'It's safe in there. I promise.'

'Go on, Jinx,' Elspeth called, giving the dragon's

neck a reassuring pat. 'It's all right. Just do as Kira says.'

Almost immediately, Kira felt a change in the dragon. Elspeth's few words had done more to reassure him than anything she could have said. Giving the loop a light tug, she felt him start to move again. 'That's a good boy.'

The further into the dark tunnel they walked, the more Kira and Elspeth had to coax Jinx forward. The light from the torch was bright, but only pushed back the darkness a few paces. It also cast eerie, flickering shadows on the walls that made them all a bit nervous.

Time seemed to stop as they journeyed in the darkness. Many times, the walls narrowed and Jinx had to squeeze through.

'Are you all right up there?' Kira called, holding up the torch.

Elspeth nodded, though fear showed on her pale face. 'We're fine, but it's so dark in here.'

The sound of her light voice seemed to echo through the tunnels as though there were a great gathering of people whispering all around them. Hearing this, Kira had an idea.

'Dragon poo!' she shouted with all her might.

The words filled the tunnel with sound and bounced back on them hundreds of times. Looking up to

Elspeth's shocked face, Kira smiled. 'Come on, Shadow, it's fun. Try it.'

'Hello!' Elspeth called. She frowned as the words returned time and time again.

'You can do better than that,' Kira teased. Raising her head, she shouted, 'Lord Dorcon smells like a dung heap!'

Again her words bounced off the walls and seemed to fill the whole tunnel with life. Smiling, she looked up at her sister. 'Well?'

'And he eats bugs for breakfast!' Elspeth finally shouted.

'And worms for dinner!' Kira added loudly.

Soon they were laughing as they shouted the worst words and curses they could think of into the surrounding darkness. When they finally grew tired of the game, Kira and Elspeth made plans for what they would do once they were out of the tunnels. At her side, Kira felt Jinx slowing down and drawing back.

'I'm tired too,' Kira agreed, lifting her arm and patting his neck. 'But we can't stop now. We don't know how far we have to go.'

'Onnie says we shouldn't be down here for more than two days,' Elspeth offered as she reached up and scratched his head where it rested on her shoulder. 'He also thinks you should ride up here with us because then Jinx can see where he is going.'

Kira looked around in the darkness and agreed. In truth, Jinx had been leading her along for some time. Handing the torch up to Elspeth, she climbed up the dragon's wing and settled on his back.

'All right, Jinx,' she called over the winds, 'let's go.'

As they pressed on, Kira noticed the tunnel changing. The walls were farther apart, and holding up the torch, she couldn't see the ceiling. Around her, the winds continued to increase, only now they were blowing wildly in every direction.

'Kira,' Elspeth called from behind her, 'Onnie says he can't remember it being like this. He says something has changed in the mountain. He thinks we should be really careful and hold on extra tight in case Jinx gets scared and bucks.'

Nodding, Kira grasped the reins tighter in one hand while she slipped the other under the leather strap tied around the dragon's girth. 'Come on, Jinx, keep going.'

After only a few short paces, Jinx stopped. Lifting his head high in the air, he snorted loudly and puffed out his cheeks.

'What's wrong, boy?' Kira shouted. Raising the

torch, she could see his eyes pinning as his pupils grew big then small countless times, faster than she'd ever seen before.

'Jinx is frightened,' Elspeth called.

This time Kira didn't need her sister to tell her how the dragon was feeling. Jinx's behaviour was telling her all she needed to know. 'I know, but of what?' she called back.

'I don't know,' Elspeth answered. 'But something is very wrong.'

Still holding up the torch, Kira gazed around in the small ball of light it offered. 'I can't see anything,' she called back. 'Ask Onnie if he knows what's wrong.'

But before Elspeth could ask, Jinx started to growl. 'He's really scared now!' Elspeth cried. 'Something is happening.'

As she finished speaking, the ground beneath them started to tremble. Startled, Kira dropped the torch. When it landed, it rolled forward a bit, then disappeared over an edge.

'There's a big hole ahead!' Kira cried over her shoulder. Suddenly they heard the sounds of cracking. 'Wait Jinx! Stop, don't move!'

But her cries were lost as the sound of cracking increased and the earth beneath them started to shake. Kira warned Elspeth to hang on as she clutched the reins tightly and pressed her body closer to the dragon.

In one final sickening break, both girls heard and felt the ground beneath them falling away. Shrieking in terror, their screams mixed with the dragon's roars as they were suddenly cast into the chasm.

Somersaulting over and over, they desperately clung to the dragon's back. Screaming all the way, Kira clenched her eyes shut and waited for the moment when they hit the bottom. But just when she thought it was over, something miraculous happened. Beneath their feet, Jinx unfolded his wings. Opening her eyes in the darkness, Kira suddenly realized they weren't falling any more. They were flying.

'Shadow, he's flying! He's really flying!'

From behind her, Kira heard her little sister starting to shout and laugh.

Their dragon was flying. Suddenly all the guilt Kira had felt for keeping him in the cave vanished. Jinx's wing beats were powerful and sure. As though he'd been flying all his life.

Lifting her head, Kira felt the wind blow against her face. They were climbing. Clinging to Jinx's back, she felt every move he made. Several times, one wing moved more than the other. When this happened, the wind on her face changed. Jinx was changing direction.

On and on they flew in the eternal darkness. Then Jinx started to roar. But the sound was tight and didn't echo; they were no longer in the giant cavern. Looking forward, she thought she saw a faint light in the distance. In the darkness, it was hard to tell how far away it was. But as Jinx flew towards it, she watched it growing bigger.

Soon, it was more than a faint light. It wasn't long before Kira realized they were heading towards daylight. Somehow, Jinx had found his own way out of the mountain. Cheering and shouting, they burst out of the darkness and rose high into the brilliant blue sky.

Thrust violently into the bright sunshine, Kira's hand flew up to her eyes as Elspeth cried out in pain. Beneath them, they could feel the dragon reacting sharply to the unexpected sunlight.

'It's hurting him!' Elspeth cried as she shielded her own eyes against the sun. 'He can't see—'

Jinx roared and started to writhe in the sky. Beneath them, Kira saw they were flying over a lake. As she clung to the dragon, she watched him losing height. 'Keep going, Jinx,' she yelled. 'Keep flying.'

But the dragon wasn't listening. Throwing back his

head, he let out a terrible, agonized roar. Looking ahead, Kira saw the shore quickly approaching, but she knew they weren't going to make it.

Jinx was going down.

# CHAPTER
## ~24~

'Elspeth, hold on!' Kira cried. Lowering her head, she curled as tightly as she could into the dragon as they struck the water. But despite all her attempts to stay on his back, she was thrown into the air and splashed down quite far from where her sister and the dragon landed.

Kira took in several mouthfuls of cold water as she rose to the surface. Coughing and spitting, she looked desperately around. 'Shadow, Shadow, where are you? Shadow?'

Her cries rose in pitch as she found no traces of her sister or the dragon. 'Shadow! Jinx! Answer me! Where are you?'

Not far from where she treaded water, she heard the sounds of bubbles. Spinning, she saw Jinx's head suddenly break the surface of the water. A moment later, Elspeth appeared, choking and gasping for air. Watching her, Kira saw that her sister's hands were still caught in the leather rope going around the dragon's back. As Jinx started to thrash in the water, he was forcing Elspeth's head beneath the surface.

'Shadow!' Kira cried. Diving deep into the water, she swam as fast as she could towards her sister. Before her, she saw the blurry blue image of the dragon. Further down his back, she saw Elspeth struggling to pull her hands free of the leather rope.

Kira forced herself to remain calm. Her lungs cried out for air. She pulled out her knight's dagger and moved forward. Reaching Elspeth, she quickly cut away the leather rope binding her to the dragon. When she was free, Kira drew Elspeth back up to the surface.

Gulping air, Kira supported Elspeth's head above the water. 'It's all right, Shadow. Calm down and breathe. You're all right!'

'Onnie?' Elspeth weakly gasped. 'Where's Onnie?'

In the confusion, Kira had completely forgotten the fox. Reaching into the pack on Elspeth's back, she expected to find him dead. But as her fingers searched the pouch, there was no sign of him – alive or dead.

'He must have been thrown free,' Kira answered. 'I bet he's already waiting for you on the shore.'

'I want Onnie!' Elspeth started to cry. 'Where is he?'

'He's over here!' An unfamiliar voice shouted from the shore. 'Over here!'

# CHAPTER
## ~25~

Dane remained in the dungeon while the plans to destroy the Rogue and his offspring were drawn up. The only way he knew what was going on was when his instructor would sneak down to his cell bringing him food and news of his mother and other bits of palace gossip.

'They've lost more men and dragons to the Rogue,' he reported late one evening. 'They sent up another ten knights, but like before, it was a blood bath. The Rogue made quick work of them. Only this time, his offspring joined the fight and managed to kill one of the king's dragons.'

Hearing this news meant little to Dane. He wasn't interested in the Rogue or his offspring. His only concern was for his two sisters.

'Did anyone survive?' he anxiously asked.

'One knight,' the instructor responded. 'His dragon was wounded, but he managed to get her away before she was killed.'

Dane was almost afraid to ask, but he had to. 'Did he mention my sisters? Were Kira and Elspeth hurt?'

The instructor shook his head. 'The survivor said he found their cave and went in. But they were gone. He doesn't think the Rogue got them. He said there were signs of packing, but it looked like they left in a hurry.'

'Where could they go?' Dane asked. 'How could they get past the Rogue?'

'I don't know. But the knight didn't stay long enough to find out. As it was, he was nearly killed by the Rogue's offspring.'

'So what's the king going to do now?' Dane asked.

'Your guess is as good as mine,' the instructor said. 'But news from the battlefront isn't good either. We're losing men faster than we can train replacements. I think the king bit off more than he could chew with this war.'

'Have you heard anything of Shanks?'

Again the instructor shook his head. 'No. We're not getting a lot from the front. Only that they need more and more fighters. But with the king going after the Rogue as well, there just aren't enough men to fight both battles.'

'They should let me out of here,' Dane said. 'I could help out somehow.'

'Lord Dorcon wants you kept where he can keep an eye on you. Now that your sisters have left the mountain, he's even more obsessed with tracking them down. But until they show themselves again, he has no idea where to search.'

'Surely the king won't let him waste time with my sisters while there is the Rogue and the war to worry about?'

'You'd think that, wouldn't you? But no, the king has given Lord Dorcon all the resources he needs to find them. No one knows why. But so far, Dorcon has come up empty handed.'

'Let's hope it stays that way,' Dane said.

# CHAPTER
## ~26~

Turning sharply at the new voice, Kira saw a figure standing on the shore. He wasn't very tall, and was wearing a long dark cloak that looked like it had seen better days. The hood was up so she couldn't see his face. Waving his arms in the air, he was calling them to him. 'Over here girls, swim over here.'

Looking from the figure back to the dragon, Kira saw that Jinx had found his rhythm and was already making for shore. Still supporting Elspeth, Kira started to swim awkwardly towards the dragon. 'Jinx, over here boy. Come here.'

At her command, the dragon changed direction and started to swim towards them. 'Good boy,' Kira praised. 'Keep coming.' When Jinx swam past, Kira caught hold of the leather reins and let the strong dragon drag her and Elspeth towards the shore.

As they approached the shallow water, Kira released the reins. When she felt her feet hit the sandy bottom, she concentrated on her sister. 'Are you all right, Shadow? Do you think you can walk?'

Still coughing, Elspeth caught hold of Kira's hand and weakly climbed to her feet. Helping her to stand, Kira glanced at the cloaked figure on the shore. She still couldn't see his face, but as he drew nearer she saw just how dirty and tattered he was. As he moved, she saw he had an older man's gait. This was definitely not a young knight.

But then Kira saw Jinx. He was already out of the water and running towards the figure. As he drew near, the dragon bared his teeth and started to growl. Quickly rearing on his hind legs, he extended his wings and let out a ferocious roar.

'Jinx, no!' Kira shouted.

Looking back to Elspeth, she quickly asked, 'Will you be all right?'

When her sister nodded, Kira dashed out of the water and ran over to the cloaked figure. Putting herself between him and the dragon, she held up her hands. 'No Jinx, don't hurt him! Sit down.' Making the sitting command, she ordered the dragon down. 'I said sit!'

Kira watched Jinx's expression change. He seemed uncertain and almost a little frightened. As he stopped

203

roaring, he lowered himself back down to all fours. Still baring his teeth, he let out a long, deep growl.

Kira crossed to the dragon. 'Good boy, Jinx, now calm down.' She reached for the reins and started to draw him towards a cluster of trees. 'Let's get you out of the nasty sunlight until your eyes adjust. I'm sure that man isn't going to hurt us.' Turning back to the figure she said, 'Are you?'

The old man took a short step forward and held up his hands. 'I'm not going to hurt them, Jinx,' he said softly. 'I promise. I could never harm Kira or Elspeth, they're far too precious to me.'

Startled by his statement, Kira watched as he pushed back his hood. He was by far the oldest man she'd ever seen in her life. His face was like a wrinkled old potato left too long in the barrel – the parts that she could see at least. The rest of his face was covered by a very long, grey beard. Like her father, he was bald on top, but had long grey hair growing down from the sides, reaching almost to his elbow.

Once Jinx was settled in the shade of a tall tree, Kira crossed to the old man. 'Who are you? How do you know our names?'

From behind her, Kira heard Elspeth squeal, 'Onnie!'

Turning quickly, she watched as Elspeth sprang from the water and opened her arms. Suddenly a flash of red flew past and launched into the air, straight into Elspeth's outstretched arms. 'I thought you were dead!' she cried, burying her face in the fox's wet fur. 'Don't you ever leave me again!'

As the fox wagged his soaking tail, he licked Elspeth's face furiously.

'I'm Paradon,' the old man answered, 'and I have been waiting for you for a very long time.'

Growing suspicious, Kira frowned. 'How do you know our names? Why are you here?'

Paradon laughed lightly. 'Please don't be concerned, Kira, you have nothing to fear from me. Elspeth already knows this, don't you?'

Elspeth turned to her and nodded. 'It's all right, Kira. Paradon is our friend.'

'How do you know?' Kira whispered back tightly, not taking her eyes off the old man.

'Trust your sister, Kira,' Paradon said gently. 'She knows about these things.'

'What things?'

'I think you've witnessed enough to know that Elspeth is special. That she has a very rare gift.'

Kira gazed into her sister's eyes and saw the trust

there. 'Is he really all right?'

Elspeth nodded. 'He's a good person, you'll see.'

Kira considered this. Then she frowned. 'That still doesn't explain how you know who we are.'

'True,' Paradon agreed. 'Well, as Elspeth has a gift with animals, I too have a gift. Sometimes, it allows me to look on to a special globe – I call it my Eye to the World – and this Eye allows me to see things that are happening to others far away from where I am. For instance, I saw you on the day when they took your family away. When I saw that Lord Dorcon was after you, I sent a friend along to help guide you girls to the mountain where I knew you'd be safe.'

Kira turned to the fox resting contentedly in Elspeth's arms. 'You're talking about Onnie, aren't you?'

Paradon nodded. 'But it seems I underestimated my little red friend. He was only to guide you there, then come back to me.' Suddenly he sighed. 'But alas, it seems that Onnie much prefers the friendship of a pretty young girl to an old man like me.'

'What is Onnie?' Kira asked, hoping to finally have some answers.

'I don't really know,' Paradon responded. 'He came to me when I was a boy. He's been with me whenever I've needed him. But then he'd go away. Sometimes I wouldn't see him for years, then suddenly he'd reappear. Now it seems he's taken a real liking to Elspeth – enough that he's actually told her his name. All these years, and I have never known it.'

'So you can speak with him too?' Elspeth asked.

'Not like you. No. It was more that I could understand what he was feeling. But from what I've seen, you can actually speak with him.'

Elspeth nodded. 'Onnie teaches me things.'

'So I've seen,' Paradon agreed.

'Just how much have you seen?' Kira asked.

'Almost everything,' Paradon answered. He turned to look over to where Jinx was resting. 'I looked into the Eye and watched when you first found him. You were both very brave taking on the responsibility of a baby dragon.'

Kira followed his glance and smiled as Jinx raised his head when he caught her watching him. He was still suffering from the bright light, but his head was tilted to the side as if he knew they were talking about him. Walking over to the dragon, she started to scratch behind his ears. 'We couldn't let him die. He was just a baby. He needed us.'

'It was still very brave of you.'

Kira shrugged as she left Jinx and returned to

Elspeth. 'Paradon, if this Eye lets you see what happened to us, can it show you what's happened to our family?'

'Kira, I don't think—'

'Please, Paradon,' Elspeth added, 'where is Kahrin? Is she all right? Lord Dorcon took her to Lasser Commons. Have you seen her there?'

Paradon shook his head, saying nothing.

'But we need to know,' Kira pleaded. 'You have to tell us, please. You don't understand. We have been alone for so long. Please Paradon, please, tell us . . .'

Taking a deep breath, the old man started to walk towards the resting dragon. He stopped when Jinx raised his head and puffed out his cheeks. The dragon let out a long deep growl.

'Now, now, Jinx,' Paradon said softly. Glancing back to Kira and Elspeth, he shrugged. 'I don't think Jinx likes me very much.'

Kira stepped back to the dragon. Again placing herself between them, she reached up to scratch behind Jinx's ears. 'He's fine. He's just not very good with strangers. He met a knight in our cave. But when he tried to hurt us, Jinx went for him. After that, I don't think he trusts anyone except us.'

Elspeth joined Kira at the dragon's side as she faced the old man.

'Please, Paradon,' she begged. 'If you've seen anything of our family, tell us. We already know there's nothing we can do to help. And that Father wanted it this way when he told us to run. But we need to know. What happened after the knights took them away?'

Kira watched Paradon closely. He seemed to struggle with himself, uncertain of what he should say. She then saw him open his mouth to speak, but close it again and turn away. Stepping away from them, he walked over to the water's edge.

Leaving the dragon, Kira and Elspeth followed him. 'What is it?' Kira softly asked. 'What did you see?'

The old man's shoulders slumped as he stood facing the water. 'I know you're anxious to hear anything of your family, but right now isn't the time to go into details. The world you knew has gone. This once beautiful land is bathed in blood. Good men are dying because of an evil king. People are starving and desperate. If anyone were to see you now, they wouldn't hesitate to turn you in for the reward the king is offering for your capture.'

'Reward?' Kira repeated. 'What reward?'

Paradon turned back to them. 'Because you two are the only ones ever to defy the king, he has offered a large reward for your capture. People who would have once helped you are now desperate to catch you and hand you back to him.'

This news chilled Kira to the bone. She had no idea how bad it had become since they'd fled to the Rogue's Mountain. 'What about you?' she finally asked. 'Will you turn us in for the reward?'

'Me?' Paradon repeated. 'Good heavens, no. I came here to help you. I have never liked King Arden. It is a foolish and wasteful war he is waging. So many noble knights are fighting for an unjust cause. No, the last thing in the world I would do is help him. So I will help you instead.'

Kira looked into the old man's eyes and wanted desperately to believe him. But it was more than herself she had to worry about. She had to look out for Elspeth as well. 'How can you help if the king is after us? Lord Dorcon has tried to get us so many times. What can you do?'

Paradon reached out and gently caught hold of Kira's, and then Elspeth's, hands. 'I can take you both someplace where you will be safe. Somewhere not even

Lord Dorcon would think to look.'

'Where's that?' Elspeth softly asked.

'My castle.'

# CHAPTER
## ~ 27 ~

Seeking the safe refuge of Paradon's castle, they started out on the long journey. Knowing that anyone who saw them was likely to turn them in, they waited for the cloak of darkness to protect them and travelled only by night, while during the day, they hid themselves in deserted stone barns to avoid being seen.

With Jinx constantly wanting to attack Paradon, Kira and Elspeth had to follow him from a safe distance. Yet despite his obvious age, he had a good stride that kept them moving.

During their journey, Paradon tried to reassure Kira and Elspeth that they were safe, but neither could fully push aside the constant fear of discovery.

On the third night, as dawn was breaking on the distant horizon, Paradon stopped and pointed. 'Over there,' he called back to Kira. 'Just past those trees where the land starts to rise again. On the top of that ridge is my castle. With luck, we should be there soon.'

Seeing their destination suddenly put a bounce back in her step. 'Shadow, wake up!' Kira called excitedly as she stepped closer to Jinx and caught hold of Elspeth's foot where it dangled down the dragon's side. Giving it a light shake, she repeated, 'Shadow, wake up.'

When Elspeth opened her eyes and sat up, she looked down on Kira. 'I wasn't asleep,' she said sleepily.

Kira chuckled. 'No, of course you weren't. So I guess I don't have to tell you that we can see Paradon's castle, do I?'

'We can?' Elspeth exclaimed, looking around. 'Where is it?'

Kira pointed. 'It's over there, where that hill rises to the ridge. The castle is at the top.'

Cheering, Elspeth reached back and petted the fox resting on her shoulders. 'Do you see that, Onnie? That's Paradon's castle and our new home!'

Kira shook her head and chuckled quietly. Her sister seemed to have completely forgotten that Onnie had come to them from that castle. Instead of mentioning it, she reached forward and patted Jinx on the neck. 'We're almost home.'

Soon both girls were gazing in wonder at the sight before them. It was the oddest place they'd ever seen in their lives.

On each of the six corners of the castle there was a tall tower. But only two went straight up. The other four lazily zigzagged their way into the sky. Fancy, upside-down staircases with heavy rope handholds led up along the outside walls. But they seemed to Kira to lead nowhere and have no entrance into the structure. Instead of windows, the high walls were dotted with doors with huge golden knockers.

Kira helped Elspeth climb down from Jinx. Walking side by side, their smiles soon turned to giggles as they pointed and marvelled at the strange castle. They had never been to the king's palace, but her father had drawn pictures. It never looked anything like this.

'Kira, look. It's floating!' Elspeth cried.

Kira opened her mouth in shock.

Ahead of them, the odd castle was suspended almost waist high off the ground. It didn't move or drift, just sat there with nothing beneath it but air.

'Paradon?' Kira called forward as he walked several paces ahead. When he turned, Kira pointed. 'Why is your castle floating?'

Paradon chuckled and shook his head. 'Well, now, you've caught me. I haven't exactly told you girls everything about myself.'

Kira frowned. 'What do you mean? What haven't you told us?'

'Do you remember I told you about how I can look into my Eye and see things?'

When Kira nodded, he continued. 'That's because I'm a bit of a wizard.'

'You are?' Elspeth excitedly called.

Paradon nodded.

'Really?' Kira asked. 'We've never met a wizard before. Father told us about them, but I never believed they existed.'

'Oh we exist all right. But I'm afraid I'm not a very good wizard. My powers don't work the way they are supposed to. My master tried for many years to teach me how to use my gifts properly. But something always went wrong. I can see the words clearly in my head, but they never come out straight. Then something goes wrong.'

'Like what?' Kira asked.

'Well, like the castle for one thing. I tried to do a bit of decorating and, well, the towers now look a little strange, as I'm sure you'll agree. Then some years ago I was doing my spring-cleaning. I only wanted to lift the rug in my chamber. I cast a spell I thought would do it. But as you can see, I lifted the whole castle instead.'

'Didn't you ever try to get it back down again?'

Paradon shook his head. 'I couldn't risk it. There is no telling what could have happened. I might have sent it away. Or so high up, I might never have got it back down again. Then after a time, I came to like it like that.'

'Does it have a moat?' Elspeth excitedly called.

'Of a sort,' he answered, turning back and smiling again. 'And considering how you've both been laughing mercilessly at my home and magic, I know you are going to like it.'

Paradon was right. They did like it. As they started to walk over the lowered drawbridge that crossed the moat, Kira and Elspeth leaned over the side and laughed. 'Is that really what it looks like?'

'It is. I don't know how it happened,' Paradon admitted, 'but then I never know how these things happen. They just do. All I wanted was some fresh water with a few fish so that on long summer evenings, I could come out here and do a little fishing. I said the words for water, imagined water, and boom! I get ice. But this is no ordinary ice, oh no. This is ice that never melts. Even on the hottest days of summer, the moat remains solid.'

'But what about fish?' Elspeth asked gazing down on the ice.

'If you look closely, you can see them dotted here and there. They are as frozen as the water.'

'Kira, look! Over there, little fish!'

Staring at the ice, Kira did see the dark shapes of fish. Closer to the shore, she found small schools of minnows that would never move. 'This is amazing. Look over there, Shadow, that's a really big one!'

'Kira, Elspeth,' Paradon said seriously. 'I know you are enjoying yourselves, but I think it's best if we get you all under cover before anyone sees you.'

'We're coming,' Kira said, drawing Elspeth along.

Once they were safely on the other side of the drawbridge, Kira watched as Paradon raised his hands in the air and started to mumble strange words. Moments later they watched in astonishment as the drawbridge slowly rose, blocking off the only easy route into the castle.

After he finished with the drawbridge, he turned and said a few more words to the heavy portcullis that blocked the entrance of the castle. It started to creek and moan and finally began to rise. While it climbed along its tracks, the large heavy oak doors behind it slowly opened.

'This way.' Paradon beckoned as he walked to a set of wooden steps leading up to the entrance of the castle. 'Just a little bit further.'

As they moved forward, before they climbed the steps, both Kira and Elspeth bent down to peer under the floating castle. They saw dirt and exposed roots hanging down from the bottom of the castle, while on the bare ground beneath it, they saw a rabbit dashing around. But they couldn't see anything to show them how the castle stayed up in the air.

'This way, girls,' Paradon called. 'There will be time for exploring later. Just get Jinx in here first.'

'He's right,' Kira agreed. 'Let's go.'

Climbing the stairs, Kira and Elspeth followed Paradon under the portcullis and through the heavy oak doors into the castle's courtyard.

Paradon led them to another huge set of doors. They stood much taller than Jinx. Looking at the old oak, Kira saw flying dragons beautifully carved into the heavy wood. Rubies blazed in their eyes and there was gold for claws.

Paradon raised his hands in the air and muttered a few words. Moments later, the heavy doors slowly swung open. 'This way, ladies.' He beckoned, bowing formally. 'Welcome to your new home. Far away from the king and Lord Dorcon.'

Following him through the doors, Elspeth asked,

'Paradon, why does the king hate us so much?'

Paradon stood in the entrance hall of the castle and turned towards Elspeth. To Kira, it looked as though he was carefully considering his words. Finally, a deep frown cut across his wrinkled brow.

'Well, it's all very complicated. But Arden isn't the first king to treat girls like this. His father did too. So did his father before him. It's been this way for many generations.'

'But why?' Kira asked. 'And what about women? They took our mother to the palace with my father and Dane, but not Kahrin.'

'Grown women are no threat to the king. It's girls and young women whom he fears above all else.'

'Fears?' Elspeth repeated and then shook her head. 'King Arden isn't afraid of girls. He just hates us. Mother always said so.'

Elspeth was clutching Onnie to her chest as she wandered around the entrance hall. While she moved, Kira watched Paradon's eyes closely following her. She had the strangest feeling that he wanted to say something more, but at the last moment, changed his mind.

'What is it?' she quietly asked, stepping closer to him.

Drawing his eyes from Elspeth, Paradon put his arm around her shoulders and quietly said, 'In a moment.' Then he turned to Elspeth. 'Onnie, how would you like to show Elspeth around the castle?'

After a short yip Onnie leaped from Elspeth's arms and dashed down the corridor.

'Just keep to the safe areas,' Paradon called to him and watched Elspeth chasing after the fox.

When they were alone, Kira looked over to him. 'Thank you, Paradon, for letting us stay here.' Then she paused, uncertain if she should say what was really on her mind. Finally she decided. 'Please don't take this the wrong way and think I'm not grateful, because I am. But I must know. Why are you doing this for us? I mean if King Arden is offering a reward, why would you risk your life to help us?'

Paradon slowly nodded his head. 'I was wondering when you might ask me. Come,' he said, drawing her forward. 'Let's get Jinx settled in his quarters with some food. He's still recovering from that fight with his father. After that, you and I must talk.'

Kira agreed and followed the wizard through the corridors of the great castle. Just ahead, they approached another set of very tall doors. Paradon stepped aside, taking care not to approach the dragon too closely. 'Take

Jinx through there. I hope it's to your liking.'

Stepping up to the doors, Kira gave them a light push. When they opened, they revealed a very comfortable chamber with two separate four-poster beds. Just opposite the beds, she found a large area where a thick layer of clean straw covered the floor. Against the wall was a large stone trough filled to overflowing with fresh meat. Beside it another trough contained water.

Almost immediately Jinx smelled the meat and moved over to eat. While he was occupied, Kira walked back to the entrance of the chamber and found Paradon.

'Do you approve?' he asked.

When Kira nodded, he caught her by the elbow. 'Very good. Now, I'm afraid we don't have a lot of time before Onnie brings Elspeth back. I have something I must tell you and I think it's best if you hear it alone.'

'Of course,' Kira agreed, shocked by the sudden mood change. Then looking around, she pointed to the beds. 'Maybe we can sit there. If I go out of here, I know Jinx will follow me and I want him to rest.'

Paradon agreed and followed Kira to the beds. When she sat down, he took a seat on the bed opposite. Leaning over, he rested his elbows on his knees and rubbed his rough hands together. Finally he looked up at her.

'Well, it all started long ago,' the wizard said softly. 'A secret prophecy passed down from one king to the next. It said that one day, a young girl astride a twin-tailed dragon would destroy the monarchy and change the world for ever.'

'Really?' Kira said.

Paradon nodded. 'It was my great-great-grandfather, Elan, who foretold this many generations ago. He was a palace wizard in the court of King Lacarian. It was his duty to tell the king of his visions. But on this occasion, telling King Lacarian was a grave mistake. Not long after Elan told him, the king had him murdered.'

Stunned, Kira's mouth fell open. 'Why would he do that?'

'Because King Lacarian was an evil coward. Just like his descendent, King Arden, is today. All he cared about was wealth and power. Not his people or their needs. And because King Lacarian didn't trust Elan, when he heard about the prophecy, he ordered Elan be put to death.'

'So he didn't believe him?'

Paradon nodded. 'Oh, he believed him all right. He

just didn't want Elan telling anyone else in case it caused his people to rise up against him. But he was too late. Elan had already told others about his vision.'

'Who did he tell?' Kira quickly asked.

'He told his wife. Then their son, my great-grandfather.'

'And so that's how you know about the prophecy?'

Paradon nodded. Then he continued, 'But Kira, there's more. You see Elan knew how evil King Lacarian could be. So when he told him the prophecy, Elan withheld the details of the girl. He was convinced if he told him everything, the king would have had all the girls in the kingdom that fit the description killed. So instead, he only told him it would be an unmarried girl astride a twin-tailed dragon.'

Kira mulled this over for a moment, not quite understanding the importance of what Paradon was saying. Then she looked up. 'Was that how the First Law started?'

'Indeed it was,' Paradon agreed. 'At first King Lacarian wanted all the palace dragons destroyed. But then his advisors talked him out of it and suggested First Law instead. It was the only thing they could think of to stop the prophecy from coming true. So as each prince is born to the ruling king, when he is old enough, he is told the secret prophecy and that wretched First Law against girls continues.'

Kira frowned. 'Why are you telling me this now?'

'Because, Kira, we don't have a lot of time.'

'Time for what?'

'Time to train you to handle Jinx properly. More importantly,' he said seriously, 'how to fight.'

'Fight?' Fear crept into her voice. 'I don't understand. Why do I need to know how to fight? Fight whom? Lord Dorcon?'

Paradon looked up to the ceiling and seemed to concentrate on a spot that wasn't there. Finally he looked back at her. 'Yes, Lord Dorcon. But you must also fight King Arden and his entire army.'

'What!' Kira suddenly rose. 'That's impossible! I'm not going to fight the king. I don't want to fight anybody. I just want to find a safe place for us to live.'

'Please understand, my child,' Paradon said sombrely. 'There is no safe place for you to live. You are going to have to learn to fight for your life. For Elspeth and for the life of that dragon over there.'

'But I can't fight, I'm just a girl! I won't!'

'You must,' Paradon said gently. 'Now please sit down and let me finish what I have to tell you.'

Kira hesitated and suddenly wondered if they had made a grave mistake in coming to the castle. Elspeth had said they could trust Paradon. But now she wasn't so sure. Slowly she took a seat and eyed the wizard suspiciously. 'Go on,' she said, 'I'm listening.'

'Kira, Elan told his wife the details of the girl he had seen in his vision; the girl who would topple the corrupt monarchy. For he had clearly seen her face.' Pausing, Paradon reached over and took hold of Kira's hand. 'And the face he saw was yours.'

Kira pulled back her hand and started to shake her head. 'No, that's impossible! You're wrong, Paradon. I'm not that girl. I can't be!'

'I swear by my oath as a wizard, I speak the truth. Elan spoke of a girl who had pale skin with sky-blue eyes and bright red hair kept in twin braids. He said she dressed as a boy and didn't wear the bands of marriage. This precious girl would be the one to finally free the kingdom from the monarch's vicious tyranny.'

Kira lowered her head, unable to believe what she was hearing. 'But a lot of girls have red hair,' she softly argued.

'True,' Paradon agreed. 'But look at yourself, Kira. How many red-haired girls do you know who dress like a boy and ride around on a twin-tailed dragon? A dragon, I might add, that loves them.'

'What?'

Paradon nodded. 'Elan described you and Jinx as clearly as if he had seen you both together.'

'But it can't be true,' Kira argued. 'There are two of us, Elspeth and me. Your great-great-grandfather didn't mention her, did he?'

'No he didn't,' Paradon admitted. 'But, Kira, you must agree that the chances of it being a different red-headed girl, dressing as a boy and riding a twin-tailed dragon that loves her, are remote at best.'

Kira wanted to argue the point, but she couldn't. 'I just can't believe it,' she said, shaking her head. 'I'm no fighter. I'm just a girl. I can't do anything.'

'Kira, you listen to me!' Paradon cut in sharply. 'You can do anything you want to! Being a girl has nothing to do with it. Just think of what you've accomplished so far. You saved your sister's life back on the farm. You saved the life of that dragon and raised him into this magnificent beast before me. You were prepared to fight Ferarchie when he was going to kill Jinx, without the least bit of hesitation or fear for yourself. So don't go telling me that you can't do something because you are a girl! Despite what the king says, girls are just as capable as boys.'

Kira's head was spinning. *Her?* The girl from the prophecy? It wasn't possible. But then she looked over to the dragon lying contentedly on the straw watching her. Jinx *did* have twin tails, and most of all, he loved her and she loved him.

'How, Paradon?' she finally asked, turning back to him. 'I don't understand how it could be me?'

'I promise you, child, I don't know either. That it is you who will bring down the monarchy I have no doubt. Certainly the Eye showing me the visions of you and Elspeth coming here reveals this to be true. It also shows me that somehow I am a part of it all.'

'But I don't know how to fight or to be that hero girl,' Kira argued. 'I just can't do it.'

'Maybe not now, but you will. I'll be there to show you what you need to know.'

'But what about Elspeth? What happens to her?'

'I truly don't know,' Paradon answered softly. 'But I think for her sake, we should keep this between you and me for the time being.'

'You want me to lie to her? I couldn't do that.'

'To protect her, you would,' Paradon said seriously. 'Kira, what good can come from telling your eight-year-old sister your destiny? She will ask what her part in this is and neither of us can give her an answer. Our silence is the only way to protect her from all that must come.'

He was right. And Kira hated it. 'Why now?' she suddenly asked. 'Why must you tell me this now, today, when we've only just arrived? Why couldn't you wait a bit to let us settle in?'

'Because we don't have the luxury of time.'

Kira saw something in his face. 'What do you mean?'

Paradon lowered his head and wrung his hands together. 'I misled you in the woods when I said you could come here and be safe.'

'Why?' Kira demanded.

'Because of Elspeth,' Paradon answered, still wringing his hands. 'She is young but has already been through more than anyone should ever have to endure. I couldn't bear to take the illusion of safety away. But the Eye has revealed to me that you and your sister will not be safe here for as long as I had hoped. I have seen Lord Dorcon and his men here at my castle.'

'What!' Kira cried, jumping up. She immediately sat again when Jinx raised his head and looked as if he was about to cross over to her. 'It's all right. Stay there.'

She concentrated on Paradon again and lowered her voice. 'What do you mean you've seen Lord Dorcon here? When? Should we leave now?'

Paradon shook his head. 'The Eye will not show me when, but it is not in the immediate future.'

'Does he catch us?'

Paradon shook his head. 'No. I have seen his rage at losing you. Therefore, I must assume you get away. But again, it is not very clear.'

'Why is it so unclear and yet you could clearly see us when we were at the farm and then heading to the mountain?'

'When the Eye showed you on your farm, everything I saw was happening at that very moment. For this, what I am seeing is the future. And like I told you before, my powers are unpredictable. I have very little, if any, control over what the Eye reveals to me.'

'Maybe you're wrong then,' Kira hopefully suggested. 'Maybe it was just like a dream and not the actual future.'

'I'm not wrong, not about this. I may not be able to tell you all the details you need, but it will happen, you can be certain.'

'So what do we do?' Kira asked, already feeling defeated and overwhelmed by it all. It seemed as though she and her sister would never find peace in their life again.

'What you do, my dear child, is learn all that you

can with this time we have left.'

Kira rose from the bed and crossed over to the sleeping dragon. At her approach, Jinx woke and raised his head. Reaching up, Kira started to scratch behind his pointed ears. Finally turning back to the wizard, she nodded. 'All right, I'll learn as much as I can. When do we start?'

Paradon also rose. 'Tomorrow.'

# CHAPTER
## ~ 28 ~

Dane stood at his cell door waiting for the instructor to arrive. The little bit of food he smuggled down to him was all that was keeping Dane alive. The dungeon guards had stopped feeding all the other prisoners in the cells around him. As it was, they were rarely given fresh water or straw for the floors.

As each morning arrived, it brought death with it. Dane regularly watched the guards dragging the bodies of the dead out of their cells. He didn't know how many prisoners were left alive in the dungeon, but it wasn't a lot. Starvation and the cold were taking a ferocious toll on all of them.

Starting to pace the confines of his cell, Dane recalled what his instructor had told him the previous day. Food was running dangerously low, so much so that supplies to the battlefront were being cut.

But what frightened Dane most was hearing that all supplies to Lasser Commons were being stopped.

Castle rumours said that the king was going to let the guards at the prison fend for themselves. As for the girls held there? Their fate was even grimmer. It seemed the king would much prefer all the girls there to die quietly so as not to trouble him any more.

But Kahrin was there. Furious that he couldn't do anything to help her, he knew it was only a matter of time before his little sister succumbed to starvation.

# CHAPTER
## ~29~

Paradon was true to his word. The day after they arrived, he had both girls out in the courtyard learning to use a bow and arrow. For Elspeth, this was turned into a game. But each time she drew back her bow Kira knew it was no game. She was in a life and death struggle. There was no time for mistakes.

The training never stopped, leaving little time for anything else. Climbing tiredly into bed late one evening, Elspeth looked over to her sister. 'Do you know what Onnie showed me last night after you went to sleep?'

Kira rose up on one elbow and looked over to her. 'What's that?'

'He showed me Paradon's special place where he keeps this really big stone ball. Onnie says it's the one he uses for his visions. You should see it, it's really pretty and it has all these colours flashing around inside it.'

Kira sat up, suddenly very curious. 'You've seen

Paradon's Eye? Where is it?'

'It's in one of the funny-shaped towers; the big one closest to the kitchen. It's kind of hard to find the way to the top with all the twists and turns. But Onnie knows a secret path. I'll take you there if you like.'

Kira did like. In fact, she really wanted to see the Eye for herself. Maybe if she looked into the stone globe, she could see what Paradon had seen. Just maybe he'd been wrong about Lord Dorcon coming to the castle. 'Do you think you and Onnie could show me tonight?'

'You don't want Paradon to know, do you?' Elspeth asked, as if she'd read Kira's mind.

'No, not really.'

'Don't you trust him?' Elspeth asked.

'It's not that,' Kira said softly. 'I do trust him. I just don't want him knowing where we are all the time.'

After drawing on their robes, Kira and Elspeth left Jinx sleeping peacefully as they quietly entered the corridor.

'It's this way,' Elspeth whispered, clutching Onnie in her arms.

Kira followed behind her sister. They had been in the castle for a while and yet she still didn't know her way around. Nor had she seen all of it. Paradon kept her too busy with training to allow her time to go exploring.

Kira also realized she didn't know where Paradon slept or spent his private time.

'Kira, come on,' Elspeth called.

Kira shook herself out of her musing and saw that she'd lagged behind. 'Keep your voice down, I'm coming!' she whispered back.

Elspeth led Kira deeper into the huge castle. Travelling along the smooth, seamless marble floors, they passed countless suits of armour and the many tapestries that adorned the thick walls. Finally they arrived at the kitchen that served the main dining hall.

'This way,' Elspeth prompted as they entered the kitchen and crossed to the rear of the room. When they left the kitchen from a door at the back, Kira followed Elspeth down a long and narrow corridor. At the end, she saw a heavy wooden door. It held nine separate panels. Each panel showed a wonderfully carved scene with a dragon. But what she couldn't see on the door was a handle or any obvious way of getting it open.

'How do we open it?' she softly asked.

'Onnie showed me,' Elspeth explained. She reached up and started to push her small index finger into the eye of the dragon on each of the panels. 'He says you have to press them in just the right order or the door won't open.'

After Elspeth pressed the final dragon's eye, Kira heard a click. A moment later, the heavy door slowly swung open. As they passed through, Kira saw that it was thicker than her hand. No one could ever break it down.

'It's this way.' Elspeth beckoned and he confidently stepped into the tower. She started up three worn stone steps, then walked along an impossibly long corridor.

From the outside of the castle, this tower zigzagged into the sky. But on the inside, it was even stranger. It had odd doors that opened to reveal other doors. Once they were opened, they led to the outer wall.

'Don't take those steps,' Elspeth warned as they walked past a spiral set of stairs.

'Why not?' Kira asked as she stood on the first step. 'You said Paradon's room was at the top.'

'It is, but you don't take those steps because they never end. Onnie says they just go up and up and up.'

'That's silly,' Kira argued. Leaning forward, she gazed up the staircase. It did seem to spiral up incredibly high, but as the tower had a roof, they simply had to end somewhere.

'Not with magic, it's not,' Elspeth said. 'If Onnie says they don't end, I believe him.'

Kira stopped arguing and looked at the stairs again.

There was a lot about this castle she didn't understand. But she had already seen enough magic not to question it any more. 'So if we don't take these stairs, which ones do we take to get up?'

'We don't take any stairs. We go through that window over there.'

Across the corridor, Kira saw what looked like a wooden window frame hung on the outer wall. Stepping closer, she peered through and saw only the wall. But when she reached her hand forward, it passed right through the stone. 'So we go through there?'

Elspeth nodded. She released Onnie who dashed forward and leaped lightly through the window. 'Just follow us,' she said as she climbed through after the fox.

When Kira followed Elspeth through the window, she looked back and saw only the wall. Touching it, it was cold and solid. There was no way back.

'How do we get out of here?' she asked nervously.

'There is a different way out. Onnie says you can only go in one direction in here. It's very strange. But it's so no one can find the way in. Or if they ever do, they can't find their way out again. It's kind of a trap.'

Hearing this made Kira very uneasy. 'Well, I hope you remember the way out.'

Nodding confidently, Elspeth started to walk. 'Come on, Kira. It's this way.'

Climbing through another window, they came upon a closed door resting in its frame. It was standing alone in the middle of the floor along a short corridor. Circling fully around the door, Kira came back to the front and reached for the handle. It was locked.

'What's this for?' she asked.

'Don't know,' Elspeth answered. 'Onnie says that Paradon's master used it. But he's never gone through it himself.'

'Used it for what?' Kira asked as she tried the knob again.

'As a door, silly,' Elspeth answered.

Kira looked at Elspeth feeling very frustrated. This tower was starting to annoy her. Stepping around the door again, she made no further comment. Not far ahead they came upon another set of stairs, this time leading down. As Elspeth was about to speak, Kira held up her hand.

'Don't tell me, I already know. These steps just go down and down and never end.'

Elspeth shook her head. 'Onnie says these do end. But we shouldn't ask what's down there. It's very bad.'

'I don't think I want to know, anyway,' Kira finally

said. 'How much further is it to Paradon's room?'

'Just ahead over there. It's through that door.'

'Wait,' Kira said, frowning deeply. 'You told me Paradon's room was at the top of the tower. We haven't climbed any stairs yet.'

'I know,' Elspeth agreed. 'But we're at the top. Look out the window over there. You'll see.'

Kira did as Elspeth suggested and walked up to a real window. Unable to trust anything she saw in the tower, she put her hand through first and felt the cool night air. Sticking out her head, she was shocked to see moonlight glistening off the ice of the frozen moat, a very, very long way beneath them.

'Told you,' Elspeth said. 'We're at the top.'

Kira pulled her head in and stood up. 'This doesn't make any sense. We didn't climb any stairs. How can we be at the top?'

'It's magic,' Elspeth answered casually. 'Paradon's chamber is here. Are you coming or not?'

Kira shook her head in bewilderment and followed Elspeth to a door. There were no panels with secret eyes to push. There were no magic words to be spoken. No windows to climb through. It was just a very ordinary, everyday, castle door.

Reaching for the knob, Kira didn't know what to

expect. But it turned easily in her hand. Pushing forward, she and Elspeth entered the torch-lit chamber.

Around them, the round tower walls were lined with countless shelves going all the way to the pointed ceiling. On the shelves were hundreds, maybe thousands of books. Covered in a thick layer of dust and cobwebs, the writing on their leather spines could no longer be read. To Kira, they looked as though they hadn't been disturbed in many years.

'Kira,' Elspeth excitedly called from her place in the very centre of the room. 'Come here and see, the colours are so pretty!'

Leaving the books, Kira looked over to Elspeth. Her sister was standing before a large, round boulder covered in brambles. As she stepped closer, she saw the rock was solid, dark grey in colour and didn't look too different from the large boulders her father and Dane were always digging up on the farm. This was Paradon's Eye?

'Aren't they beautiful!' Elspeth breathed.

Kira's eyes passed from the rock to her sister then back to the round rock again. 'Aren't what beautiful? That's just a big old rock.'

'No it's not,' Elspeth said. 'Look right there, it's full of colours. Just like a rainbow after a storm, only better.'

Kira stepped closer to Elspeth and strained her eyes to see what her little sister was seeing. Try as she might, all she saw was cold grey rock. 'I don't see anything.'

'Of course you do, right there!' Elspeth pointed. 'See, the red and baby blue, oh and there, bright green . . .'

'Shadow,' Kira said suspiciously, 'if you have brought me here as some kind of joke, it's not very funny.'

The wounded expression on her sister's face was enough to tell Kira that Elspeth wasn't playing.

'Can't you see the colours?' she softly asked.

Kira looked at the grey rock again. Turning to Elspeth, she shrugged. 'Maybe if we move some of these brambles away . . .' As Kira's hand moved forward, the brambles covering the rock started to quiver. Gasping, she looked to her sister. 'Did you see that?'

Elspeth nodded and held her hand over the thorny plants. As her fingers drew nearer, the brambles actually moved as if to cover the rock. She looked up to Kira. 'They don't want us to touch it.'

'Why? Shadow, this is nothing but a dumb old rock.'

'No it's not,' Elspeth said sincerely. 'This is Paradon's Eye. Those brambles are here to protect it. They won't let anyone but Paradon touch it.'

'That's crazy,' said Kira. 'Those weeds can't stop me from touching it.' To prove her point, she reached for an area of the rock that didn't have any of the green vines covering it. But before her fingers went anywhere near the surface, the brambles had moved in and sharp thorns stabbed up into her approaching fingers.

Kira cried out in pain and snatched her hand back. Inspecting it, she pulled several sharp thorns from her fingers and saw dark beads of blood rising to the surface.

'I told you,' Elspeth said. 'They will only obey Paradon.'

'Kira! Elspeth!' boomed a voice from behind them. 'What in the stars are you doing in here!'

Startled, both girls turned to see Paradon at the entrance to the chamber. He was standing with his hands on his hips and an expression like thunder on his face.

'Paradon . . .' Kira stammered. 'We, um, we just wanted to, well, we couldn't sleep. So we came for a walk.'

Storming into the room, the wizard crossed to the Eye. 'This area is off limits to you girls. It's far too dangerous. You could have been badly hurt coming here. How did you find your way up?'

From the corner of the room came the light sound of scurrying. Turning sharply, all three watched as a flash of red dashed across the floor and out of the chamber.

'That damn fox!' Paradon cried in a fury. Running after Onnie, he stood in the corridor and raised his fist in the air. 'How many times must I tell you? Stay out of here!'

Returning to the chamber, he stepped up to Elspeth. 'He led you here, didn't he?'

Too frightened and ashamed to speak, Elspeth weakly nodded.

'I thought so.' Leaving the Eye, Paradon started to pace the confines of the chamber. 'I have warned him time and time again not to take you girls into certain parts of the castle. There are areas here guarded by very powerful magic. Some of the spells even I can't break. If you'd got into trouble, I might not have been able to help you.'

'But it's your castle,' Kira said bravely. 'How can there be spells that you can't break?'

Paradon stopped his pacing and walked over to her. His immediate temper seemed to have ebbed as he softened his tone. 'This isn't my castle. It belongs to my master. I am only living here until he gets back.'

'Where is he?' Elspeth timidly asked.

Taking a deep calming breath, Paradon looked at her. 'I don't know. Many seasons ago, I watched him pass through the door in the corridor. He has never returned.'

'What is that door?' Kira asked.

'It's a portal. It leads from one place to another. For as long as I can remember, it has been here. Many times I asked him to show me how it worked, but he always refused. Sometimes, he would pass through and be gone for days and days. Then he would come back bearing many strange and wonderful items. In fact, most of the books in this chamber came from his journeys through that door.'

'What are the books about?' Kira asked.

Paradon lowered his head and his shoulders slumped. Finally he shrugged. 'I don't know. My master tried to teach me to read, but somehow, like my magic, it never worked. I used to spend entire days struggling to learn, but I couldn't. So all these books you see in here – I can never read them.'

Kira felt a sudden sympathy for him. Reaching out, she gently grasped his hand. 'We can't read either. Girls aren't allowed.'

'I know,' Paradon agreed. 'Believe me, if I could teach you, I would. But I'm afraid I can't.' Suddenly he snapped his fingers. 'Good heavens, I nearly forgot the reason I followed you up here.'

'You said it was because it isn't safe for us,' Elspeth weakly offered.

'Yes, of course,' he agreed. 'But also, that dragon of yours is down there ruining my kitchen!'

'Jinx?' Kira said. 'He tried to follow us?'

'That's what got me up,' Paradon exclaimed as he ushered the girls out of the chamber and led them down the corridor. 'I heard him roaring and racing through the corridors of the castle. When he couldn't get through the kitchen door, he broke it down and forced himself inside and that's where I found him. Now he's stuck in there and tearing the place apart.'

'He could hurt himself,' Kira said. 'We've got to get down there!'

'It's this way,' Paradon said as he led them through a door at the end of the corridor. Pausing, Kira stared at it for a moment. She was certain it hadn't been there before.

'Come along, child,' Paradon called as he held the door open.

Passing through it, Kira glanced back and was shocked to discover it was the very same door with the carved dragon panels that she and Elspeth had entered when they first arrived at the tower.

'How did we get here?' she asked, feeling very

perplexed. 'I just don't understand this place at all. We were at the top of the tower. Now after one door, we are back where we started at the base.'

'This is why you and Elspeth must never venture in the castle alone; not unless I have shown you which doors you can use and which ones to avoid. You may enter a door that I have never used before and that may lead to a part of the castle that I can't find.'

Kira was about to ask him another question when a loud crashing and roar from the kitchen stopped her.

'Quickly, go to him,' Paradon ordered. 'Before he brings down the castle!'

Catching Elspeth by the arm, both girls raced down the corridor towards the kitchen. 'Jinx!' Kira called. 'Jinx, we're coming!'

Immediately the crashing stopped and they heard their dragon starting to whine.

Entering the large kitchen, Kira's heart sank at the damage. Every flour barrel had been torn open and its contents spread all over the floor. A cloud of white still hung in the air. The centre table was overturned, its contents spilled all over the floor and trodden on. The oak washing basins had been torn from the walls and smashed apart. Cooking pots had been pulled down from where they hung and crushed under the dragon's massive weight. Every dish, every cup, anything remotely breakable had been destroyed. The only thing left undamaged was the fireplace, but even that had smoking logs lying outside the hearth.

'Jinx!' Elspeth scolded as she stepped up to the flour-covered dragon and started wagging her finger in the air. 'Look at this mess. Shame on you!'

'Shame on you all,' Paradon added as he turned to leave. 'Now I want you both to clean up this mess. And don't you ever let me catch either of you up in that tower again. Do I make myself clear?'

Shamed, Kira lowered her eyes and nodded. 'Yes Paradon. We're sorry. We won't do it again.'

'No, we won't,' agreed Elspeth. 'We're sorry.'

It was late in the day when the girls saw Paradon again. At some point after they'd gone to bed, Onnie had returned to Elspeth and now as they walked down the long corridors towards the kitchen, he hid himself in her arms.

With Jinx trailing obediently behind them, they returned to the kitchen expecting to see, the remains of the disaster in daylight. But when they entered Kira's eyes and mouth flew open. She glanced over to Elspeth who was equally shocked. Everywhere they looked everything that had been broken was repaired.

Standing in the back corner, Paradon crossed his arms over his chest and smiled broadly. 'Never underestimate the power of magic,' he said softly.

Striding over to him, Kira could barely speak. 'How?' she finally managed.

'I told you, magic.'

'Yes, but Paradon, your magic doesn't work!' She suddenly realized she might have offended him. 'I'm so sorry, what I mean to say is, well . . .'

The old wizard chuckled. 'I told you, child. It doesn't work most of the time, but sometimes it works just fine. Today I was lucky,' he raised one eyebrow, 'and so were you.'

Days passed. Training followed more training until both Elspeth and Kira ached from head to foot. But rising one morning, they didn't go to the courtyard. Instead Paradon directed them to the banquet hall.

'Today,' he said, 'I thought I might teach you girls how to put a real bridle and saddle on Jinx. After that, once the sun has set, if weather permits, we'll take our blue friend outside where I can show you how to direct him.'

Kira's heart started to race with excitement. This was

what she was really interested in. 'We couldn't really figure out how to put a saddle on Jinx, not with those bony plates running down his back. Father once told me they cut them off at the palace. But we could never do that to our boy.'

'That's right, they do,' Paradon agreed. 'And because of it, the poor creatures are in constant pain, especially when they have riders on their back. Which partly explains why palace dragons are so dangerous. And why I have had to design a new kind of saddle.'

'But we still don't know how to ride him properly,' Kira said.

'Indeed, which is why I am doing this now.' He then looked to Elspeth. 'I want you to stand at Jinx's head and tell him not to be frightened. It's time we put the saddle and bridle on him.'

Kira looked around the banquet hall but could see no traces of a saddle or bridle. Finally she glanced back to the wizard. 'Where are they?'

'Stand back and watch.'

Stepping a safe distance away from the dragon, he raised both his hands in the air. 'I have been thinking about this design for some time. Let's see if it works.' He said some strange words aloud, and suddenly the air around them started to snap and sparkle.

'Easy boy,' Elspeth said as Jinx's eyes started to pin in fear. He then began to fidget restlessly. Petting his face and neck, she continued softly, 'It's all right, Jinx, nothing is going to hurt you.'

When the sparkling increased, Kira started to see a shape coming together on Jinx's back as well as around his head. As each moment passed, the objects became more and more solid. Finally, the saddlebox and bridle just seemed to pop into existence.

# CHAPTER
## ~30~

Late one evening, after a long day of training on Jinx, and after Elspeth and Onnie had gone to bed, Paradon asked Kira to stay up and join him in the lounge. Seated together before a roaring hearth, the old wizard dropped his head and sighed.

'I've been to the Eye,' he said. 'It's not good.'

Suddenly frightened, Kira asked, 'What have you seen? Is it Lord Dorcon? Is he coming?'

Paradon shook his head. 'The war isn't going well. The king is losing knights at a terrifying rate. He is also wasting men launching fruitless attacks on the Rogue.'

'Why is he still going after the Rogue?'

'It's not the Rogue he's after, it's his offspring. When Lord Dorcon attacked you on the mountain, he saw Ferarchie's baby. When the king found out about the twin-tailed offspring, he became terrified that this was the time of the prophecy.'

Kira felt a shiver running down her spine. 'Does he know about Jinx?'

'No,' Paradon answered. 'But very soon, he will.'

'Why?' Kira asked. 'Because Lord Dorcon is coming here and will tell him about us?'

Again Paradon shook his head. 'No. He will learn of Jinx long before then. Because of what you and Elspeth are about to do.'

'Paradon, please,' Kira pleaded, 'just tell me. What have you seen?'

'Kira, because the king is losing so many knights to the war and to Ferarchie, he is pulling fighters from anywhere he can. But he is also very aware of the prophecy. He suspects you, but he can't be certain. So he is going to do the only thing he can to protect himself.'

'What's that?'

Paradon lowered his head. 'He is going to execute all the girls at Lasser Commons.'

'What?' Kira cried. 'He can't!'

'He'd planned to starve them to death by withholding their food shipments. But that's not working fast enough so he's sending men to kill them. Then once they're dead, he'll pull the guards away and use them for the war.'

'He can't do that!' Kira cried.

'Unless you stop him,' Paradon continued, 'he can and he will.'

'No!' she shouted.

'Kira?' Elspeth said as she sleepily entered the lounge. 'I heard shouting. What's happening?'

Jinx was standing right behind her. When he saw the wizard, he started to growl.

'Not now, Jinx,' snapped Kira. She then looked to Elspeth. 'You'd better come in here. We have something to tell you.'

Kira, Elspeth and Paradon stayed up all night discussing the upcoming execution of the girls of Lasser.

'We've got to stop him,' Elspeth said as she clutched Onnie to her chest.

'We will,' Kira agreed. She then turned pleading eyes to Paradon. 'Please tell me you'll help us?'

'Of course I will,' the wizard said. 'I'll do all I can.'

'Will you use your magic?' Elspeth asked.

Paradon shrugged. 'Perhaps. But I'd rather not. It's just too unpredictable. There are girls' lives at stake. One mistake on my part and I could end up doing the king's work for him.'

'But without you, how can we rescue Kahrin and

free the girls in Lasser?' Kira asked.

'I didn't say I wouldn't help,' Paradon corrected. 'I just won't use a lot of magic.'

'What else is there?' Elspeth asked.

'You have many things on your side. You've got your new skills with the bow and arrow. You've got the element of surprise. Then there's the fact that most of the able-bodied men have already been pulled away from Lasser. All that's left are either too old to fight, or too wounded.' Paradon paused and then looked over to Jinx. 'Not to mention you have a very large dragon who would do anything to protect you.'

'Jinx?' Kira said.

Paradon nodded. 'We are used to thinking of him as a baby. But your blue friend over there isn't a baby anymore. He is a very large, very ferocious dragon. The fact that you can control him will make him a very strong ally.'

'But Jinx doesn't even know how to fly.' Kira said remembering his plunge into the lake after their escape from the Rogue's mountain. 'How can we expect him to help us with this?' Kira said.

'We can teach him. Believe me, by the time you leave here, you and your dragon will be well prepared.'

'How long have we got?' Elspeth asked.

'From what I saw, the executions won't start until after next full moon.'

Kira panicked. 'Wait! There's a full moon tonight! How do you know they won't execute the girls tomorrow?'

Paradon raised his hands and motioned her to calm down. 'Believe me, Kira, it is the next full moon, not this one. I have seen a very heavy snowstorm giving you the cover you need.'

'Snow?' Kira said. 'That's impossible. Winter snows are over. It's spring. The most we can hope for is rain.'

In Elspeth's arms, Onnie started to yip. Everyone turned to him. 'Onnie says that you are going to make it snow,' she said to the wizard.

'Now that, I can do,' Paradon agreed. 'And I will. In fact, it might be an idea to start the storms early so that it doesn't look too suspicious. Besides, it might slow the king and his men down a bit. We might even give ourselves more time.'

'So we've got at least one moon cycle to plan our attack?' Kira asked.

Paradon nodded. 'We can't waste a moment of it.'

# CHAPTER
## ~ 31 ~

With so many men going off to war, Dane was finally allowed out of the dungeon during the day to work in the dragon stables. His job was to help care for the young dragons before they were trained and went off into battle.

The other workers in the stable never spoke to him and kept well away, as though the brand on his face was some kind of curse that would bring the wrath of Lord Dorcon down upon them. Dane didn't care how they felt. All he cared about was finding out anything he could about his sisters.

'I doubt Lord Dorcon will ever find them,' the instructor said to Dane as they walked together to the stables. 'He's just back from another fruitless search. It's like your sisters have vanished right out of the kingdom. Mind you, this weather isn't helping. I've never seen snow this late in the season before.'

'Well, if it's helping my sisters stay hidden, I'm glad for it.'

'So am I,' the instructor said. 'I've been called back into active service. When the storm breaks, I'm off to the front.'

'They can't do that!' Dane protested. 'If you go, who will teach the new knights?'

'Actually, Dane, I wanted to talk to you about that.' The instructor stopped walking and turned to face Dane. 'You know we are losing a lot of knights to this war?'

When Dane nodded, he continued. 'The king needs more men. So they are calling back all the guards from Lasser. Those that can still fight will go into battle. Those that can't will come here. That's where my replacement is coming from.'

Dane frowned, unsure of what he'd just heard. 'But if all the guards are leaving Lasser, are they going to release the girls?'

The instructor shook his head slowly. 'I'm so sorry, Dane. I know your sister is there. I really wish I could do something, but I can't.'

Fear constricted Dane's throat. 'What do you mean? What are they going to do?'

'From what I've heard, they are not waiting for

starvation to kill them. They're going to execute the girls instead.'

Dane's face went deathly pale. 'They're going to kill Kahrin?'

'They're going to kill everyone. The king is keeping it quiet because of all the girls' families here at the palace. I'm sure if they knew, they would turn against him.'

'I'll tell them!' Dane cried. 'I'll tell everyone! Then maybe they'll fight the king and we can stop it.'

The instructor reached out for Dane's arms. 'You mustn't! Believe me, I feel the same. But the moment we tell anyone, the king will have every family at the palace put to death. He'll do it, Dane. Believe me he will, and he'll enjoy every bit of it.'

'But we've got to do something,' Dane cried. 'We can't let him kill the girls just because he needs the men.'

'I've been trying to think of something, anything we could do to stop it. But there is nothing. Dane, you're Lord Dorcon's prisoner. I'm supposed to be going to the front any day now. We're just two people. There is nothing we can do. I'm so sorry, Dane. But the girls of Lasser are doomed.'

# CHAPTER
## ~32~

When Onnie said Paradon could make it snow, Kira had no idea just how powerful the wizard really was. After he cast his spell, it was as though a heavy winter was upon them, with large flakes falling steadily from the sky.

With the tension of the upcoming battle taking a heavy toll on Kira, the only relief she felt was the fun she had watching Elspeth taking a break from training. They were in the courtyard playing with Onnie and Jinx. The young dragon had never really experienced snow before. His first evening out in the storm, he lifted his head and opened his mouth to feel the flakes falling gently on his tongue.

Taking advantage of his distraction, Elspeth made a snowball and threw it at him, hitting him squarely on the head. Jinx jumped in surprise and then loped after Elspeth like an excited puppy. Unable to resist the game, Kira quickly joined in and also threw a snowball at the dragon. Before long, they were running around the courtyard as an all-out snowball fight began.

But just as quickly as it had begun, the fun ended when Paradon called them forward to begin their training again. He quickly had both girls firing arrows out in the snow, shooting at targets while racing through the corridors of the castle – anywhere and everywhere he could.

'Tonight,' Paradon said from his place just inside the safety of the castle doors, 'we've got to get Jinx into the air again.'

'How?' Kira asked. 'He rarely opens his wings. How are we going to teach him to fly?'

'I'm not really sure,' Paradon admitted, rubbing his beard. 'At the palace stables, the younger dragons learned to fly by watching the older ones. As Jinx is the only dragon here, we have to approach the problem differently. So, I was thinking. Back on the mountain, Jinx flew because he had no choice. You fell into that chasm. It was fly or die! So he flew.'

Kira frowned. 'What are you thinking?'

'I'm thinking that we create the same situation here. Just for the first time until he gets his wings beneath him.'

'How? You know I would never do anything to hurt him.'

'We won't have to! Now, I must ask you to leave.'

'Why?' said Kira.

'Because it could be a touch dangerous for you to remain here.'

'Dangerous? Paradon, what are you going to do?' Kira nervously asked. 'You aren't going to use magic are you?'

Paradon grinned widely and nodded. 'Of course I am! And with a little luck, this might just work. Now, go and get Elspeth and Jinx. This shouldn't take me too long.'

As the wizard started to walk away, Kira jogged after him and caught his arm. 'Wait, please, I know we've got to train Jinx, but—'

Paradon turned back to Kira and patted her reassuringly on the hand. 'Yes we do, it's very important.' Grinning again, a twinkle rose in his eyes. 'Besides, it's been a long time since I've done anything with the old castle. The place could use a little changing.'

'But, Paradon—'

'I know, I know,' the wizard agreed. 'Which is why you and your sister are going to wait outside the castle grounds just in case something doesn't quite go to plan. Now don't you fret. I'll come for you in a short time.'

Kira opened her mouth to protest. Then closed it again. There just wasn't any point arguing. As she watched him walking to the castle doors, he called back to her, 'Remember, wait on the other side of the moat. That should be safe enough.'

When he disappeared inside, Kira trotted over to where Elspeth was standing with Onnie and Jinx.

'Where's Paradon going?' Elspeth asked.

'You don't want to know,' Kira answered as she patted Jinx's thick neck and reached for his reins. 'He said he has an idea for how we can teach Jinx to fly. But he says we need to wait on the other side of the moat while he makes some changes to the castle.' Kira gave the reins a light tug. 'Come on, Jinx, let's go for a little walk.'

'He isn't going to do magic is he?' Elspeth nervously asked as she fell in step beside her.

Kira nodded. 'I'm afraid so. I tried to talk him out of it, but he wouldn't listen to me. He got this strange expression on his face and seemed really excited by what he was planning.'

Clutched in Elspeth's arms, Onnie started to yip and threw back his head in a long howl.

'What's his problem?' Kira asked.

Elspeth looked down into the fox's face. After a few

short yips and another long howl, her expression darkened. 'Onnie says we should do more than just go over the drawbridge. He said we should get as far away from the castle as we can. Then be ready to run.'

Kira looked from Elspeth back to the fox. For a change Onnie didn't squint or scowl. Instead, his eyes were showing genuine fear. Catching her sister by the arm, Kira gave the reins a tug and started to run.

With Jinx at their side, Kira and Elspeth ran until the castle was far behind them. Turning around, they huddled closely together as they watched and waited.

Nothing happened.

'Now what?' Elspeth asked.

'I don't know,' admitted Kira. 'I really thought Paradon was going to do something big—'

No sooner were the words out of her mouth, than they saw a sudden flash of light and heard a huge explosion coming from the castle.

'There!' Elspeth shouted as she pointed to the castle's north tower.

Unable to believe her eyes, Kira watched as debris shot up into the air and a blinding white light sprang up from the top of one of the two straight towers. Roaring thunder mixed with the horrible groaning sounds of the castle until Elspeth was forced to release

Onnie from her arms and cover her ears.

Beside them, Jinx roared in fear as the light hurt his sensitive eyes. He slammed his head down on the ground and started to whine. Finally he tucked his head under his wing.

Kira shielded her eyes to block out the terrible light as she tried to see the castle. Her ears were ringing from the thunder roaring from the north tower. But as she listened, it slowly started to soften. The bright light started to fade as well, until it went out completely. With the light gone, they were cast back into darkness.

They ran back to the castle, passed under the portcullis and entered the courtyard. All the torches were still lit, revealing the melted snow and scorched grounds. The walls of the castle were burned black and still smouldering. But as Kira's eyes scanned the area, she couldn't see Paradon anywhere.

'Stay with Jinx,' she said nervously. 'I'm going to look for him.'

Desperately calling his name, Kira ran across the courtyard to the blackened entrance doors. As she was about to knock, they slowly opened.

'Paradon!' she cried, filled with relief. 'I thought you were dead!'

'Almost, but not quite,' the wizard said sheepishly.

Throwing her arms around him, she felt heat coming from his cloak. He smelled of fresh smoke and she saw that he was actually smouldering. His face was black with soot. His eyelashes and eyebrows were gone. His long beard was burned off and he was now completely bald.

'Paradon, you're on fire!' Kira exclaimed as she saw flames rising from the hem of his cloak. Quickly stomping them out, she looked back to the wizard.

'My, my,' Paradon coughed. 'That was a wild one!'

'What happened?'

'Onnie says Paradon blew up the castle,' Elspeth answered as she and the fox stepped up to the doors. Jinx trailed a short distance behind, growling lightly when he saw the wizard.

'Not *all* the castle,' Paradon defended. 'Just the north tower. But it's much better now. Come along and I'll show you girls what I've done.'

Wary of the dragon, Paradon stepped into the burnt courtyard. 'As you can see, the north tower is much bigger now. It has a flat roof and large doors for Jinx to fit through. It should be everything we need to get him to fly.'

Elspeth looked up to the top of the tower and

frowned. 'It's very high. How are we going to get Jinx up there? Magic?'

'No,' Paradon answered. 'I've put in a set of stairs that should be easy for him to climb.'

She then asked, 'Paradon, where did the bright light come from?'

'Well, now, that's a very good question,' he chuckled. 'I'm not really sure. All I did was say the words to make the tower bigger and change the stairs and roof. Instead I seemed to capture a lightning storm in the palms of my hands. I threw it away just as quickly as I could, but, well, as you know, it blew up the tower . . .' Paradon then lowered his voice and finished, 'and half the castle with it.'

'I'm just glad you weren't hurt!' Kira said.

Paradon held up his hands. Kira hadn't noticed before, but they were both so badly burned there was hardly any skin left on them. 'Well, I didn't get off that lightly,' he admitted. 'But when I saw what was happening, I quickly cast a spell of protection. Lucky for me, that one worked. The fire storm passed right over me without actually killing me.'

'Lucky for all of us,' Elspeth added.

'Indeed,' Paradon agreed. 'Now, girls, this old wizard is extremely sore and very tired. If you don't mind, I'm going to go to bed. I suggest you do the same.'

'What about your hands?' Kira asked. 'Let us help you with them.'

Paradon's blackened face lit with a warm and affectionate smile. It made his teeth glow even brighter in all the soot. 'Thank you, child, but you needn't worry about me. I've lotions in my chamber that will fix this up in no time. I will be as right as rain in the morning.'

It took a full day before the castle was back to normal. Much to the girls' amusement and Paradon's frustration, most of the wizard's spells went wrong during the course of repairs. But finally the job was finished.

'Well, now that that's done,' Paradon said as he dusted nonexistent dirt off his hands, 'I think tonight we should take Jinx up into the new tower and try to get him to fly.'

When evening arrived, Paradon led Kira and Elspeth through the courtyard and into the newly changed tower. With Jinx following behind them, still growling and puffing out his cheeks at the wizard, they approached the base of the stairs.

'I've never actually seen a dragon climb stairs before,'

Paradon admitted, 'I just hope our boy can do it.'

'He will,' Elspeth said confidently. 'You'll see. Jinx can do anything.'

'I believe you're right,' Paradon agreed. 'But if you don't mind, just to be safe I'll go up first. It will also give me time to light the torches. Then you girls can follow me.' Paradon paused, and then said, 'I think it's best if Jinx comes up last. If he slips and falls back down, I don't want either of you near him.'

Kira nodded and waited for Paradon to get a good distance ahead before she and Elspeth started to follow. Gazing around the tower, the changes were amazing. The stairway was much wider than it had ever been, with each step being particularly deep to allow for the dragon's long claws.

'Come on, Jinx,' Kira coaxed as the dragon waited at the base. 'You can do it. Just follow us.'

Hesitant at first, Jinx finally started to climb, up and up until he came to the top of the tower. At the top, they found Paradon waiting.

'Girls, stand back, I'm going to do this very quickly.'

'Do what?' Kira asked.

The wizard raised his arms in the air and cast his spell. Suddenly, in a move quicker than their eyes could follow, Jinx was pushed forward by invisible hands and shoved off the top of the tower.

'Paradon, no!' Kira cried as she watched Jinx going over the edge. Racing forward, they both saw the dragon tumbling down the side of the tower as his terrified howls filled the air.

'Fly, Jinx! Fly!' Kira shouted.

'Open your wings and fly!' Elspeth ordered. 'Do it now! Jinx, open your wings and fly!'

Both girls watched in terror as Jinx continued to fall. They were convinced it hadn't worked. But moments before their beloved dragon crashed to the ground, he spread his wings. Soon his howls of fear turned to roars of triumph as he soared above the singed grounds of the courtyard. Giving a light flap of his wings, he climbed assuredly into the night sky.

Instantly going from horror to jubilation, Kira and Elspeth clung to each other, shouting and cheering.

'Isn't he beautiful!' Kira cried as tears of joy sprang to her eyes. 'Shadow, that's our baby up there! He's really flying!'

Jinx's roars filled the dark sky as he circled around the castle. Testing himself, he rose higher in the air and then lower. But all the while, he never ventured so far that Kira or Elspeth couldn't see him.

'Call him back to you,' Paradon instructed. 'He's got

to learn to come back when you need him.'

After several more successful flights, Paradon called the girls forward. 'Kira, Elspeth, I want you to climb into the saddlebox. It's your turn to learn to fly with him.'

Kira looked at Jinx and felt her stomach clench with fear. She knew she had to do it. But the tower was awfully high, and Jinx had only just learned to fly. But beside her, Elspeth fearlessly climbed into the box. Once she was settled, she held open her arms and called to the fox, 'C'mon, Onnie, you can fly too.'

'Go on, Kira,' Paradon said. 'You've got to lead Jinx to Lasser.'

Swallowing back her fear, Kira took a deep breath. 'You can do this,' she muttered softly to herself. 'It's what you've always wanted.' Finally she climbed up the dragon's wing and took the lead seat in the saddlebox.

'Don't forget your harnesses,' Paradon warned.

Quickly fastening their safety harnesses around their waists, Kira took hold of the reins. Turning back to her sister, she said, 'Remember, Elspeth, hold on really tight and don't let go.'

'I will,' she excitedly responded.

Immediately Kira heard her sister giving the same instructions to Onnie. From behind her she heard a sharp yip. To Kira it sounded as though the fox was as frightened as she was.

'Ready everybody?'

'Ready!' Elspeth called forward, followed by another short yip. 'Onnie's ready too.'

'All right, Jinx,' Kira cried, flapping the reins. 'Go!'

Beneath them, they felt subtle movement as the dragon tensed to fly. A moment later, Jinx was spreading his wings and launching himself off the top of the tower.

Terror and exhilaration filled Kira as Jinx climbed assuredly into the sky. Behind her she could hear Elspeth's cries of excitement mixing with the yips of Onnie. Stealing a glance over the side of the saddlebox, Kira felt she'd swallowed her heart when she saw just how high Jinx was taking them over the castle grounds.

'Make him go around,' Elspeth called. 'Use the reins and make him go around!'

Pushing aside her fears, Kira gave the reins a gentle tug to the right. Immediately Jinx responded. Tilting his wings, they were soon flying to the right.

'Good boy!' Kira shouted, though she doubted if the dragon could hear her over the rushing wind. After that, she drew the reins to the left. With equal agility,

Jinx easily changed directions and flew where Kira directed him to go.

Initial fear soon turned into exhilaration as Kira and Elspeth cut through the night sky astride their dragon. Feeling unmatched joy, Kira wondered what her father would think if he could only see them now.

After they had circled around the castle several times, Kira suddenly realized they had one very big problem. In their training, they had taught Jinx how to turn left, to turn right, to run, stop, and even fly, but the one thing they hadn't taught him was how to go down on command.

'How do we get him down?' Kira called over her shoulder.

'Just tell him what you want!' Elspeth responded.

'No,' Kira corrected, turning back in her seat. 'You tell him to land in the courtyard. He'll understand you!'

Kira saw doubt shining on her sister's face. Finally, Elspeth's tiny voice called, 'Fly down, Jinx. It's time to go down to our play area.'

Immediately the dragon responded and changed directions. Soon they were losing height as Jinx smoothly came in for a landing. Lightly touching down in the courtyard, both girls started yelling and cheering in their seats. Unable to contain her excitement, Kira undid her harness, opened the saddlebox and quickly climbed down to the ground.

Running up to the dragon's big head, she threw her arms around him and kissed his snout. 'What a good boy!' she cried. 'Jinx, you're wonderful!'

Elspeth soon joined her and together they praised and fussed over the dragon. But as they shared their excitement, Kira caught a glimpse of Onnie. Sitting quietly on the ground, the fox looked like he was about to be sick.

'I don't think Onnie is feeling too good. I guess flying doesn't agree with him.'

Crossing over to the fox, Elspeth knelt down on the ground beside him and lightly stroked his head. 'You'll get used to it, Onnie,' she said. 'You'll see. Soon you'll love flying with Jinx.'

Kira watched the fox tilt his head to the side. She could almost hear his thoughts saying that he never would. Smiling, she returned to scratching Jinx.

That night, after Elspeth had gone to bed, Kira sat up with Paradon sipping her evening drink.

'Jinx is beautiful, isn't he?'

'Indeed he is,' Paradon agreed. 'You and Elspeth

have done a wonderful job rearing him. If King Arden weren't such a blind fool, he'd see it too and have both you and Elspeth working at the palace in the stables. You could teach new ways of handling dragons.'

'With First Law?' Kira said ironically. 'There's not a chance of that ever happening.'

'Not yet,' Paradon agreed. 'But soon.'

Kira felt a shudder running down her spine. He meant after she brought down the king. Finally she turned to him. 'I sure hope so.'

Falling silent, Kira and Paradon watched the fire roaring in the hearth. After a while, Kira turned back to him. 'Paradon, do you know how Elspeth does what she does?'

'What do you mean?'

'Lots of times, including tonight, when she speaks with Jinx, he seems to understand everything she says. She's always had this talent with animals, but it seems to be growing stronger.'

'It is,' Paradon agreed. 'That's because she is growing up. The older she gets, the stronger her powers will become.'

'How?' Kira asked. 'There have never been any wizards in our family. How can she do it?'

'Are you sure there haven't been wizards?' Paradon asked.

Kira thought back on all the family stories her parents had told her when she was growing up. 'Mother and Father never mentioned anyone.'

'That doesn't mean there weren't any. Some families hide their heritage, like it is a deep shame. Or perhaps, there haven't been wizards in your line. In which case, it would make Elspeth even more special.'

Paradon paused for a moment to take a sip of his drink before he continued. 'Kira, I think it's time you realized Elspeth has as much power in her as I do. Which is why she could see the colours in the Eye when you couldn't. The only difference between us is that hers comes out in one form. Mine another. She will never be able to conjure things or do the things I can. But then again, I could never do as she so easily does. And hers is without any training at all.'

Kira nodded thoughtfully and then said, 'I think Onnie might be teaching her a few things.'

'True,' Paradon agreed. 'And I must warn you, they won't all be good. That furry red friend of ours has his own idea of what's right and wrong. Promise me that you'll watch closely over your sister. For as much as he helps her, don't let Onnie's hold over her grow too strong.'

'How can I stop it?' Kira asked.

'I'm not sure,' Paradon admitted. 'Just love her and be there for her. Show her the difference between right and wrong.'

Kira nodded. 'All this time together and I still don't know who Onnie really is.'

After a long pause, Paradon said, 'To be perfectly honest, neither do I. I've known him for more years than I care to remember. But still, I have no idea who or what he is, where he comes from or where he goes to when he disappears. I do know that until he met your sister his only priority in life was himself. Now I truly believe Onnie would do absolutely anything for her.'

'And she for him,' Kira added.

'Indeed,' Paradon agreed. He then climbed from his chair. 'Now, I don't know about you, but I'm getting rather tired. How about we call it a night? We've got a busy day tomorrow.'

After she bid Paradon good night, Kira did what she had done every night since he had told her of the approaching executions at Lasser. She quietly climbed the stairs of the tallest tower and looked up into the sky, searching for the moon.

Most nights, Paradon's snowstorms hid it from her sight. But occasionally she could see it and watched in fear as it progressed from full, to half, to quarter, to new moon and make its way back to quarter and half again.

Each passing night brought her that much closer to the next full moon. But she knew they weren't going to wait for the moon to get full. They would be attacking Lasser long before then.

'Soon,' she called up into the night sky. 'Soon.'

# CHAPTER
## ~33~

There wasn't much time now. Both girls knew it, and so did Paradon. Kira and Elspeth spent every free moment practising their archery. During this time, Paradon would disappear to the chamber of the Eye. He never said what he was doing in there, and they never asked.

But when he emerged late one afternoon, he called Kira and Elspeth into the banquet hall. Arriving in the large hall, they found the banquet table covered in parchments.

As she approached the table, Kira looked down on the pages and saw a confusing collection of drawings. 'What's all this?'

'These are the layouts of Lasser,' Paradon softly responded. 'I have been using the Eye to see what it's like on the inside.'

'Did you see Kahrin?' Elspeth asked as she inspected the plans.

Kira expected Paradon to say no, or at least give her the signal that they would speak privately later. Instead the old wizard dropped his eyes and nodded.

'I have seen horrors beyond belief,' he said softly. 'I knew it would be bad, but I never imagined just how bad it was.'

Both Kira and Elspeth crossed to Paradon. 'What did you see?'

'They are treating those poor girls worse than animals. They are filthy, cold and starving. Most of them are ill and from the looks of things, countless girls have died.'

Paradon took a seat and put his hands on his head. To Kira, it looked like the old wizard was crying.

'It's all right, Paradon,' she said, rubbing his back. 'We're going to save them.'

'No, it's not all right,' Paradon moaned. 'I started the storms to slow the king down. But in their weakened condition, the cold is now beginning to threaten them. It's my fault. I've got to stop the storms immediately and warm the air up.'

'You're wrong, it's not your fault,' Kira said. 'The king is the one to blame, not you. Please, listen to me. You can't stop the snow, not yet. It hurts me to say this, but you must keep it up just a bit longer.

We need the protection it will give us.'

'But I'm killing those poor girls.'

'Then we'll go tonight. We won't wait another moment. We'll destroy that wretched place and then you can warm the area up. Please, give us one more day of storms.'

Onnie was clutched in Elspeth's arms and started to yip. When Paradon and Kira looked over to her, she said, 'Onnie says Kira is right. We need the snow. We're ready. Let us go tonight.'

Paradon sat still for a long time. Finally, he lifted his head. 'If you both think you are ready, we'll do it tonight.'

'We are ready,' Kira agreed. 'Now, please show us these plans.'

Lasser Commons was the biggest, most imposing prison in the kingdom. It wasn't just one building, but actually four. These four large cellblocks stood side by side and were connected by a large central corridor that ran across the front of each individual building.

A thick, fortified outer wall and then a second inner wall surrounded the whole area. There were bars on the few windows that the prison did have. But what made Lasser unique and able to withstand attacks from the outside was that there was only one way in. That was through a huge impenetrable door that had been made of the thickest trees in the kingdom.

Back when the designers first drew up their plans, they never made provisions for an air attack. As every dragon in the kingdom belonged to the king, they had no cause to consider it. This was what Paradon, Kira and Elspeth hoped to use against the notorious prison.

It had taken Kira and Elspeth the better part of the afternoon to memorize the layout of Lasser. But as the night drew in and darkness fell, they all felt the tension building.

'Remember, girls,' Paradon said, 'you will only get one chance at this. We have got to make the most of it.'

'I still wish you were coming with us,' Kira said, looking over to the wizard.

'So do I,' Paradon admitted. 'But I can best serve you from here. I can use the Eye to watch everything that is happening all around the prison. Then, whether it works or not, I will use every bit of magic I possess to help you free those poor girls.'

Paradon stopped speaking and reached into the pocket of his cloak. He pulled out two pendants. He handed one to each girl. 'Here, I want you to have these.'

Kira received the pendent in her hand and saw a fine gold chain suspending a beautiful golden dragon's claw clutching a pebble.

'It's beautiful,' she said.

When Elspeth received her pendant, she beamed. 'This is from the Eye. I can see all the pretty colours in it.'

'Really?' said Kira as she inspected her pendant. 'I can't see anything in mine.'

'Elspeth is correct,' Paradon said. 'These are the children of the Eye. They have been born of magic and empowered with magic. With these, we will be able to hear each other whenever I am at the Eye, no matter how far apart we are. This way, even though I am not with you, we can still reach each other.'

'Thank you, Paradon,' Kira said excitedly. 'So, it will be like you are with us even though you aren't.'

'Believe me, Kira, I will be with you all the way,' Paradon said. 'Though, I must warn you, there is one catch.'

'What's that?' she asked, still admiring the pendant.

'Once you girls have put them on, there is no taking them off again. No amount of tugging, cutting, or even magic will ever be able to remove them. They will remain with you for the rest of your lives.'

Elspeth's smile became even bigger. 'Then you can always be with us.'

'Indeed I will,' Paradon agreed.

Without hesitation, both Kira and Elspeth excitedly drew the pendants up to their necks. Helping each other with the clasps, the chains were quickly sealed closed. After admiring the pendants a final time, they each tucked them under their clothing.

'Well,' Kira said, taking in a deep breath. 'I think we had better get ready to go.'

'We still have to load Jinx,' Elspeth said.

'Then let's get started.'

As a general rule, Jinx was always kept saddled. It never seemed to bother him, and was easier than struggling to get the saddlebox on and off. Packing their arrows in leather quivers, they soon had everything loaded into the saddlebox.

Then they all walked to the doors of the castle. Kira felt her stomach clench with nerves. Stepping out into the cold winter night, she saw that more snow flurries were starting. Gazing at the heavy, silvery-grey clouds above them, it looked like it was going to be quite a storm.

'I thought it best if we had a big one tonight. It will throw the guards off,' Paradon said as he followed behind them. 'But the moment Lasser falls, I'll stop it and warm up the air.'

Kira turned back to him and smiled weakly. 'Thank you, I'm sure it will help.'

Walking to the centre of the courtyard, before they climbed into the saddlebox, they said their goodbyes to Paradon.

'I'll go straight to the Eye and start watching the moment you leave here,' Paradon said with a lump in his throat. 'You won't be alone, I promise you.'

Tears were in Kira's eyes as she embraced the wizard. 'I know. And don't worry about us. We'll free the girls and then come right back with Kahrin.'

'Please be careful,' Paradon said. 'Don't take any foolish risks.'

'We won't,' Elspeth said, also embracing the wizard. 'Onnie is with us, he'll help.'

Paradon sniffed and gave the girls a final squeeze. Then he handed a torch to Elspeth. 'Don't forget this. You'll need it to light the fire arrows.'

When she received it, he looked at Kira. 'And remember, Kira, Jinx is there to help. Let him do what he can for you. Don't hold him back.'

Kira knew exactly what Paradon meant. He was telling them to use Jinx as a weapon. Hearing what was happening to the girls at Lasser, Kira felt no guilt in agreeing with him. 'I understand,' she said.

Finally drawing away from the wizard, Kira, Elspeth and Onnie climbed into the saddlebox. After she fastened her harness, Kira turned back to her sister. 'Are you sure you're ready? Because if you are frightened, now's the time to tell me. I won't be mad if you want to stay here.'

'All I'm frightened about is that we won't be able to find Kahrin,' Elspeth said. 'And I'll shoot anyone who tries to stop us.'

Inhaling deeply, Kira nodded. 'Me too.'

After saying her final farewell to Paradon, Kira turned in her seat and caught hold of the reins. Giving them a light tug, she ordered Jinx up into the sky. Feeling none of the thrill she usually felt when flying with the dragon, Kira had Jinx take a final pass around the castle to wave at Paradon as he made his way back to the front doors.

When he was gone from sight, she took another deep breath and set Jinx on course for Lasser.

# CHAPTER
## ~34~

As they travelled through the night, Kira was shocked to see that there were no firelights rising from any of the homes or villages passing beneath them. Paradon had said the king had ordered almost everyone to the palace. Looking at the darkness beneath them, she realized it was true.

'It's over there!' Elspeth called as she tapped Kira on the shoulder.

Following Elspeth's finger, rising in the distance, Kira saw the glowing light from the tall torches surrounding the outer walls of Lasser Commons.

As they approached the prison, Kira realized that looking at the plans on parchment was nothing like the real thing. Lasser Commons was massive.

'How are we ever going to find Kahrin in there?'

'You will,' came Paradon's strong voice. It seemed to be coming from the pendant beneath her clothing. 'Just trust yourself and you'll both do fine.'

'Paradon, can you hear us?' Kira called.

'Quite clearly,' he said.

'Hi Paradon!' Elspeth called.

'Hello, child,' Paradon responded. 'How is Onnie?'

'He doesn't like flying,' Elspeth called. 'But he says he'll be fine once we land.'

'Kira,' Paradon continued, 'I want you to fly around the prison a few times. Become familiar with it. You'll see the large entrance doors. That is where you will land once you start the fires.'

Directing Jinx to fly a little bit lower, they started to circle the confines of the prison. Beneath them, they saw the four large cellblocks that Paradon had mapped. Then a little further along they saw the large entrance doors and the main courtyard with horse stables and hay barn.

'Kira, remember what I told you,' Paradon said. 'Most of the able-bodied men have been called away to war. You shouldn't encounter a lot of resistance.'

'I hope not,' Kira said. Then she turned back to Elspeth. 'Remember, Shadow, when we land, you stay in the saddlebox with Onnie. I'll go down on the ground and open the cell doors. Do you understand?'

'Kira, we've gone over this a hundred times. I know what to do!' Elspeth cried. 'You just open all the doors and let the girls out. I'll keep firing arrows from here.'

Kira nodded. Looking back down on the prison, she suddenly saw the insanity of their plan. She was thirteen. Elspeth was eight and Paradon's powers were unpredictable at best. What could they possibly do against the might of Lasser Commons? It wasn't too late to turn back. They could still get back to their castle without anyone ever knowing they were here.

But then what? In a few more days the king's men will arrive at the prison to kill the girls. Steeling herself, Kira realized they were their only hope. Despite her fears, she knew she couldn't let them down.

Reaching for several fire arrows, Kira pulled out her bow. 'All right, I'm going to bring Jinx in closer. Once the place is burning, get ready to fire your bow. This is probably going to happen very fast.'

'Onnie and I are ready,' Elspeth said confidently.

Using the reins, Kira brought Jinx in much closer to the prison. Circling around to the open courtyard again, she quickly loaded a fire arrow in her bow. 'Light it,' she called to Elspeth as she leaned back and offered the paraffin tip to her sister.

Once the arrow was burning, Kira leaned over the side of the saddlebox. Drawing back the bow, she aimed for the hay barn and then released the arrow. Suddenly, all the long days and nights of training bore fruit as the first arrow accurately hit its mark. By the time a second arrow was fired, the barn was ablaze.

Almost immediately the main doors to the prison burst open and guards poured out into the snow to fight the fire. Running and shouting, they never thought to look up to see the dragon descending from the sky.

'Now!' Kira shouted as she directed Jinx to land in the open courtyard.

The moment they touched down, chaos erupted. Jinx immediately roared at the sight of the men. Rearing up, he lurched forward and started to chase the terrified guards.

'Down, Jinx, down!' Kira ordered as she pulled back the reins and got the dragon under control. When he stopped, she quickly unfastened her harness and threw open the saddlebox. Climbing down on to the dragon's wing, she looked up to Elspeth. 'Remember, Shadow, whatever happens, whatever you see, don't leave this box! Stay with Jinx and Onnie!'

Elspeth had already dropped the torch and was loading an arrow into her bow. 'I will, you just be careful. We'll try to protect you from here!'

Reaching for her bow and quiver, Kira leaped down from Jinx's wing. Fixing an arrow, she started running at the scattering guards. Almost immediately, she saw that Paradon was right. The main guards were gone. All that remained at Lasser were old men. The only young men she saw were wearing bandages or had missing limbs. Yet despite their age or wounds, when the guards caught sight of her, they looked very angry and ready for a fight.

'A girl?' the nearest guard cried. 'It can't be!' Drawing his sword, he started to charge her.

Reacting instinctively, Kira drew back her bow and fired. The arrow struck the guard in the thigh and dropped him immediately to the ground. Racing around him, she fixed another arrow and downed a second guard, then a third and a fourth.

From behind her, Kira heard Jinx's roars as he continued to chase and attack the fleeing guards. Stealing a quick glance back, she watched Elspeth encourage the dragon while firing arrows at anyone she could. Before long, the courtyard was littered with fallen guards.

'Kira, look!' Elspeth suddenly shouted. 'They're closing the doors!'

Turning towards the entrance, Kira saw several

guards fleeing inside the building and drawing the tall doors closed.

'No!' she angrily cried. 'Shadow, get Jinx over there, see if he can stop them!'

Racing as fast as they could, they were still too late. By the time they arrived at the entrance, the heavy doors were tightly secured.

'Elspeth,' Paradon called. 'Have Jinx tear them down. He can do it.'

Standing beside Jinx at the doors, Kira kept her bow at the ready as she looked over the wounded men in the courtyard. Those that could still move were watching them fearfully and crawling further away. Lowering her bow, Kira saw that they were no longer a threat.

'Kira, stand back,' Elspeth warned. Then she called to the dragon. 'Go on Jinx, tear them down!'

Jinx reared up on his hind legs and let out a roar that shook the very foundations of the prison. Suddenly he lunged forward and tore into the thick wood of the heavy doors with all the strength he possessed.

'That's it, Jinx, keep going!' Elspeth called. 'You can do it!'

'Good boy!' Kira cried as she watched the heavy doors being torn to splinters under the dragon's sharp claws. When he had ripped a hole in the doors, he forced his head through and started to tear at the heavy wood with his teeth. Again and again, the dragon's head entered the growing hole and tore into the wood.

As Kira watched, she could see the scars on Jinx's snout being scraped along the sharp wood and start to bleed. But if he felt any pain, the dragon didn't show it. Instead he kept tearing at the wood until finally, the impenetrable entrance of Lasser Commons was shredded down to nothing.

When their way was clear, Kira raised her bow and called Jinx forward. 'Be ready with your bow,' she warned Elspeth.

Stepping into the entrance of the prison, Kira saw more guards standing with their swords drawn, prepared to fight. Immediately Jinx reared up on his hind legs and his roars filled the wide corridors of the prison. Firing her bow at the nearest guard, Kira's arrow struck him in the side and he went down.

Quickly loading another arrow, she started to advance on the men. 'Back off!' she roared as she moved. 'Back off or I swear I'll let my dragon have you!' The viciousness of her own voice shocked her as she raised her bow. 'I said back off!'

Staring in shock and fear at the sight of Kira and the rearing dragon behind her, the men immediately abandoned their posts and ran deeper into the prison. With her confidence building, Kira led Jinx forward.

'Kira,' Elspeth called. 'There's the first cellblock over there.'

Following Elspeth's pointing finger, Kira looked down the corridor to their destination. She then turned back to Elspeth. 'Let's go. Keep your eyes and ears open. Shoot anyone who comes near us.'

As they approached the first large cellblock, Kira saw it was a long corridor with heavy, locked doors running along each side. Kahrin was behind one of those doors, but which one?

'Kira, beside you!' Elspeth cried.

Turning left, Kira saw two older guards running at her. Without hesitation, she raised her bow and fired at the nearest man. Elspeth hit the second. Both men fell together and were still. With more guards appearing from behind them, Kira reached back into her quiver for another arrow – but found it empty.

'Shadow, I'm out of arrows!' she called back to Elspeth. 'How many do you have left?'

'I've got lots,' Elspeth responded as she fired at the approaching men. 'Start opening doors. Jinx and I will take care of the guards.'

With the cellblock ahead of her, Kira watched

Elspeth turning Jinx around to face the guards. 'Get them, Jinx!' Elspeth cried, rage filling her light voice.

Kira was stunned and unable to move as she watched her little sister use Jinx as a vicious weapon. Without hesitation, he followed Elspeth's orders and lunged forward to attack the guards. The sounds of the men's agonized cries mixed with the roars of the dragon as Jinx caught hold of them and quickly dispatched them.

'Kira, don't just stand there. Go!' Paradon's voice shouted from the pendant. 'Leave Elspeth to do what she must. Free the girls!'

Suddenly coming back to herself, Kira turned away from the horrible sight and started to move down the corridor of the cellblock. As she approached the first door, she was sickened to find it locked.

'Paradon, it's locked!' she cried. 'We don't have a key.'

'You don't need one,' the wizard called. 'You've got me.'

As she stood before the door, Kira heard the wizard casting a spell. When he finished, she looked again, but nothing happened.

'It's not working – the door is still locked!'

Paradon cursed. Then he repeated the spell. This

time, something did happen. Before her eyes, she watched the lock turning into water.

'Well?' Paradon called.

'It's not neat, but it will work,' Kira responded as she pulled the door open.

When she entered the cell, Kira sucked in her breath at the first glimpse of the girls of Lasser. Unable to count how many were jammed in the tiny cell, she saw their pitifully thin bodies huddled together for warmth as their filthy faces looked warily at her.

'Get up!' Kira cried. 'You're free. Get moving.'

The girls seemed too stunned to move. Finally Kira ran forward. Catching the nearest girl by the arm, she hauled her to her feet. 'Come on, get moving. We don't have a lot of time.'

As if waking from a dream, the girl looked at her and weakly asked, 'Are you a girl?'

Kira looked down at her clothing and realized she looked more like a boy than a girl. 'Yes I am,' she answered. 'So is my sister on that dragon out there. Listen to me. The king is sending men here to kill you. You've got to get away!'

None of the girls moved as she spoke. Unable to believe what she was seeing, Kira dragged the girl towards the open cell door. 'Come on, all of you. Do you want to die? Believe me, they'll kill you if you stay. Please, get up and get out there!'

Leaving the first stunned girl, Kira moved to the back and pulled a second older girl to her feet. 'Gather all the weapons you can from the fallen guards. You've got to fight for your life. You're free now. So get out there and prepare to fight.'

'But what about First Law?' one of the younger girls protested. 'We'll be punished if we break it.'

'First Law?' Kira repeated. 'Are you mad? Didn't you hear me? The king is sending men to kill you. Why? Because you are girls, that's all. Do you want to die? Is that it?'

Suddenly realizing the truth, the girl before her turned to her cellmates.

'She's right!' the girl cried. 'We've been victims of the king long enough. They've beaten us, starved us and killed us. But no more! If she can fight for us, so can we! We're strong. We've survived everything they've done. Now let's show them what we can do!' Moving to the door, the girl called the others forward. 'Come on, let's get moving!'

'Finally!' Kira cried. 'Now, get out there and help me with the others. My sister and dragon are at the end of the corridor. Stay well away from them. Wait until we move on to the next cellblock, then go and gather as many weapons as you can find. You are going to have to fight if you want to live.'

As the girls climbed unsteadily to their feet, they followed Kira out of the cell and into the corridor.

'All right, when the second cell is opened, I want you to help me convince the others. We've got to work together if we are to win this.'

'We will,' said the oldest of the girls gathering around her.

As Kira approached the second cell, she called to Paradon and waited for him to cast another spell to open the lock. Immediately more water flowed down the door from where the lock had been.

Pulling the door open, Kira entered and was once again struck by the sight of the starving girls within. With several girls from the first cell following her in, she was able to get them moving faster.

When the third cell was opened, Kira looked down the corridor of the cellblock and realized it was going to take all night just to open the cellblocks' doors.

'Paradon,' she called, grasping her pendant. 'This is taking too long! Can't you open all the doors at once?'

'I don't know,' the wizard replied. 'But I'll try.'

From down the corridor, Kira kept hearing

Jinx's roars as he and Elspeth continued to fight with the guards.

'Hurry up, Kira,' Elspeth's light voice called. 'I'm almost out of arrows!'

'We're trying,' Kira replied. 'But all the doors are locked.'

Suddenly there were multiple loud bangs as all the locks on the doors exploded and water flew into the air.

'Paradon, you did it!' Kira cried.

'Thank heavens,' responded the wizard. 'Now get the girls moving!'

Directing the girls forward, Kira ordered them into the cells to free the other prisoners. Working together, the corridor of Cellblock One was soon filled with the shocked occupants of the cells. Kira looked at the collection of girls. She had never seen anything as horrible as this in all her life. But even as she watched, she saw the stronger girls moving to protect and support the weaker and younger ones.

Older girls then moved forward to collect swords from the dead guards. Forming a small army, they gathered behind Jinx and prepared to move with the dragon into the next fight.

Running forward, Kira approached Jinx. 'Shadow, the first cellblock is empty. Take us to the next.'

With Elspeth on Jinx leading the way, the girls of the first cellblock followed closely behind Kira as they moved down the main corridor towards Cellblock Two. As they approached, shouts of guards came from deep within the second cellblock. Not waiting for Jinx to defend them, the older girls with swords rushed forward. Without any training at all, they raised their swords high and started to fight with all the energy they had left.

When the fight ended and all the guards were dead, the girls cheered triumphantly.

'Paradon,' Kira called over their cries, 'we're in the second cellblock. Unlock the doors.'

Everyone was prepared this time as the locks exploded into water. Without hesitation, the girls from the first cellblock raced down the corridor, entering cells and freeing the occupants.

As the newly freed girls entered the corridor, Kira desperately searched among their filthy faces, looking for her missing sister.

'Kahrin! Kahrin!' she called above the din of escaping girls. 'Kahrin, where are you?'

With all the girls of the second cellblock free, Kira followed Elspeth and Jinx and the new fighters to the third. They were building up quite an army of girls. Once again, the same scene was repeated as Paradon cast a spell to open the locked doors. Yet no matter how many cells were opened, Kira could find no trace of Kahrin.

As they approached the fourth and final cellblock, Kira tried to keep the fear that Kahrin was dead out of her heart. But as each cell was emptied and she saw no signs of her sister, she began to fear the worst.

Just as despair was settling in, at the end of the final cellblock, Kira opened a cell door and almost immediately recognized a filthy face.

'Kahrin!' she cried as she raced over to her sister. 'Kahrin, it's me, Kira!'

Huddled in the corner, Kahrin weakly opened her eyes. Looking up into her sister's face, she frowned. 'Kira?'

Tears rushed to Kira's eyes as she looked down on the wreck that had once been her pretty little sister. 'Yes, Kahrin, it's me. We've come to get you out of here!' Reaching forward, she pulled Kahrin into a tight embrace and was shocked at how weak and thin she was. Helping her to stand, Kira supported Kahrin and led her out of the cell.

'Shadow, I've got Kahrin!' she cried.

'Kahrin!' Elspeth howled. Throwing off her harness,

Elspeth and Onnie jumped free of the saddlebox and climbed down to the floor. Running around Jinx, she ordered the dragon to stay as she pushed through the crowd of girls and ran forward to help Kira with her sister.

'She's so weak,' Kira said as she helped Kahrin walk over to Jinx.

Seeing the stranger drawing near, Jinx started to growl and rear up.

'No, Jinx!' Elspeth shouted. 'Kahrin is our sister. Don't hurt her!'

At her command, Jinx immediately calmed and let them approach.

'You've got a dragon?' Kahrin said weakly as her eyes grew large at the sight of Jinx.

'He's your dragon too,' Elspeth said. 'He's going to take us home.'

It seemed to take ages getting Kahrin up on to Jinx's wing and into the saddlebox. Settling her in the back seat, Elspeth and Onnie took the lead seat and Kira stood on Jinx's wing.

Suddenly, from further down the main corridor, they heard girls shouting and the sounds of more sword fighting.

'Take Jinx,' Kira ordered. 'See if they need your help,

but don't let him hurt any of the girls.'

'He won't,' Elspeth said. 'I told him to leave the girls alone. He's not happy about it, but he'll behave.'

'Get going!' Kira said as she jumped down from the dragon's wing. Jinx raced down the long main corridor. His roars drowned out the sound of the screaming girls as they quickly parted to let the angry dragon through.

Leaving Elspeth to take care of the last of the guards, Kira helped the other girls open the final doors in Cellblock Four. Once open, the corridor overflowed with the surviving girls of the prison. Around her, Kira heard cries of pain mixed with shouts of joy as sisters found each other and were reunited.

One of the first girls stepped up to her. 'Who are you?'

'I'm Kira,' she said. 'My sister is Elspeth and that's our dragon, Jinx.'

As she spoke, more girls gathered around to listen. Soon Kira was answering all kinds of questions about where they came from and how it was that they had a dragon. But of all the questions, the biggest one was what the girls of Lasser were supposed to do now.

'You're free,' Kira answered. 'You can do what you like, go where you like.'

'But we're starving. We've no food,' the first girl said.

'Look around you, Kira. Most of these girls are too weak to go anywhere. We may have the prison right now, but without food, we'll starve before the king's men arrive.'

'No you won't!' came the booming voice from Kira's pendant.

Jumping back in fear, the girls looked at Kira as though she had two heads.

'It's all right,' she said holding up her hands. Then she reached inside her top and pulled out the pendant. 'This lets me speak to a friend of mine. Paradon. He's a wizard and was the one who opened the cell doors.'

'Girls of Lasser,' Paradon began. 'Your ordeal is over. I know you are cold, hungry and most likely, very frightened. But believe me, you are free. And as for food, I can help you with that.'

As she listened, Kira heard Paradon casting another spell. Then from behind her, she heard a girl call, 'Look!'

Everyone turned and stared into the main corridor. The air was sparkling. Moments later, a large black cauldron appeared. A fire was burning beneath it, and steam was coming from its contents. Beside the cauldron appeared a large stack of fresh bread. Racing forward, the girls tore off chunks of bread and dipped them into the stew.

Watching as the starving girls started to eat, Kira had never been so grateful that Paradon's spell had worked on the first attempt.

'Kira,' Paradon called, 'tell the girls not to worry or fight over the food. The cauldron will never empty. They can eat as much as they want. It will always be full.'

When Kira passed along the message, everyone in the corridor cheered. But quietly she asked, 'They have food, Paradon, but what about medicine? A lot of them are sick. And what about the king's men? How can they defend themselves against them?'

'Kira, calm down,' Paradon said. 'Tell the girls you'll be back with all the medicine they need. As for the king's men, by the time they make it there, the girls of Lasser will be gone. Tell them I will find them somewhere safe to live. But for now, go and get Jinx and get back here. Kahrin doesn't look well. She needs help.'

Saying her goodbyes to the girls, Kira promised to return with medicine and clothing. She then raced down the main corridor searching for Elspeth and Jinx. At the very end, she found her sister standing at Jinx's head and stroking his neck as some of the fighter girls stood back asking questions.

Most of the girls still had swords in their hands and their filthy torn clothing was covered in blood. As Kira looked around the area, she saw the bodies of guards as well as a few fallen girls from the final battle.

'Kira!' Elspeth cried as she approached. Running forward, she wrapped her arms around her.

'We did it, Shadow,' Kira said softly as she returned the embrace. She then looked up to Kahrin sitting silently in the saddlebox. Her sister's eyes were haunted and yet vacant as she clung to Onnie.

'How is she?' Kira asked.

'I don't know,' Elspeth answered. 'She doesn't seem like Kahrin any more.'

'It'll take time,' Kira said. 'Let's get back to the castle. Paradon's got some medicine for her.'

Kira and Elspeth walked on either side of Jinx along the route back to the entrance. Around them, the girls offered their thanks and parted to allow the large dragon to pass. Looking at their starving faces, Kira made a silent vow. The horrors of Lasser Common would never be repeated. Somehow, someway, she would fulfil the prophecy and bring down King Arden and his wretched monarchy.

Finally drawing up to the remains of the tall doors, Kira ordered Elspeth back up into the saddlebox. Once she was settled, she caught hold of the bridle and started to lead Jinx forward. Walking out into the snowstorm, Kira failed to notice movement coming from the shadows behind the ruined door.

Suddenly a thunderous battle cry roared out. A wounded guard lunged forward and thrust his sword into her back. Standing perfectly still, Kira looked down on the sword blade that protruded from her front. She felt no pain. All she could feel was the strange sensation of cold steel where the sword had cut through her warm flesh.

Just as quickly as it had been thrust into her, the guard pulled his sword free, shouting again in triumph.

Kira turned to face him and felt her legs buckle. As she fell to the ground, she was dimly aware of the madness erupting around her. She thought she heard Elspeth's cry, and then Jinx's roar. But for some reason, it all seemed very distant. Right before she closed her eyes, she saw Jinx rearing up and attacking the guard. Blackness quickly swallowed her and she was unable to see any more.

# CHAPTER
## ~35~

Dane paced the confines of his cell, waiting for his instructor to appear with news from the palace. He had been returned to the dungeon several days before, without being told why. But while he was being escorted back to his cell, he'd heard some of the guards talking about the king and how he was calling a legion of fighters away from the war to launch a massive assault. But Dane hadn't been able to hear where the assault would take place, or when.

Part of him wondered if this was to do with the king's plan to kill the girls at Lasser. No, the king wouldn't make such a terrible plan public. No one was supposed to know about the executions. It had to be something else.

That night, Dane lay awake, unable to sleep. It had been days since he'd seen the instructor. It wasn't like his friend not to visit. While he was trying to figure out why, he heard the muffled sounds of a scuffle coming from outside his cell.

Standing quickly, Dane crossed to the door and peered out through the bars. But he couldn't see much of the corridor. He heard the sound of hushed voices and the soft tread of feet on the stone floor.

'Dane?' a voice softly called. 'Where are you?'

Dane instantly recognized that voice. 'Shanks! I'm over here.'

Suddenly Dane saw the grinning face of his best friend appear at his door. 'Shanks!' he cried. 'You're alive!'

'What did you expect?' Shanks teased. 'I'm the best dragon knight the king's got! No one can catch me.'

Beside him, Dane saw another face he recognized. 'Marcus?'

'Aye, lad,' the old dragon knight said. 'We've come to break you out of there.'

'But the door is locked, I can't get out.'

Still grinning, Shanks held up the key. 'We borrowed this from the guards down there. They'll be asleep for a while.'

Shanks inserted the key in the lock and opened the cell door. Free, Dane quickly embraced his best friend. 'I didn't think I'd ever see you again.'

'And you wouldn't have if it weren't for Marcus. He was the one with the ideas.'

Marcus blushed and shuffled on his feet. 'Not me, lad. It was my Beauty. She said I had to help you.'

'This old goat hasn't stopped talking about that bloody dragon since this mess started,' Shanks said, laughing lightly and shaking his head.

'And I won't stop talking about her until you believe me,' said Marcus affably. 'She says I have a job to do, and I'm doing it.'

Dane's eyes passed from Shanks to Marcus and back to Shanks again. For all the teasing, he could see that Shanks really cared for the old knight.

It was only then that Shanks noticed the brand on Dane's face. 'Ouch!' he said as he lightly touched the burns. 'That must have hurt. You think Lord Dorcon made it big enough?'

'Well, at least he left me one side of my face,' Dane said darkly. Finally he asked, 'How did you find me?'

'Are you kidding?' Shanks answered. 'The whole kingdom is in an uproar because of your sisters. Everyone knows Lord Dorcon had you put back down here. I'm just glad he didn't have you killed.'

'My sisters?' Dane repeated. 'What have they done?'

Marcus stepped forward. 'The girls have gone and sacked Lasser Commons, that's all. Somehow, they've got themselves a dragon and used it to take over the prison. Most of the guards were killed, but a few escaped to tell the tale. I would have loved to see their faces when your little sisters arrived on their big blue dragon and tore down the doors to that wretched place.'

Dane could hardly believe his ears. 'Kira and Elspeth have a dragon?'

'Aye, they do. Some claimed it was a twin-tailed dragon. The son of the Rogue. They're also saying the girls controlled it. That it did everything they told it to. Let me tell you, the king is not best pleased about it!'

Dane recalled the day he saw the Rogue's offspring. 'No, wait,' he said, shaking his head. 'I saw the Rogue's baby. It was purple, not blue.'

'A dragon can have more than one baby in a clutch,' Marcus said lightly. 'Believe me, there is no mistake. Your sisters attacked Lasser with a blue dragon.'

'So all the girls are safe?' Dane asked. 'Kahrin is safe?'

'I imagine so,' Marcus said. 'Though we can't know for sure.'

'Why?' Dane asked, looking to Shanks.

'Because the place up and disappeared!' Shanks answered. 'All of it, gone. There's nothing left but a big hole in the ground. They say a wizard moved it. In fact, that's why we're here.'

This was all too much for Dane to take in. 'What do you mean a wizard? What wizard?'

'His name is Paradon,' Shanks explained. 'It seems your sisters have been living with him since they left the mountain. He's the one who helped them sack Lasser. Now the king has called back a legion from the front. As soon as they arrive here, Lord Dorcon will lead us to the wizard's castle to get them.'

Panic filled Dane's heart. 'We've got to warn them!'

'I know,' Shanks agreed. 'Which is why we are here. Our old instructor has called an emergency strategy meeting of the dragon knights. He's done it so we could sneak down here and break you out. He's going to keep the knights occupied for as long as he can.'

'But we need dragons,' Dane said. 'How else will we get to the wizard's castle?'

'Don't worry, Dane,' Shanks said brightly. 'It's all worked out. Harmony and Rexor are tied up in the training field. The instructor has given me a map to Paradon's castle. All we have to do is get there. Now, do you want to go, or stay here and wait for those guards to wake up?'

Dane lightly punched Shanks in the chest. 'What do you think I want to do, you idiot? Let's go!'

Falling silent, the three quickly moved down the

corridor to the unconscious guards. They dragged them back to Dane's cell. When they were dumped on the floor, Marcus drew out his dagger and ordered Dane and Shanks out of the cell. 'Leave me a moment and I'll take care of these too.'

When Dane frowned and started to protest, Marcus continued, 'I'm sorry, lad, but we can't have them waking up and setting off the alarm. This has to be done.'

'Come on, Dane,' Shanks said drawing him from the cell. 'He's right. Think of your sisters.'

Dane nodded and followed Shanks. Soon Marcus reappeared. 'Even with that, we won't have a lot of time. We've got to get moving.'

Creeping unseen through the palace was not easy. Activity was at fever pitch as guards and soldiers alike prepared for the assault on Paradon's castle. Heading down to the dragon stables, they kept well hidden as they skirted around the antechamber. Coming from inside, they heard the instructor's voice going over the planned attack. Dane hoped that one day he would have the chance to thank him for all his help.

The stables were filled to overflowing with all the dragons called back from the battle.

'All of this is for my sisters?' Dane quietly asked.

'Aye, lad,' Marcus answered. 'Those two girls have some very powerful enemies. Lord only knows why, but the king has actually stopped the war for them.'

Shaking his head, Dane continued to follow Shanks and Marcus through the stables. They reached the doors leading to the training field, pushed them open, and stepped out into the warm spring evening air.

'It was snowing last time I looked,' Dane said as he looked around the clear field.

'Rumours around the palace say it was Paradon who made it snow. The day after your sisters sacked Lasser, it stopped and spring returned,' Shanks offered.

Dane was in shock. 'A wizard can control the weather?'

'Paradon can,' Marcus said. 'I remember when he was here at the palace. Most of his spells never worked, but when they did, they were very powerful. Your sisters were lucky to find him.'

'I just hope we reach him in time,' Dane remarked.

Entering the darkened field, Dane could barely make out the shapes of the two dragons tethered there. 'I thought dragons wouldn't fly at night?'

'They don't like to, but they can,' Marcus explained. 'And under the circumstances, it's the only chance we've got. So like it or not, those dragons are going to fly tonight.'

Suddenly from the palace came the sounds of alarm bells ringing and the shouts of angry men. Then the doors to the dragon stables burst open and men poured out.

'Looks like they found the guards!' Marcus said, and he quickly drew his sword. Turning to Shanks, he said, 'Get on your mounts and go. I'll slow them down.'

'Marcus! No, there are too many. You'll be killed!'

'I know that, you daft lad,' Marcus said kindly. 'This is what Beauty and I have been waiting for. Now don't miss this chance. Get on those bloody dragons and get out of here!'

Shanks started to follow the old knight. 'Wait, Marcus, please,' he desperately cried. 'Come with us.'

Ignoring Shanks's pleas, Marcus held up his sword and started charging the approaching guards. 'I'll be with you soon, my Beauty!' he shouted as he plunged headlong into the group of men.

'Shanks, come on,' Dane cried as he quickly undid Rexor's restraints. 'Don't let him die in vain. Get on your dragon!'

Shanks watched for a moment longer as Marcus engaged the guards in swordplay.

'Shanks!' Dane repeated, climbing on to Rexor's back and preparing to fly. 'We've got to go!'

Finally turning away, Shanks raced up to Harmony and undid her restraints. Climbing into the saddle, he caught hold of the reins.

'Come Harmony,' he angrily called. 'Get moving!'

# CHAPTER
## ~36~

Kira woke in her bed. She was lying on her side, but as she tried to roll over and stretch out her legs, she found she couldn't. Weakly lifting her head, she looked down to discover Jinx's snout taking up the lower half of the large bed.

'Kira!' Elspeth squealed.

'Shadow?'

Suddenly Elspeth was at her side. Kneeling on the floor, she stroked back hair from Kira's face. Looking at her, Kira saw tears shining in her sister's eyes.

'I thought you were going to die!' Elspeth cried.

'What happened?' Kira weakly asked. 'I feel awful . . .'

'I would suspect so,' Paradon said from his place at the entrance of the chamber. 'Considering you were run through with a rather nasty sword.'

'Sword?' Kira repeated. Then it all came flooding back. They were leaving Lasser when a guard surprised her from behind. She looked back to Elspeth. 'Where's Kahrin?'

'I'm here,' her younger sister softly said.

Looking over to Elspeth's bed, Kira saw Kahrin sitting there, stroking Onnie. Her face and clothes were clean, but she was painfully thin and her eyes were still haunted.

'Are you all right?' Kira asked.

'She will be,' Paradon answered. 'In time. All that Kahrin needs right now is a lot of rest and good food. As do you.'

Taking a tentative step closer to the bed, he looked at Jinx before continuing. 'That was a terrible wound. If it weren't for my master's healing lotion, we'd have lost you. As it is, even with the lotion, it was touch and go. That medicine was never intended for such severe wounds. I can't tell you how worried we've been!'

Kira lay her head down on the pillow and shut her eyes. 'I should have seen him coming. I let that guard sneak up on me.'

Paradon smiled gently. 'You and Elspeth did a remarkable job at Lasser. You should be quite proud of yourselves. There were very few casualties on the girls' side. Even now they are recovering from their terrible ordeal.'

When Paradon took another step closer, Jinx raised his head from Kira's bed and started to growl. Elspeth ordered the dragon silent. Grunting, the dragon looked at Kira before laying his snout down again.

'He hasn't left your side since you got back,' Paradon chuckled. 'We couldn't get him to move. That silly dragon hasn't eaten a thing and let me tell you, it's made caring for you very difficult.'

Looking back down at Jinx, Kira smiled gently. 'I'm all right, baby,' she said softly. 'I just don't feel very well.'

In response, Jinx moved his head closer and started to whine. As Kira reached to stroke the end of his snout, her mind replayed the events at Lasser. Frowning, she looked over to Elspeth. 'How did you get me back in the saddle to come home? I can't remember anything.'

'We didn't,' Elspeth explained. 'You're too heavy for us to lift. Jinx carried you home.'

'In his mouth, I might add,' said Paradon. 'It nearly scared the life out of me every moment you were in the air. Watching you through the Eye, I kept imagining him dropping you or closing his mouth too tightly.'

'But he didn't,' Elspeth added. 'Jinx saved you.'

Kira's heart swelled with love for the dragon as she

patted his head. She looked over to Paradon and saw the pain in the wizard's eyes. She turned to Elspeth. 'Do you think you could take Jinx and Kahrin out of here for a while? I need to speak with Paradon.'

Elspeth glanced at Paradon and then back. She nodded. Rising, she stepped back to her bed and reached for Kahrin's thin hand. 'Onnie and me are starving. Do you want to go down to the kitchen with us to get something to eat?'

'Yes please,' Kahrin softly answered. Climbing from the bed, she crossed to Kira and kissed her lightly on the cheek. 'I'm sorry you were hurt because of me.'

'I'm not,' Kira answered as she reached up to stroke Kahrin's hollow cheek. 'I'd do it all again if it meant keeping you safe. Now go on with Shadow and get something to eat. You're far too thin.'

Kahrin nodded then joined Elspeth and Onnie at the door.

'Come on, Jinx,' Elspeth called. 'Kira is fine. Come with us and eat.'

Kira watched the dragon. Jinx seemed unsure of what to do. Reaching down, she patted his snout again. 'Go on, baby. Go with Shadow and eat.'

Finally Jinx raised his head and stood. Moving

slowly around the bed, he crossed the chamber and joined Elspeth and Kahrin at the door.

'We'll be back soon,' Elspeth promised.

'I'll be here,' Kira responded with a smile. But when they were gone, the smile faded and she closed her eyes as pain overwhelmed her.

'Is it very bad?' Paradon asked.

Kira nodded.

'I'm sorry. I'll check again to see if my master left anything to diminish pain. But he hasn't got a lot.'

'I'll be fine,' Kira said. 'But Paradon, the girls of Lasser won't. Thanks to you, they've got food. But if the king's men arrive there, there's nothing to stop them from killing everyone.'

Paradon raised his hand to calm her. He then crossed over to Elspeth's bed and sat down. 'The girls of Lasser are fine, Kira. Once I was sure you would live, I went to the Eye and cast another spell. It didn't quite work as I had planned, but now, the girls are quite safe.'

'What happened?'

'What always happens with my powers? I say one thing and another thing happens.'

'And,' Kira prodded.

'Well, I wanted to put a spell of protection around the prison, one that would keep the king's men out.

Only instead of protecting the prison, somehow I moved it.'

'Moved it?' Kira repeated. 'Where? Are the girls all right?'

'Quite all right,' Paradon said. 'In fact, I don't think they even realize they've been moved. As for where, well, they are on the opposite side of the kingdom. In an area I believe the king would never think to look for them. They have fertile land to plant up and plenty of food. I believe they will do just fine until the time comes when King Arden is gone and we can go to them.'

Kira felt a heavy responsibility lifting from her tired shoulders. 'Thank you, Paradon.'

'You don't have to thank me, child,' Paradon said softly. 'Your job is to get well as quickly as possible.'

There was something in the way he said the words that bothered her. 'Paradon, what's wrong?'

'I think we should wait a bit. At least until you are feeling better.'

Kira shook her head. 'No. Whatever it is, tell me now.'

Paradon sighed and reached out to take her hand. 'Kira, we all knew when we attacked Lasser, it would send a message back to the king. A redheaded girl with a twin-tailed dragon was out there and ready to fight.'

Kira nodded. 'And you think he knows this is the prophecy?'

Paradon nodded. 'He'd be mad not to. So he's drawing up his own plans against you.'

'Have you seen what he's doing?'

'Kira, Lord Dorcon and the king have also figured out I am helping you. They are calling back men from the war and will soon be marching on our castle. It's only a matter of time before they arrive.'

Kira threw back her covers and struggled to rise. 'Then we've got to get going!'

'You aren't going anywhere,' Paradon warned as he leaned over and pushed her shoulders back down on the bed. 'Not in this condition. We have a little bit of time. Use it to get well. Then we can think of our next plan.'

Kira stopped struggling. Her body hurt. Even if she wanted to get up, she knew she couldn't. Finally she said, 'Do Elspeth and Kahrin know they are coming?'

Paradon nodded. 'I told them the moment I knew. There was no point keeping it secret, not with so much at stake. Though I still haven't told them of the prophecy. Again, there seemed no point.' Rising from the bed, he walked slowly to the door. 'Try to rest, Kira. You need to rebuild your strength. Ready or not, those men are coming and you need to be prepared.'

After several days in bed, Kira's health slowly started to return. But she was still very weak and even more uncertain of the days ahead. The prophecy said she would bring down the monarchy, but it never said how. The Eye showed Lord Dorcon marching on the castle, but it didn't show when.

Late one evening as she lay in bed, Kira kept asking herself the same question over and over again. How? How was she supposed to bring down a king?

Her wound was aching and she just couldn't get to sleep. Just before dawn she gave up trying. Looking over to Elspeth, she saw her sister sleeping peacefully with her arm draped over Onnie. On the other side of the chamber, Kahrin was in her own bed, soundly asleep. Across from her, Jinx was awake. Lifting his head, he looked over to her.

Climbing slowly to her feet, Kira crossed to the dragon and kissed him lightly on the end of his snout. 'Now, I want you to stay here, Jinx,' she softly whispered as she held up her hand. 'Stay here and keep watch over Elspeth and Kahrin.'

Backing away from the dragon, Kira continued to hold up her hand while ordering him to stay. Making it to the door, she crept from her chamber and walked silently through the castle corridors. Entering the large kitchen, she was surprised to find Paradon seated at the oak table quietly sipping a warm drink.

'Couldn't sleep?' he announced without turning to her. Rising, he went to the fire to draw off some boiling water to make another drink.

Kira took a seat at the table. 'No. I just can't shake this feeling that Lord Dorcon is on his way. Right now.'

'Me too,' Paradon agreed darkly.

'Have you visited the Eye to see where he is?'

Stepping back to the table, he offered the drink to Kira. 'I was just about to do that when you arrived. Would you like to come up with me and see what we can see?'

Kira nodded. Staring into the swirling drink in her cup, she made a confession. 'Paradon, I'm really frightened. I know I've got to be strong, and that the prophecy says I'll do it. I just don't know how.'

Paradon sighed heavily. 'I don't know how, either. To tell you the truth, I have been searching the Eye for ages, but it will show me nothing.'

'Did you ever think that maybe it's not me? I

mean it could be someone else who brings King Arden down.'

'Of course I have,' Paradon answered gently. 'But Kira, it has to be you. There aren't a lot of other girls out there riding twin-tailed dragons. In fact, apart from the Rogue's other baby, there aren't any other twin-tailed—'

A sudden urgent banging on the castle doors cut short Paradon's comment. He and Kira stared at each other. 'This is it!'

Wild with fear, Kira stood and started to move. 'I'll get the girls and Jinx ready. Do what you can to hold them back! I don't know where we are going to go, but we aren't staying here!'

Clutching her wound, Kira raced back to her quarters and threw open both doors. In the chamber, she found Elspeth and Kahrin already up and dressing. Onnie was at Elspeth's feet yipping loudly. 'I know, Onnie,' Elspeth cried, 'I'm dressing as fast as I can!'

Crossing over to Jinx, Kira reached for his bridle before glancing at her sisters. 'Hurry up you two, we can't waste a moment!'

After checking the bridle, Kira inspected all the other straps and harnesses on Jinx's saddlebox. She then loaded their bows and quivers filled with arrows. When she was certain that Jinx was ready, she moved over to her bed and threw off her robe.

'What about these?' Elspeth asked as she held up two knights' daggers.

'Take them, take everything you can!' Kira ordered. 'They are not taking us without a fight!' Dressing as quickly as her wound would allow, she reached for her heavy wool cape.

'Let's go!'

Crossing to Jinx, Kira waited for Elspeth and Kahrin to take their places in the new saddlebox. While she had been recovering, Paradon had redesigned it to hold all of them. Once her sisters were settled, Kira painfully climbed up the dragon's wing and took the lead seat. Fastening her harness, she called over her shoulder. 'Hold on everyone. This is going to get rough!'

Kira gave the reins a flick. 'Come on, Jinx, we've got to go!'

Jinx started to run at a full gallop down the castle corridors towards the internal entrance to the north tower. If the men were in the courtyard and at the doors, she planned to escape using Jinx's tower.

Halfway there, Paradon appeared in the corridor telling them to stop. His unexpected appearance made Jinx rear up and start to roar violently. Flung back in their seats, Kira cried out in pain as her wound twisted against the straps of the harness. But despite the pain, she was grateful for the restraints. Without them, she and her sisters would have been tossed right off the dragon's back. 'Down, Jinx!' she cried, pulling back on the reins. 'Down!'

After several more tugs, Kira finally regained control of the dragon. When he lowered himself back down to the ground, she saw two young men standing a safe distance behind Paradon. One was dressed in the armour of a dragon knight while the other was clothed in rags. They both looked absolutely terrified as they watched the enraged dragon growling before them.

Frowning, Kira noticed that one of the two had bright red hair and looked strikingly like her father.

'Kira? Kahrin? Elspeth?' the redhead called as he took an unsteady step forward. 'Is it really you?'

Kira's eyes flew wide with recognition. 'Dane!' Looking over her shoulder, she called back, 'Shadow, Kahrin, look. It's Dane!'

Kira's hands were shaking as she undid her harness. Climbing out of the saddlebox, she raced past Paradon and threw herself into her brother's outstretched arms. 'Dane!' she cried over and over again as she buried her head in his chest. Finally she released him enough to look up into his face and see Lord Dorcon's brand covering his cheek.

'What did he do to you?'

'It's all right,' Dane assured her. 'It doesn't hurt any more.'

'But he branded you!'

'Yes, and he tried to kill you on the mountain,' Dane said as he embraced her again.

'Dane!' Elspeth squealed as she ran up behind Kira.

'Elspeth, is that you?' Dane laughed. Taking her in his arms, he gave her a big hug. 'Look how tall you've grown. Oh Elspeth, how I've missed you!'

Kira watched Elspeth's face light with love as she hugged her brother.

Still in shock from her long ordeal at Lasser, Kahrin hung back. When Dane released Elspeth, he dashed forward and wrapped her in his arms. 'I'm so glad to see you!' he cried as he kissed her face. 'I've been so frightened since Lord Dorcon took you to Lasser!'

Finally Kahrin started to cry and put her arms around her brother.

'How did you find us?' Kira asked, touching him to convince herself he was really there.

Suddenly remembering the reason he came, Dane looked urgently at his sisters. 'The king has got a whole legion of men coming for you,' he warned. 'We've got to get away. They can't be more than a couple of days behind us.'

'A full legion?' Paradon repeated.

'At least,' came the answer from the young man standing back. 'Not to mention every dragon knight at the palace.'

Remembering his friend, Dane called him forward. 'Everyone, I'd like you to meet my best friend, Shanks-Spar. But you can call him Shanks. We trained as dragon knights together.'

Kira looked over to Shanks suspiciously. He was older than Dane and wearing the same kind of armour as the knights who'd attacked them on the mountain. Across his breastplate blazed the crest of the king.

'Hello Shanks,' Elspeth said, not sharing her sister's reluctance. 'Are you and Dane really dragon knights?'

Shanks nodded, but then added, 'Not any more. They know I helped break Dane out of the dungeon and escape from the palace to warn you. I get the feeling we're in as much trouble as you are.'

Kira turned to Dane. 'Why were you in the dungeon?'

As Dane was about to answer, Jinx moved closer to the group and started to growl.

'Calm down, Jinx,' Elspeth said. 'It's Dane. He's our brother.'

Both Dane and Shanks looked over to where Jinx was standing. He was puffing out his cheeks threateningly and growling. Shaking his head, Dane turned back to Kira. 'I couldn't believe it when I heard you had your own dragon. And now, seeing him right there, I still can't. But Kira, keeping an unsecured dragon is dangerous. With his mouth free, he could eat all of you.'

'No he wouldn't,' Kira said as she walked over to the dragon. Jinx stopped growling and lowered his head for her to scratch behind his ears. 'See?' she said to her brother. 'Jinx is special. We found him when he was just a baby. He's been with us ever since.'

Dane stood with his mouth hanging open. 'If I hadn't seen it for myself, I would never have believed it.'

'Me neither,' Shanks agreed.

Clearing his throat, Paradon stepped forward. 'I do hate to interrupt this wonderful family reunion, but I'm afraid I must.' He turned his attention to Dane. 'Exactly how far away are Lord Dorcon and his men?'

Dane scratched his head. 'It took us four days to get here. But they know we escaped, so they would have left soon after. I don't think they'll be that far behind us. Maybe a day or two at most.'

Kira gave Jinx a final pat, then stepped back to her brother. 'How did you know we were here?'

'After what you did at Lasser Commons?' Dane asked. 'The whole kingdom is talking about you and that dragon of yours. Some people are even calling you heroes for what you did for their daughters.'

When Dane finished speaking, Shanks stepped forward. 'I was fighting at the front when we were all called back to the palace. When I heard what Lord Dorcon had done to Dane, a good friend helped me break him out of the dungeon.'

'Where is your friend?' Elspeth asked.

Shanks lowered his head. 'He didn't make it.'

'He gave his life to save us,' Dane added. 'Marcus was a good man.'

'Then we mustn't waste this opportunity,' Paradon said.

Kira looked desperately over to the wizard. 'Paradon, what are we going to do?'

The wizard started to pace the area. 'The first thing we do is not panic. We do that and we've already lost. Girls, please take Dane and Shanks into the kitchen. They must be tired and hungry from their long journey.'

'I must also ask if you have any meat you can spare for our dragons,' Shanks said. 'They didn't eat before we left and we haven't stopped to feed them.'

'Of course,' Paradon answered. 'Go with the girls. I'll sort out your dragons.'

Gathered in the main kitchen with Jinx sitting just outside the door, Elspeth and Kahrin prepared a large meal for everyone. With her wound badly aching, Kira sat at the table with Dane and Shanks. Together Kira and Elspeth explained everything that had happened to them from the time of Lord Dorcon's arrival at the farm, to the sacking of Lasser and rescue of Kahrin.

When they finished, Shanks shook his head appreciatively. 'I just can't believe it. I don't know which was scarier – living on the Rogue's Mountain, or attacking the most notorious prison in the kingdom!'

'Or getting run through with a sword,' Dane added. 'Are you all right now?' he asked worriedly.

'Getting there,' responded Kira. Standing, she lifted her top to show her brother the deep scars from the sword wound. 'It still hurts, but I'll live.'

'Not for long if the king and Lord Dorcon have their way,' Shanks said.

'But they won't get their way,' Elspeth added as she

beat several eggs in a bowl. 'We won't let them.'

Shanks sat back and whistled. 'You two do have powerful enemies! Rumour has it you and Elspeth are the first ever to get away from Lord Dorcon. He's almost insane with rage. Says he won't stop until he's caught you.'

'Killed us, you mean,' Kira corrected.

Quickly changing the subject, Elspeth reached forward and gently stroked Dane's scarred cheek. 'Did Lord Dorcon do this to you because of us?'

A shadow entered Dane's eyes. Shanks looked down into his lap, knowing what was coming.

'What is it?' Elspeth asked. 'Dane, tell us.'

Dane took a deep breath and held it. Finally he let it out again and started to tell the girls the events of his life up until the moment he and Shanks made it to Paradon's castle.

'No!' Elspeth cried.

'Lord Dorcon killed Father?' Kira repeated in a hushed voice.

Dane sniffed loudly and nodded.

'Father is dead . . .' Kahrin weakly said. Leaving the hearth, she crossed over to a corner and crouched down to the floor. Wrapping her arms tightly around her knees, she started to rock.

She looked just like she did when Kira first found her at Lasser. Quickly leaving the table, Kira crossed to Kahrin and crouched down beside her. Pulling her into a protective embrace she stroked her delicate sister's hair.

Dane was soon at their side and wrapping his arms around her as well. 'Lord Dorcon will pay for what he's done to us,' he sobbed.

As tears streamed down her face, Kira looked at her brother's burned cheek and then into the tormented eyes of her sister.

'He will. I promise you all, he will!'

# CHAPTER
## ~37~

After breakfast, everyone gathered in the great hall with Paradon. Sitting together, they struggled to find a solution. But the more they talked, the further away a solution seemed.

'I don't understand,' Dane challenged. 'Why can't we just get on our dragons and go now? We've got a day's head start on them. We could get away. Maybe even get to Lasser?'

'What if Lord Dorcon follows us?' Kira challenged. 'Dane, we'll lead them right back to those girls. We can't do that. We have got to stay as far away from Lasser as we can.'

'All right, we don't go to Lasser. But we can still go. There has got to be somewhere safe for us.'

'With three dragons?' Kira asked. 'It was hard enough keeping Jinx hidden. How can we do it with two more?'

'Besides, you can't leave now,' insisted Paradon. 'I

hate it, but we must wait until Lord Dorcon is on our doorstep before we take action. I have seen it countless times in my Eye.'

'But he's got a legion with him!' Dane cried. 'We'll be slaughtered!'

Everyone fell silent. Dane and Kira continued to pace the great hall as they tried to figure out a solution.

'What about magic?' Shanks finally suggested. 'You're a wizard. Why can't you just cast a spell or something?'

Paradon shook his head. 'Yes, I'm a wizard. But I'm an awful wizard. None of my spells ever work. Ask the girls. They've seen enough to know my powers can't be trusted.'

'So we're stuck waiting here until they come?' Dane asked.

Elspeth spoke for the first time. Clutching Onnie in her arms, she crossed over to Paradon. 'Shanks is right. You've got to use your powers.'

'What?' Paradon said. 'I just told you, it's far too dangerous. Look what happened with the tower.'

'What happened with the tower?' Dane quietly asked Kira.

Kira leaned over to her brother and whispered, 'Paradon blew it up and nearly killed himself.'

'I know you don't like to use it,' Elspeth continued. 'But magic is the only way. Lord Dorcon is coming for us with dragons. We can't fly away from here when they arrive. Kira and I can shoot arrows—'

'So can we,' Shanks added, indicating Dane as well.

'I can't,' Kahrin softly added.

'It doesn't matter,' Elspeth insisted. 'There's just us. We can't fight everybody.'

'But my magic,' Paradon pleaded, lowering his head. 'We can't trust it.'

'We don't have a choice,' Elspeth insisted. 'Your magic worked fine at Lasser, didn't it? Paradon, you fed all those poor girls and moved them to somewhere safe. It will work, you've just got to believe.'

Kira stepped forward. 'Shadow is right, Paradon. There are too many coming at us. It's not just Lord Dorcon now. It's the king's legion. No matter how good we are, we can't fight them all.'

Paradon stood and held out his hands. 'But I might hurt you.'

Kira crossed to the wizard and hugged him. Resting her head on his chest she sighed, 'I would rather die by your magic, than face Lord Dorcon and his men. Please Paradon, isn't there something you can do?'

'I just don't know,' the wizard admitted.

'What about that door?' Elspeth suggested.

'Door?' Shanks said.

'Yes, up in Paradon's tower. There's a door standing in the middle of the corridor that his master walked through and disappeared. Maybe we could bring it down here and go through it.'

Paradon smiled gently at Elspeth. 'A good idea, but I'm afraid it won't work. I don't know how to use it. Besides, the dragons wouldn't fit through it. I'm sure you wouldn't want to leave your baby behind.'

Elspeth shook her head and sighed. 'No.'

In her arms, Onnie started to yip excitedly. Leaping free of Elspeth, he raced over to Paradon and started to jump at the wizard's feet. He then ran back to Elspeth and leaped back into her arms and began to lick her chin.

'What is it with Elspeth and that fox?' Dane whispered to Kira.

'You wouldn't believe it if I told you,' Kira said dryly. 'Just don't try to pet him. Not if you want to keep all your fingers.'

Dane nodded but said nothing more.

'Onnie has a really good idea,' Elspeth said excitedly.

'I gathered that,' Paradon said lightly as a smile crept to his face. 'What does our red friend suggest?'

'He says that you should use your magic, Paradon,' Elspeth quickly explained. 'But not the door up in the tower. He says you should make your own door. Up in the sky. Then we could all fly through it and be safe.'

'A door to where?' Kira asked Elspeth.

'A door to the future,' Paradon said softly. Stroking the growing stubble on his chin, he started to walk around the hall. 'Not far into the future, say, just a season or two. We could let Lord Dorcon see you go. That should satisfy him that you are gone. Then after a time, you would reappear without him ever knowing it.'

Shanks frowned. 'Paradon, I've heard you've done some amazing things. But time travel? That's impossible. No one can do that.'

Beside him Dane nodded in agreement.

'Paradon can,' Elspeth said as trust shone in her eyes. 'Paradon can do anything.'

When she finished, Paradon smiled, but it was a sad smile. 'My master used to travel across the ages. Past or future, it didn't matter. It was easy for him. If I were a proper wizard, it would have worked for us too.'

'But you are a proper wizard,' Elspeth defended.

'Proper wizard or not,' Shanks said, 'you're all we've got. Paradon, if you say Lord Dorcon must see us go, then magic is the only way any of us will survive this. You've got to at least try.'

Kira's gaze passed from Paradon to the fox. Then back to Paradon again. 'Onnie's idea really could work. If you sent us into the future, Lord Dorcon would never find us. Then we would be free to come back and finish this.'

The wizard sadly shook his head. 'It would work if I had my master's control. But I don't. My powers are too unstable. I might kill you.'

'We'll all die anyway!' cried Dane, stepping up to Kira's side. 'Paradon, I don't really know who you are, but my sisters trust you. So do I. Please, isn't there some way you could do it?'

Paradon wrung his hands together and started to pace. 'I just don't know,' he said, shaking his head. 'I don't have the control to do what you ask of me.'

'You can do it, Paradon,' Elspeth offered. 'I believe in you.'

Kira watched a deep sadness enter the wizard's eyes. 'Thank you, child,' he said gently as he stopped pacing and stood before Elspeth. 'But you see, I don't believe in myself.'

'Well, you're going to have to start!' Shanks said with his voice full of authority. 'Because that legion is coming here soon and you are our only way out of here.'

Paradon raised his eyes up to the ceiling. 'Stars protect us,' he said. Then he looked back to Kira. 'I have no choice, do I?'

Kira shook her head. 'None of us do.'

# CHAPTER
## ~38~

The balance of the day was spent preparing everyone for Lord Dorcon's arrival. Harmony and Rexor were brought into the castle and housed in the great hall and fed as much as the dragons could eat.

After that, Paradon assigned Dane and Shanks the first watch up on the tallest towers of the castle. Once they were settled with their duties, he led Kira, Elspeth and Kahrin to the banquet hall. With Jinx trailing behind them, they entered the hall to find the long table filled with supplies.

'Girls, I don't know how this is going to work out. I'm not convinced that I have the control to send you away very accurately. If something goes wrong, I want to make sure you have enough food and supplies to see you through.'

'It will work, Paradon,' Kira said as she stepped forward to start packing. 'It has to.'

While they worked, Paradon called Elspeth over. 'I

have a special job for you. I want you to come with me to Rexor and Harmony. You need to let them know we need their help and cooperation.'

'Paradon, wait,' Kira said. 'You can't take Elspeth to those two dragons. They're not like Jinx. They're palace dragons. They'll kill her.'

'No they won't,' Paradon said. 'Remember Ferarchie. He had every opportunity to kill Elspeth, but he wouldn't. It will be the same with Rexor and Harmony. They'll do anything she asks them to. Trust your sister, Kira. She can do this.'

'It's all right, Kira,' Elspeth said lightly. 'They won't hurt me.'

Kira felt her stomach lurch, but nodded. 'Please be careful. Don't turn your back on them.'

While they were gone, Kira worked in silence with Kahrin to fill Jinx's saddlebox with as much as it would hold. But with every passing moment, she worried more and more about Elspeth.

Finally she could take it no longer. 'Kahrin, would you stay here a moment. I'm going to go check on Elspeth.' Catching hold of Jinx's reins, she led the dragon forward.

As she walked down the long corridors of the castle, Kira expected to hear dragon roars or at least growls.

343

But when she arrived at the great hall and pushed open the doors, she was shocked to see her sister standing between Harmony and Rexor. Both dragons had their heads bowed and were enjoying having their ears scratched.

When Jinx saw the other dragons, he started to puff out his cheeks and growl.

'Easy Jinx,' Kira calmed. 'Be nice.'

'Kira,' Paradon called. 'I'm glad you're here. I want you to bring Jinx in to meet these two. If they are going to be travelling together, it's best if they meet now.'

Drawing Jinx forward, Kira could hear his heavy breathing and saw the pinning of his eyes as he nervously watched the two armoured dragons. Stroking his strong neck, she praised him as they approached.

'Good boy, Jinx,' called Elspeth as she crossed over to him. 'I want you all to be friends. This is Harmony,' she said as she led him forward. 'And that is Rexor.'

Kira looked from the palace dragons to Jinx. Though he was much younger, Jinx was almost the same size as Rexor. Standing amongst them, Elspeth looked so small and vulnerable and yet Kira saw how all the dragons were watching her. Paradon was right. Elspeth had complete control over all of them.

Kira crossed to Paradon. He was holding the vicious

bits from the two palace dragons. She reached for one and held it in her hands. Turning it over, she saw the horrible spikes that pressed into the dragons' tongues.

'These are awful,' she said. 'No wonder palace dragons are so mean.'

'Indeed,' Paradon said. 'The moment Elspeth saw them, she asked me to replace them with bits like Jinx has got. But I'll tell you now, if we didn't have Elspeth, I would never dream of replacing them. These terrible bits are a knight's only way to control his mount.'

'Do you think Dane and Shanks will be able to control them now?'

'Dane won't have a problem. Elspeth tells me Rexor actually likes your brother.'

'But what about Harmony?'

'Unfortunately, Harmony is another story. She doesn't like Shanks. I don't think she likes anyone but Elspeth.'

'But if Harmony doesn't like Shanks, what are we going to do? He needs her to get away from here.'

Giving Jinx a final pat on the neck, Elspeth joined Kira and Paradon. 'I'm going to ride Harmony,' she explained. 'Shanks can ride with Dane on Rexor and you and Kahrin can go on Jinx.'

Kira looked from Paradon back to Elspeth. 'Is that

safe? Shadow, you've only just met Harmony. Now that she doesn't have her bit, can you really trust her?'

Instead of an answer, Elspeth stepped back to the three dragons standing together. She stroked Jinx first, then Rexor and finally approached Harmony. As Kira watched, the large red dragon behaved just like Jinx did around Elspeth. She lowered her head and lightly nudged Elspeth, inviting her to pat her.

'I don't think I'll ever understand how she does that,' Kira said softly to Paradon.

The old wizard turned to her. 'It's pure magic,' he finally said. 'And thanks to that, we now have two more dragons who will do anything for your sister. Including not attacking us.'

Before long, Jinx became accustomed to the other two dragons. Though he seemed to tolerate their company, the moment Kira and Elspeth left the great hall, he quickly followed. The bigger surprise came when Rexor and Harmony also entered the corridor behind Jinx. Any attempts to keep them in the great hall failed as the dragons insisted on staying with Elspeth.

'This is going to get awkward,' Kira finally said as she stood with her hands on her hips before the three large dragons. 'How are we going to fit you all in our chamber?'

* * *

That night, further preparations for battle continued. Quivers were stocked to overflowing with arrows, Dane and Shanks were given swords by Paradon and Kira made certain everyone had daggers.

When they finished as much as they could, it was agreed they should all spend the night together in the great hall with the dragons. With Lord Dorcon and the legion of knights due to arrive at any time, they had to be prepared to move on a moment's notice.

As they settled down to sleep, Paradon took his turn on watch. Unable to settle, Kira quietly left her brother and sisters in the hall and joined him on the north tower.

'They're close, aren't they?' she asked as she stepped out on to the flat roof.

'I'm afraid so,' Paradon said. 'I've seen the Eye. By all accounts, they will be here tomorrow. I just wish we had a better plan. Relying on my powers is dangerous.'

'Not as dangerous as those men coming to kill us,' Kira said.

'Perhaps,' Paradon agreed. 'I still wish I could see how all of this turns out.'

Standing together, they stared out over the darkened grounds surrounding the castle. 'Paradon,' Kira said softly. 'I don't want you to stay here. It's just too dangerous. Come with us, please.'

Paradon slowly shook his head. 'I wish I could, but I can't. I've got to work the spells with the Eye, just like with Lasser. You've been to the tower and you know how difficult it is to find your away around. I promise you, I will be perfectly safe.'

Saying nothing more, Paradon put his arm around Kira and together they stood, staring out into the night. Waiting for the arrival of Lord Dorcon.

# CHAPTER
## ~39~

Kira and Paradon were still keeping watch as the first pink rays of dawn crept across the sky. When the sun finally lit the horizon, Kira saw dark specks moving in the distance. Before long, the specks became solid. With her eyes wide, she realized the sky was filled with dragons.

'They're here!' she cried.

Paradon said, 'Go downstairs and wake everyone up. I'll be there in a moment. I'll cast a spell to try to slow them down.'

When Kira hesitated, he smiled. 'Go on, it will be fine. I'm just going to get them a little wet.'

Leaving Paradon to cast his spell, Kira ran down the stairs of the north tower and through the castle until she came to the great hall. Throwing open the doors, she saw Elspeth and Kahrin feeding the three dragons while Dane and Shanks finished packing up the weapons.

'They're here!' she breathlessly cried.

'They're early,' Dane cursed.

'Let them come!' Shanks said as a broad smile lit his face. 'We're ready!'

While everyone finished preparations, Kira saw the haunted expression returning to Kahrin's face. Crossing to her, she gave her a gentle hug. 'Don't worry, Kahrin. I won't let Lord Dorcon come anywhere near you. You're safe now.'

Saying nothing, Kahrin hugged her again and nodded.

When Paradon arrived in the hall, Kira noticed his cloak was soaking wet and he was leaving large pools of water around him.

'What happened to you?' Elspeth asked.

'Well, I had a bit of a problem with a spell,' he said as he wrung water out of his sleeves. 'But never mind. Are you all ready to go?'

When everyone nodded, Paradon continued. 'Good. Now, Dane, I want you to go up to the north tower and keep watch. Come back when Lord Dorcon arrives at the castle. We can't make a move until that monster is here.' He then turned to the others. 'Everyone else, get your dragons ready. We're going to wait by the front doors.'

As Paradon stood back, Kira helped settle Kahrin in the saddlebox. Then she caught hold of Jinx's reins and moved him forward. Walking single file out of the great hall, they moved carefully down the corridors of the castle. Behind Kira and Jinx, Elspeth was holding on to Onnie while leading Harmony. Taking up the rear, Shanks led Rexor forward. As they walked, Shanks kept a nervous watch on the black dragon's mouth.

'You sure he won't attack us now his bit is gone?' he called forward to Elspeth.

'No he won't. Rexor likes you and Dane,' Elspeth said lightly. 'It is just Harmony who hates you. But even she won't attack you now. Not unless you do something silly.'

'Thanks,' Shanks said dryly. 'That makes me feel so much better.'

When they arrived at the castle doors, Paradon pulled them open. Immediately everyone saw the dragons in the sky over the castle.

'They're here!' Shanks cried. 'It's too late!'

'No it's not,' Paradon said calmly. 'You're a knight. You should know dragons can move faster than horses. These knights are here to keep us from leaving. They won't attack until Lord Dorcon arrives by horseback.'

'I sure hope you're right,' Shanks said.

'So do I,' Paradon agreed as he looked over to Kira. 'So do I.'

Time seemed to stand still as they waited before the castle doors for Dane to announce Lord Dorcon's arrival. It was late into the afternoon before they heard him shouting and running down the castle corridors.

'He's here,' Dane breathlessly announced, as he ran up to the group. 'He's leading hundreds, maybe thousands of men. They're at the drawbridge.' He paused for a breath before saying, 'They're preparing a battering ram to knock down the outer doors.'

'Fine, let them waste their time with the portcullis and outer doors,' Paradon said. 'All of you get ready to go. The moment I give the word, go out into the courtyard and get your dragons into the sky.'

'Then what?' Shanks asked.

'Then you wait for the door to open. When it does, I want you to fly right through it. Don't hesitate. I don't know how long I can keep it open. Do you understand?'

'Don't worry about us,' Kira quickly said. 'The moment we see the door, we'll go.' Before climbing on Jinx's wing, Kira ran to Paradon and hugged him fiercely. 'Please take care, Paradon. Don't let Lord Dorcon get you. And remember, whatever happens today, good or bad, it was what we wanted.'

'Take care, child. Now get ready!'

After Kira gave him a final hug, Elspeth stepped forward to embrace the wizard. Onnie was sitting in the pack on her back with both his paws on her shoulder. 'Please be safe, Paradon,' she cried.

'I will,' he promised. He then looked to Onnie and patted him on the head. 'Take good care of her, Onnie. She's a very special girl.'

In response, Onnie threw back his head and howled mournfully.

'He will,' Elspeth sniffed.

After the last of the farewells, everyone climbed on their dragons. As Kira took the lead seat, she looked back to Kahrin and smiled reassuringly. 'We'll be fine.'

Looking past her, Kira saw Elspeth sitting confidently on Harmony's back while Dane settled on Rexor with Shanks sitting behind him.

From Rexor, Kira's eyes trailed down to Paradon. 'I'm going up to the Eye to get things started. Don't make a move until I tell you to.'

'What about the other dragons?' Dane asked.

'I'll take care of them. You just concentrate on getting through that door,' the wizard called as he started to run through the castle.

As she watched him go, Kira felt a lump develop in her throat. She hated that he was staying behind. Catching hold of Jinx's reins, she tried to suppress the fear that she might never see him again. Looking over to Elspeth and then Dane and Shanks, she asked, 'Are you all ready?'

'If you mean, are we ready to go flying into a sky filled with hundreds of dragon knights wanting to kill us, waiting for a spell to be cast by a wizard whose spells never work, then I guess I am,' Shanks said from behind Dane.

'Ignore him,' Dane said to Kira as he elbowed his friend in the stomach. 'We're ready.'

'Us too,' Elspeth agreed. 'Aren't we, Onnie?' From his place on her shoulder, Onnie started to yip.

'All right, I'm at the Eye,' Paradon's voice announced from the pendants around Kira and Elspeth's necks. 'Get ready to move. When I tell you to, take your dragons into the air and wait for the door to open.'

Feeling terror building up in her stomach, Kira reached forward and nervously patted Jinx's neck. 'Get ready baby. We're going flying.'

'Go now!' Paradon cried.

Giving the reins a quick snap, Kira directed Jinx through the castle doors and out into the courtyard.

'Fly, Jinx!' she cried as she pulled up on the reins. Spreading his wings, Jinx flew confidently up into the sky. Looking wildly about, Kira saw the dragon knights around the castle start moving away as if being pushed by unseen hands. Their riders were shouting and pulling on the reins, but it wasn't working. The dragons had no control.

'Yes!' Kira cried triumphantly. 'Paradon, it's working. Keep going!'

From behind her, Kira could hear Elspeth laughing and shouting at the departing dragons while Dane and Shanks cheered.

Keeping Jinx within the area above the courtyard, Kira brought him around for a second turn.

'Kira, look,' Kahrin said softly from behind her.

Following her eyes as they approached the front of the castle, she gasped. Just beyond the outer walls she saw the legion of king's men. Some were on the ground and charging the portcullis with their ram, while others looked like they were building catapults. Even more sat on horseback with their swords drawn and staring up at them in the sky.

But at the very front of the assault, seated on his large black warhorse, was Lord Dorcon. He was staring right at her and pointing. Soon hundreds of his men lowered their swords, raised their bows and fixed them with arrows.

'Paradon, open the door!' Kira cried, as she drew Jinx around again. 'They're loading their bows. Open the door!'

Drawing her eyes away from the legion, Kira saw Shanks fixing arrows into his own bow and firing at the men below. Nearby, directing Harmony with words only, Elspeth was doing the same.

Stealing a glance back to Lord Dorcon, Kira felt a cold shiver run along her spine as their eyes suddenly locked. 'Keep watching us, you monster!' she muttered angrily. 'Watch, and see us go!'

Just as she finished speaking, the first round of arrows shot past them. Some came dangerously close to hitting Jinx. Turning her attention back to the wizard, she cried, 'Hurry! Paradon, open the door!'

As the second round of arrows shot past them, the sky before them started to crackle and change. Very soon it began to glow as a small round circle of intense colours suddenly appeared. From everything Elspeth had ever told her about the Eye, Kira realized this was exactly what she was seeing. Somehow, it was Paradon's Eye!

Suddenly the Eye grew larger and its colours

intensified. Soon, great peals of thunder echoed in the sky while bright swirling tendrils of energy shot out of the core.

At the sight of the tendrils, Jinx roared and tried to shy away. But clutching the reins, Kira ordered him to keep moving. As she struggled to keep him under control, she heard Paradon shouting, 'Kira, go into the Eye! Tell everyone to enter the Eye!'

Looking back to the others, Kira waved them forward. 'Fly into the Eye,' she called. Facing forward again, she watched more tendrils come shooting out of the core and reaching for them. But as they wrapped around Jinx, there was no heat, no burning and no pain. Instead, the world around them turned to brilliant colours as they rode within the safety of the Eye's energy.

Taking a quick look down, Kira watched in grim satisfaction as Lord Dorcon shielded his eyes against the blinding light. She could almost hear him cursing as he bore witness to their amazing escape.

'Keep watching us!' she cried.

Drawing closer to the Eye, Kira felt no fear. But when she and Jinx entered the core, her ears started ringing with an almost unbearably loud whooshing sound.

All around her, the sky was alive with swirling,

flashing colours. Looking over the side of the saddlebox, it was like a river of colour flowing wildly beneath them. Turning behind her, Kira saw Kahrin's glowing and fearful face. Further back, Dane and Shanks looked around in wonder. While at the very back, Elspeth and Onnie on Harmony cheered.

After what seemed an eternity, Kira noticed the colours changing, growing paler. A moment later there was another tremendous peal of thunder and Jinx burst out of the Eye and into a world of dark grey clouds and rainy skies.

'It worked!' Kira cried joyously. Reaching forward she patted Jinx's thick neck in excitement.

'We're free!' she cried to Kahrin. 'Now we can go back and finally stop King Arden once and for all!' Cheering in her seat, Kira heard Dane and Shanks's joyous shouts mixing with her own.

Soaring through the dark, stormy skies, everyone celebrated their triumphs. Kahrin and the girls of Lasser were finally safe. Kira had her very own dragon that loved her. She knew how to fight. But best of all, she had beaten Lord Dorcon once again.

Kira was still cheering as she heard Dane shouting her name. Looking to her right, she saw Rexor drawing up beside her.

'Let's get back to Paradon's castle,' he cried. 'Then we can go and get Mother!'

Kira was still cheering as she started to direct Jinx through the thick dark storm clouds. Paradon was waiting for them below. With her family around her for support, she felt her confidence growing. She would fulfil the prophecy. King Arden's cruel monarchy was about to end!

# EPILOGUE

Paradon was in his tower, staring into the depths of the Eye. As he had cast his spell, he prayed it would work. Kira and her family were counting on him.

Then realizing the full truth of what had happened he drew his hands to his mouth. 'What have I done?' he cried.